BYRON'S WORKS

A NOVEL BY RICHARD RABICOFF

Writers Club Press
San Jose New York Lincoln Shanghai

Byron's Works

All Rights Reserved © 2002 by Richard Rabicoff

No part of this book may be reproduced or transmitted in any form or by any means, graphic, electronic, or mechanical, including photocopying, recording, taping, or by any information storage retrieval system, without the permission in writing from the publisher.

Writers Club Press
an imprint of iUniverse, Inc.

For information address:
iUniverse, Inc.
5220 S. 16th St., Suite 200
Lincoln, NE 68512
www.iuniverse.com

Any resemblance to actual people and events is purely coincidental.
This is a work of fiction.

ISBN: 0-595-21415-0

Printed in the United States of America

Contents

Chapter 1 1
Chapter 2 29
Chapter 3 49
Chapter 4 73
Chapter 5 91
Chapter 6 113
Chapter 7 131
Chapter 8 155
Chapter 9 177
Chapter 10 203
About the Author. *229*

CHAPTER 1

My first thought is that my Ex–Fiancee did this, to get back at me. I could call her and ask her point blank, but I know what she'd say. "Shove it." That's all she has said to me in the two months since I jilted her, left her at the altar so to speak. I bear her no ill will, nor do I seriously suspect her, because any package from my Ex–Fiancee would have detonated on contact, blowing me to smithereens or at least South Dakota. Besides, I think Sheila realizes deep down that she's technically to blame for our breakup, though it was my fault.

Whoever sent me this knows I'm home during the day, because they knocked twice and split. The address label is not in my Ex–Fiancee's handwriting. The small square box, which bears the insignia of a department store that went out of business years ago, might once have contained an imported clock, a music box, a set of coasters, a paperweight, a wedding gift. Osterloh's was a high–class establishment. Six narrow strips of cellophane tape fasten down the mashed–in lid; I slice through them with my fingernails, which I notice could use paring. (I have a date tonight.) I tear through a newspaper wrapping and drop what I find like a hot potato. It bounces on the carpet and rolls.

It is, after all, a baseball.

- 1 -

I go queasy at the yellowed hide, the once crimson stitches faded to rust. It is tattooed with swirls of ink. I land on the sofa and droop my head between my thighs, one of those classic first–aid maneuvers that never works. So I lie back with my arms stretched out and my head thrown back like a dental patient and wait for the nausea to subside, meanwhile ransacking my memory for the name of any foe who could hate me this much. I am a master of probabilities, made my living at it for twenty–five years, but I draw a complete blank. I avert my one working eye from the object that infests the middle of my living room and stay like this for a while, till my alarm clock buzzes to remind me of my two o'clock appointment.

❦   ❦   ❦

Over half of us are black or Mexican, the rest white like me. The usual ratio. The woman in front of me is so fat the nape of her neck ripples, the rivets on her jeans seem to turn purple from the stress. I admire plump women immensely, but this one is immense beyond admiration. The baby on her shoulder grins and swivels its head, playing peekaboo. The kid keeps doing it, refuses to accept that I don't do peekaboo. The woman has two other kids, a girl and boy. Standing stiffly at their mother's side, their whole bodies the width of her pillaresque thighs, they look like spare limbs ready to take over in case mama's legs cave in to battle fatigue.

The man behind me cradles a Bible, swaying and muttering to himself in a south of the border inflection. Behind him stands one of my fellow regulars, but he doesn't acknowledge my neighborly nod. He takes this whole thing very seriously and is the only man, other than the ones who work here, wearing a tie. One hand clasps a smooth leather attache case, while the other wanders over his face in surveillance for any unshaved patches. He looks like he's preening for a job interview, which shows that for all his dapperness he has lost his hold on reality.

The fat lady is summoned and she lumbers up to the grilled window. She snatches a handful of lollipops from a Dixie cup and hands them to her children. This used to be a branch of a bank which merged with some larger bank from out of state and changed its name and vacated many of its buildings, putting up those little drive-throughs and ATMs instead. I suppose the county got the building cheap, in exchange for a handsome tax write-off for the bank. The place retains a bank atmosphere, with its high arched ceilings, marble floors, and hush hush acoustics, as if what's being transacted here is of the utmost intimacy and financial importance. So it's not an absolute lie when I tell my mother that I go to the bank every other Friday.

The baby is still ogling me and I flutter my hand under my chin like Curly of the Three Stooges, which elicits peals of laughter. I can't even muster a smile. That package has discombobulated me.

At the call of "Next" I amble two windows down. A woman behind the cast iron bars chews gum rapidly, cracking it in her jaws as she looks over my stuff, stamps it. I've never had her before. I never get the same person twice. The state must rotate these people or dispose of them like Q-Tips.

She directs me to desk number eight, inhabited by a thin, peaked man in green tinted designer frame glasses, with the nameplate Ryan McSweeney centered on the front of his desk. I say thank you and pluck a cherry sucker from the Dixie cup.

"Please sit down, Mr. uh" (glancing down at my manila file) "Mr. Miller. Now, Mr. Miller, have you been actively seeking employment since your last visit here?" He leans toward me but stares at my chest, which leads me to run my fingers along the shirt front to make sure all the buttons are done.

I tell him yes, I have been looking desperately. I mention I've responded to several help wanted ads and I can't wait for the results. My arms are folded with my fingers crossed under my armpits. He wheels his chair sideways and clicks away on a computer keyboard.

How hard it is to look dignified at a computer keyboard. The old manual typewriters at least involved some wrist action. Of course, if I knew how to use one of these things, maybe somebody would hire me.

Mr. McSweeney thumps the last key and the right hand springs up with a little Liberace type flourish. "There's not much, uh, activity, in your field, Mr. Miller," he says.

"That's an understatement, Mr. McSweeney."

He's not used to hearing his name. His eyes crimp at the corners. "There is a part–time job in Merriam, but you're terribly over–qualified. I think it would be a waste of time to send you over there."

"I'm willing to give it a whirl," I say, though this job in Merriam pays less than what I just received for doing nothing.

Mr. McSweeney looks over my shoulder and I hear the footsteps of his next customer. "Have you ever thought of getting retrained? Learning Basic of Fortran might make you more employable. You follow up on those want ads and we'll see you in two weeks. Goodbye, Mr. Miller." His chin rises slightly, a signal for me to scram.

Outside three men patrol the public sidewalk distributing leaflets. One of them accosts me and waves a blue sheet in my face. "Check it out," he says. "It's time for a change." The leaflet advertises a rally, sponsored by a group called the Coalition for the Unemployed, to take place next Monday at noon at bank branches all over the city. One of the other men approaches me. "You ain't got a job, you can't own your own home," he says. "That's what these banks are telling people like us. No job, no mortgage."

"I rent," I tell the man, as I move briskly away. Down the road a young boy leaps into a deep puddle left by last evening's thunderstorm. I hand him the leaflet, which he converts into a paper airplane.

Normally I drop in on Goode at his movie theater to shoot the breeze and bum some Milk Duds. It's just a few blocks from here and he's expecting me. But that ball of poison on my living room floor is still eating away at me, and I've got this craving to call my Ex–Fiancee.

I see two pay phones, one occupied by a woman, the other with the phone dangling on its metal cord, which usually means it's out of order and ate the coin of the poor soul who has left the cord dangling as a thoughtful advisory to the rest of us. I cast a harried look at the woman, who shows me her back. Finally she slams down the receiver, rattles the change slot and calls me a lousy bastard.

"She's at the lot on Forty–fifth Street," says Ward, then catches his breath, suddenly remembering that he's under strict instructions to hang up the minute he hears my voice. Ward is my Ex–Fiancee's secretary.

"Can you give me the number over there, Ward?"

There's a pause. Ward has always liked me. "I can't give you the number. Ms. Crenshaw wouldn't like that."

"Ward, I could always say you wouldn't give me the number so I had to look it up in the phone book."

"Okay." He gives me the number and hangs up. Ward is not too swift. In a few minutes he'll realize that he's committed the unpardonable sin of telling me his boss's whereabouts. He'll be terrified that he'll get canned. I make a mental note to call later and reassure him as best I can.

"What is it, asshole? How the fuck did you know I was here?" yells my Ex–Fiancee.

"I got this package today. I thought you might know something about it."

"I wouldn't send you shit. I don't ever want to talk to you again. Who told you I was here?" She is shouting, half out of rage and half in order to be heard above the grinding gears and roaring engines. The forty–fifth street lot is one of her biggest.

"I hope your customers can't hear you, Sheila. I just tried all the lots till I got this one."

"Damn that Ward. I'll bust his ass," she screams. I hear a sharp click.

At least she didn't say "Shove it."

Not that I have any right to call her, any more than I have a reason to suspect her. I've never done her justice.

Goode does not look happy. Only a sparse gathering mills around in the lobby for the matinee. For one dollar you get a double feature. Goode started this policy several months ago, but it's done nothing to improve business. His one employee, other than a projectionist, is a kid from the community college who, out of the corner of my right eye—the eye that works—I see pacing behind the concession counter. He salutes when he sees me.

"Popcorn or Milk Duds?" he asks.

I get some Milk Duds, paying for them with the cherry lollipop from the unemployment office, then stroll over to Goode.

"I really thought this would draw," he says. He's playing Casablanca and Watch on the Rhine. "How's your mother?" he asks.

"Batso. She called me Alfred the other day." Alfred was her fourth husband, who died twenty plus years ago.

I don't remind Goode that most people have seen Casablanca on TV twenty times. It was on just a week ago. He would only say, "But this is a new print, better quality." All he ever wanted to do, since we were kids, was run his own movie theater.

But he's never made a go of it. He weighs over two–fifty and not an ounce of it is business sense.

Goode smiles at one of his patrons, then turns to me. "You got any plans for the weekend?"

I shake my head. Goode knows nothing about Joanne.

I remark that he's looking rather svelte and he brightens for a moment. Goode likes hearing that a woman in line at the unemployment office weighed twice as much as he does. He gains and loses sixty pounds on a quarterly basis. He's now enjoying a slim phase, but blubber and heart trouble run in his family, neither his father nor his father's three brothers made it past sixty and Goode is nearing fifty, like me, and he hears his coronary clock ticking. Justifiably, from what I know of morbidity rates. He has a wonderful wife, thin as a pipe cleaner, and an adorable little boy, the only child I've ever felt comfortable with. I've made a secret vow to take care of them if anything happens to Goode, though it would help if I found someone to take care of me first.

"Artie, some anonymous donor sent me a baseball. In an old Osterloh's box."

"But you hate baseball. You have a goddamned phobia about baseball." Goode sucks in his cheeks, which takes some doing. "This person knows that and wanted to upset me."

"A baseball? Just a regular baseball?"

"It had writing on it. Probably autographs."

"You didn't look at it?"

"I couldn't stand looking at it."

"What if there's some important message scrawled on the ball? Or maybe it's a collector's item."

"Tomorrow it's going to be a garbage collector's item."

"Could it be Sheila?"

"I called her. She cussed me out."

"Your mom?"

With that blinking disarray that has become her life my mother is capable of anything. But also incapable of remembering. She might have done it and then forgot about it.

"This took calculation, Artie. I doubt Mom's up to it."

"It beats me," says Goode.

Most things do beat poor Artie Goode. This theater is an example. He's owned it for eight years and tried every conceivable gimmick, short of bringing Clark Gable back from the dead. One of the most successful was the Yul Brynner film festival, to which all bald men were admitted free. This year he re-named it Theater 50 and exclusively shows movies made fifty years ago, all double features with vintage newsreels (accurate to the week, fifty years ago) and shorts and cartoons. He read in some trade magazine that nostalgia for old films is rampant, even if they've been on TV, because they're only shown at late hours and chopped up with ads, and colorized beyond recognition. Many aren't available on videotape. The savvy proprietor can obtain them cheaply, reduce your ticket price, deal in volume, and clean up at the concessions. It hasn't worked so far and the year is half over.

"If I don't make ends meet by November, I go X–rated," he says.

"Gloria would divorce you. Mickey will be ashamed of you, if he ever finds out. I, of course, will still stop in for free Milk Duds, despite my moral outrage."

"Then maybe I'll just open a video store. I've got to find a niche," he says.

"It will happen," I say lamely.

"Could Caspary have sent it to you? The ball."

"I doubt it." Warren Caspary, a member of our Tuesday night men's group, specializes in tactless jokes. But he's more punster than prankster. He advised Goode to name his theater The Dead Horse. "Have you reached a decision about the reunion?" Goode asks.

"Not yet."

"We'd love to have you come with us. Have a good weekend."

"Till Tuesday."

I get a bus to Joanne's for my Friday Night Special. She welcomes me with a kiss after which I strip down to my black bikini briefs and plop down on her sofa. Sheila gave me a three–pack of the briefs, which resemble panties and hug my genitals too insistently, but they turn Joanne on so I wear them for her. Joanne brings me a Jack Daniels on the rocks in one of those imitation antique Coke glasses. She has white wine in a long stem glass for herself. She fondles me while we talk.

"So you called Sheila today?" she asks. I nod, spilling a drop of bourbon on my bare chest. Joanne blots it with her finger and then flicks her tongue over the fingertip. She switches on her telephone message machine, which emits Sheila fuming about my call.

"I thought I'd hear your side, before I call her back."

Joanne is Sheila's best friend. They grew up together and have always competed fiercely, though neither will admit it. They say they're vastly different people with vastly different personalities—which doesn't mean a fruit cup can't compete with an eclair for your dessert. The two women are inseparable but no one will ever play Tweedledee to Sheila's Tweedledum.

According to Joanne, Sheila used to rave about my prowess as a lover, probably more to make Joanne envious than to report an accurate truth. When I abandoned Sheila, Joanne tried to play peacemaker, but she turned out to be a double agent, hoarding Sheila's confidences and then sharing them with me, no doubt in expurgated form. I think Joanne relishes this opportunity to one-up Sheila, who is prettier, more successful and, until a few months ago, had a more secure domestic future than Joanne will ever have.

"So what possessed you to call Sheila, Jerry?"

"I don't know. Just trying to keep in touch." I accentuate the last word as a subliminal signal to Joanne to start caressing me again.

"You still love her."

"No."

"But you still want her."

I deny the charge with utter truthfulness. Everything I felt for Sheila died in one millisecond, months ago. I can't believe Joanne is really jealous. I give her Friday nights.

We both live in fear of being caught by Sheila, so we never stray from Joanne's apartment. The extent of my commitment is that I have to show up every Friday night. She has to have that guarantee and as far as I can tell she has no interest in me beyond that. Her true love is an older married man who lives in Iowa and she only sees him once a month. Joanne will tell me nothing about him, except that his name is Edward and he's an investment banker, and not even Sheila knew much about him. Joanne maintains a rigorous fidelity to this guy. She and I don't go all the way, though we do everything but. Joanne doesn't feel she's technically betraying Sheila and Edward, plus in this time of plague one can't be too cautious. I completely concur in the arrangement: limited ecstasy is about all I can handle right now, and it's always pleasant with Joanne.

Dinner is grilled salmon with fennel orange salsa, so says Joanne. Salmon I like but the perky topping stings my tongue and with apologies to the chef I brush it to the outer reaches of my plate. There's also asparagus with some butter sauce, and a small salad. The recipe no doubt derives from one of the seventy cookbooks that clog the shelves in Joanne's kitchen, most of them nobly stained, with little colored toothpicks sticking out of them to mark successful recipes.

Can't help comparing Joanne to Sheila, who never cooks and gorges herself on fast food. Sheila eats fast, drives fast, reads fast, talks fast and generally conducts herself in a manly style, which explains why she's made a killing in the traditionally male preserve of parking lot proprietorship. My Ex–Fiancee would rather change a tire or put up storm windows than whip up a fricassee. She is a man's man. She will charge across a street in defiance of oncoming traffic, leaving her embarrassed companion to wait for the Walk sign.

Joanne takes everything slowly, sometimes too slowly. Like her dissertation. "My research is getting screwed up. I can't tell my controls from my subjects." I love the husky coating her voice assumes on Fridays after a week of hectoring students at the community college, where Joanne teaches psychology. Nightly she slaves over her dissertation, now in its seventh year.

She originally intended to track ten teenage girls with eating disorders over a three–year period, in an attempt to determine the relationship between the girls' body image, their home environment and their anorexia or bulimia. What started as a three–year project has been protracted because: 1) new data keep flooding in and Joanne is required to factor in those revelations; 2) her adviser retired to Scottsdale last year and his successor dislikes Joanne and belittles her research; 3) several of the girls died and she had to find new ones; 4) several of the girls' families consider Joanne's study to be intrusive and refuse to cooperate; and 5) Joanne procrastinates like hell. So now the department is cracking down. One more year or else.

"It continues to amaze me, Jerry, how normal these families are. They mostly voted for Reagan and Bush, hold down white collar jobs, love their children. They could be you or me." None of the above applies to me, except the white–collar job, which I no longer hold down anyway.

After dinner Joanne disappears into the bathroom, soon to emerge nude. I ready myself for love making that will be full–bodied if somewhat half–hearted. She yanks off my underpants and we sink onto the soft chocolate crushed corduroy bedspread. It's like sliding down the back of a gigantic cat, a sensation at once so sensuous and comforting that I might go on with Joanne an extra six months (if they can extend my unemployment insurance six months, then I can certainly extend a love affair) just for the way this material soothes my pores.

I commence to inch my body down hers. Her breasts are wonderful, her only undeniably exceptional feature, and for that very reason I ignore them and tend to the rest of her. Before I can do much damage she grabs me by the elbows. "Your turn to go first, remember?" she says. My going first means that I finish first. Joanne is phenomenal, at once ginger and efficient, like those nurses who extract a pint of your blood and you never feel the needle. All the while, presumably, her thoughts run to Edward, as mine tonight run to and away from a baseball.

I please Joanne well enough, but probably not up to the level of Sheila's ballyhoo. Each time I can sense her disappointment in the subdued cry that escapes during her orgasm. Although I don't trust her any more than she trusts me, I usually rest peacefully beside Joanne, but tonight I'm on edge. The digital clock by her bed clicks off each minute and annoys me to high hell. I hate digital clocks. Time should move as a series of ticks and tocks, not in stealthy clicks. I like things to go round and round. I still have an old black rotary phone at my apartment, which doesn't have a lawn, but if it did I'd mow it with one of those old reel jobs rather than noisy electrics that shave rather than thresh the grass.

Ward! I forgot to call Ward and alert him to the wrath of Sheila. I could have at least helped him cook up a story. Knowing Sheila, I won't be surprised to see Ol' Ward soon sidling up to me at the former bank, his hound's eyes in doleful distress. I feel terrible. When I was a kid my father told me, after I complained to Mac and Bernie that I didn't like the new barber they'd hired, "The worst thing you can do to a man is cost him his job." Well, now that I've been laid off I realize that there are worse things, but getting canned ranks right up there.

I sleep only a brief spell and wake up antsy. On my side of the bed the fitted sheet has been wrenched from the mattress. At breakfast Joanne seems eager to be rid of me, as she is every Saturday morning. She's jittery about her dissertation, Saturday marking another week shot without discernible progress. She's also guilty about betraying Edward and Sheila. But even on automatic pilot she delivers two impeccable straight up eggs, a toothsome rasher of bacon, and hazelnut coffee to make you weep. Then I go. From the foyer of Joanne's building I look both ways, for Sheila.

As I'm fiddling with the keys to my apartment the phone starts ringing. When I finally burst in I trip and go sprawling, fortunately landing on the fleshy part of the rump. I'm prone to pratfalls on account of what experts term my "lower vision," but even the keenly sighted could have tripped on the baseball, which now ricochets against the wall and comes to rest against the baseboard.

The phone stops ringing and I don't have a clue as to who called. I crawl toward the ball as if stalking a Gila monster. At close range recognition throws me back on my heels. I can't believe it's the same one I once wanted more than anything in the world. The way some guys coveted a Thunderbird or Anita Ekberg, I coveted that smooth white horsehide with its antic black scrawls. I had long ago forgot the object and the coveting of it, and the deed I committed against the man who possessed it. Suddenly memory breathes his name in my ear. After all these years is he calling me to account? Isn't there a statute of limitations on a youthful mistake? This is no prank but an act of vengeance.

And it could only be the work of John Byron.

Today, the theme is my ring. Every five minutes or so, after little interludes of meandering talk, she asks for my left hand and she folds it within her own, the palms mothering me with a softness borne of magic creams. She rubs the tip of her index finger over the protruding diamond, then the silver block letters of my father's monogram, which I share. She seems to be mouthing something and if she were Catholic I'd reckon on hail Marys.

She remains, I'm proud to say, a pretty woman. From widow's peak to cupid's bow, her face binds the beauties of her generation, and it's a surprisingly fresh and smooth face, sparked by blue eyes gone a tad hazy but by no means faded. A face that has driven five husbands and no doubt countless others, wild. Her white hair is stringy in places but deftly coiffed. She has no competition on this ward. Those who still have eyes to see or the mental faculties to make comparisons must shudder in awe of her. Even if it would bring her sanity back, I would not have her hideous.

She sits in a worn red leather armchair, imported from home, to which she remains anchored all day like a dowager queen. Lionel, her fifth and final husband, hovers over her. He's a robust eighty-three, except for a touch of arthritis in the knees and some stomach problem that nobody has ever explained to me. In contrast to Mom Lionel is hyperactive. He darts about the room but he can only stray so far, till the leash of love jerks him back. He evinces that same mixture of guilt and superiority as all the spouses whose mates lay ravaged in this place. If it were not for Lionel, I'd have to perform a constant vigil here. I've detested him for ten years but really he's a godsend. My mother has no one but Lionel and me, because with each new marriage she took on her husband's family and friends and cast off the old ones. She also assumes her husbands' values, tastes and, in the case of husband number three, his flatulence.

After some prattle about the weather Mom takes my hand again. "That's a beautiful ring. So elegant, isn't it Victor?" Victor was husband number three. They're all interchangeable now, except my own father. I don't know if it's because I resemble him, or am her only child, or if, as I'd like to believe, he was the love of her life—but sometimes when she mentions the period that included him, clarity returns. He has been dead over thirty years.

"You keep it so shiny. Like you polish it. You like my new rings, by the way?" She extends a slightly arched left hand as if for a continental kiss. Two enormous gemstones—one the color of vanilla custard the other of raspberry jello—gleam at me neonlike. They were gifts from Lionel. Mom did not adorn herself

like this in the days of my father, when two slim silver bands with pinhead diamonds satisfied her well enough.

"You polish that thing, Jerry?" asks Lionel.

I shake my head no, but my mother intones, "With an old toothbrush and soap. The bristles get into the crannies. I taught you that myself, didn't I, Little Humming Bear?"

"You taught him well, Laura, ring looks as good as new," chirps Lionel. He has roved to the window, drawn by the sound of sirens. Using his hand as a visor he crooks his neck below the window sash.

My mother's roommate, Annette Western, toddles in on the arm of her full–time attendant. Annette suffers such extreme curvature that she looks like a walking letter C. Lionel nominated her to be the poster child for osteoporosis. Annette is also quite deaf. She has frequent visitors, who shout at her and at each other. She and my mother are as oblivious of each other as two newborns in adjoining cradles in a hospital nursery. "So nice of you to take time off from work, Jared," Mom says. "I hope you don't get behind in your work."

"Looks like a three–alarm fire up the street, that's what all the commotion is about," says Lionel, his nose pressed to the window.

One of the shouting relatives has blared a greeting to Annette. My mother's ears perk up. "Lord, is that Henry come to see me?"

She means Henry Blasingame, the best friend of her first husband. Henry died some time back during the Carter Administration. "I've always had a little crush on you, Henry," she calls to Lionel, who stands at the window captivated by the catastrophe across the street. "Me too," he says.

"Such a beautiful woman, to die so tragically," says Mom.

"Is it Princess Grace you're talking about?" asks Lionel.

"No, Victor honey, it's that busty blonde you always secretly had a yen for. Not that you'd admit it, but I knew. Marilyn Monroe. The one that married that baseball player. Jared here knows everything about baseball, he can tell you how many hours they took to play a World Series game back in 1929, long before he was born. He's got his daddy's head for numbers. He got an A in algebra last year from Ida Tauber, the same old battle axe that flunked me and Lucy Thornton. Of course, Miss Tauber was a <u>young</u> battle axe when she flunked me and Lucy Thornton. Jared's not going to have any use for algebra when he grows up, but it's good to have an A on your record. They can never take those high marks away from you, no matter what you do in life. Unless they find out later somehow that you were cheating. Lionel, honey."

"Yes, dear?" he says, practically flouncing to her bedside. I have spent much of my life pitying and tending to my mother and now, when she most deserves pity, I have none to give. This incoherent being is not my mother but some exquisitely crafted waxwork with a head full of smooth enamel.

"Lionel, would you see somebody about getting us another berth? I'll be damned if I want to ride all the way to Chicago in a berth that flops to and fro."

"But Laura, you know as well as I do that the train is sold out, and they're liable to make us stand if I complain. Anyway, Chicago's only a few hours away."

"Who said anything about Chicago?" screams my mother.

"Did you say Chicago?" shouts one of Annette's shouting relatives from across the room. "We just came in from Chicago." He strolls over to our side of the room, a hand in his pocket jingling some change nervously.

I softly inform him that my mother visited Chicago many years ago and was reminiscing about it. He seems insulted, and returns his attention to his deaf aunt or grandmother or whatever she is.

It's time for my mother's round of soap operas and I can take my leave in good conscience. As I kiss her goodbye she asks to see my ring one more time. "Come again soon. I know you can't come much, seeing as how busy you are."

Lionel follows me into the hall. He squeezes my shoulder.

"Jerry, you might want to avoid taking Elm Street. A building blew up over there. Looks like traffic will be blocked off."

"I'm taking the bus, Lionel."

"Oh, right, you can't drive, can you?"

"Lionel, I know this sounds weird," and Lionel's face relaxes because weirdness has become the norm and nothing will surprise him, "but did my mother send me a baseball?"

"A baseball? Where would she get a baseball?"

"Never mind," I say.

He calls after me. "You know, if she did something like that, I'd be sure to know about it."

I move through the winding corridors toward the elevator,

averting my eyes from the rooms in which people lay petrified in their barless cages. Outside the doors their names appear on little handwritten cards slipped inside a narrow black frame. I never look at these nameplates, fearing that someone I once knew or cared about might be trapped here.

I sign out at the horseshoe shaped nurses station and pass through the lounge with its wheelchaired minions. A loud blare comes from the television monitors suspended at both ends of the lounge, but people sit in stony silence. Not that they all look desolate. One couple, their wheelchairs so close they seem to be joined at the axle, sit with hands entwined and gaze off cheerfully, perhaps at a sneak preview of heaven. A woman with her mouth agog, her face a doily made flesh, waves a pinky at me, as I slant through this withered human hedgerow to the elevator. I haven't been Little Humming Bear for forty years.

Tonight we're all buying for Skretch. He got himself profiled in today's Style section, as the owner of a successful dry cleaning chain. I spotted the article at the library, where I've spent much of the past three days researching the whereabouts of John Byron. My efforts have been futile, but the librarian has taken pity on me. She even gave me a slug to use in the library's xerox machine, so I could bring copies of the article for our group tonight.

My favor goes for naught: Skretch brought umpteen copies to distribute, not just to our table but the manager of the Cattleman, our waitress, and strangers. Skretch loves the picture of him standing arms akimbo in front of this huge vat. He has spent thirty years in the dry cleaning trade, ever since he entered the family business as a teen–ager. He takes pride in his achievements and the photo conveys it.

In the interview Skretch lambastes what he calls "fly–by–night" dry cleaners who go into the business just to make a fast buck. "Any joker with $75,000 can buy a franchise," he says, "and then dupe the public with sales and gimmicks." As to the Chinese, "They do sloppy work. Every Chinese cleaners ought to be named Hoo Cares."

"You might get some nasty letters about that," I tell Skretch.

"I call them as I see them," he snaps.

"It's not too smart to call them as you see them in a large daily newspaper," offers Goode.

"It's in the public interest to know that they can't get decent service from certain businesses. It's my duty, to myself and the dry cleaning industry, to set the record straight," argues Skretch. He tweaks the bill of his Oakland A's baseball cap and takes a swig of the Bud which my un–earned money has helped to purchase. "Besides, that twat hated me. One of these feminists. Like, this nasty question here about why women's clothing costs more to clean than men's. She asked that with a regular snarl."

"I like your answer, though," says Caspary, pointing to his copy, whose edges are weighted down by two beer bottles. "'Our machines' clamps and presses are designed for standard men's shirts—not for ruffles, puffed sleeves, shoulder falsies and Peter Pan collars. It takes me another twenty minutes to hand press a woman's cotton blouse.'" Caspary sells chemicals and Skretch buys perchloroethylene from him by the metric ton.

"That twat did at least save me the last word," says Skretch, pointing to his personal copy, an original mounted on cardboard. "'Convenience is the one true God where dry cleaning is concerned.' I wouldn't mind having that on my tombstone."

"Cost is most important. They'll take price over convenience any time," says Malcolm, a real estate agent.

"Then how do you explain the success of convenience stores?" asks Caspary. "People will pay the extra quarter for a candy bar, if they can buy it when they want it."

Goode pounds the table. "Price and convenience are no substitute for quality. Deep down people want quality, but they've been conditioned by advertising to care only about superficial things." Goode had a terrible day.

I toss in, "My father used to say money isn't everything—but it's convenient."

Malcolm, our newest member, is a master at changing the subject at the first sign of friction. He announces that his ophthalmologist has urged him to consider some new surgery to correct myopia. He doesn't want to get glasses. One thing he learned is that one eye is dominant over the other. He is right–eyed as much as he's right–handed. He tells us to make a circle with our thumb and forefinger, focus on an object, and then try each eye. The eye which sees the object dead center is dominant. "Miller, you're ineligible," says Skretch.

Goode worries my feelings might be hurt. "You guys," he starts to say, but I interrupt. "You're right, Skretch, I'll have to exempt myself. I guess my right eye is dominant by default."

"Sort of like my Barbara. She's dominant by default, too," says Caspary.

Beth Ann, our waitress, hustles over to the table.

"Everything all right here?" she asks.

Malcolm explains that we're doing a test to see which eye is dominant. Beth Ann performs the exercise, concentrating on the clock above the bar, then rushes off to spread the game among the rest of the crew.

I recount to my friends the time I was in third grade and we were learning the parts of the eye. The school nurse brought in a vision chart and we all took the test one by one. When it came to me I went along with it and covered my one working eye. The class was in stitches. They would whisper the letters to me and of course they were all completely wrong. The nurse, ignorant of my medical history, was horrified. "Jerry Miller, you might as well be blind in that left eye. We're going to contact your parents and get you to the eye doctor as soon as possible. And it's not funny," she shouted at my tittering classmates.

Beth Ann swings by with a round of beers and another platter of complimentary barbecued chicken wings and miniature egg rolls.

"How about them Royals, won three straight?" she roars.

Taboo! Taboo! We have each picked one forbidden subject and mine is baseball. Beth Ann laughs and flips us the bird.

"It's called radial ker–a–tot–o–my," says Malcolm. "The surgery, I mean."

"I always knew carrots were great for eyesight," says Caspary.

Skretch wants to know how much this carrot–thing will cost.

Malcolm estimates three thousand dollars or more, none of it covered by insurance. Elective surgery. He'll have to weigh the cost against the joy of never having to wear glasses.

"So here we have it again," blurts Skretch. "Cost versus convenience. I bet Malcolm here will opt for the surgery. Convenience is God."

Goode gives me a lift home. The radio plays The Supremes and Goode switches it off instantly, knowing how most music, especially from a car radio, irritates me. We rehash tonight's meeting. Goode says he tried to give me several openings and wonders why I didn't mention the phantom baseball. I tell him I see no purpose in it, and it might set me up for ridicule, especially since I'm the one who has banned all mention of baseball from our weekly gathering. Goode still suspects Caspary, but Caspary gave no indications of guilt, and I don't think he could have held in the joke for the length of a club meeting. Goode doesn't think the club is fulfilling its purpose, we seem to be getting on each other's nerves. Every week Goode expresses concern about the waning of the group and each week I reassure him. Goode takes a glance back at the empty car seat, perhaps a reminder of his son.

A woman hunkers down on the stoop of my building, not anyone I recognize, but I'm especially blind at night.

"You have a rendezvous, Jerry?" he asks, giving me an elbow.

"Artie, I wish."

Goode drives off. The woman rises from the stoop and I do recognize her, though I'm amazed to see her.

"I came here right after we closed," says Karen, the librarian at the neighborhood branch. I have been running her ragged for three days in search of information about John Byron. I would think the last thing she'd want would be to see more of this pest.

"How did you know where I live?"

"Librarians have ways of finding out anything," she says. Her eyebrows raise a notch and I notice in the glare of the sodium–fed streetlights that she has embellished her eyes and lips and done something different to her hair. Before I can utter another word two little bodies hurtle themselves between us up the steps and through the front door, quick as mice.

"Were those children or midgets?" asks Karen.

"Dwarfs." The Kapinski twins, who live above me on the third floor.

"You have dwarfs in your building," she says, as if they were roaches or Neo–Nazis.

"Now, if we can rewind this conversation, nice to see you, Karen, but why are you here?"

"I have news," she says, and my heart leaps vehemently. "Mr. Miller, I think I've found your John Byron."

I grab her elbows and pull her toward me, gasping against her forehead. I quickly collect myself and release her, but I still feel as if the wind has been knocked out of me. Karen's lips are fluttering with excitement. I think I understand why.

Karen is a pleasant woman in her thirties. I've been putting in some long hours at the library and Karen has, even beyond her professional call of duty, translated my burning urge to know into her own special project.

At first she told me it would be easy. When the information proved elusive she accepted the challenge with relish. We rummaged in the library vault like two kids in grandma's attic, skimming through the past ten years' worth of telephone directories and newspaper obituaries. I was unsettled by the ornamental "D" that heads the death notices, which reminded me of the Detroit Tigers home uniforms. Our excavations were frequently disturbed by the chiming bell at the desk and Karen would rise from her knees, the joints sweetly creaking, and hustle out to answer some query about the capital of Sri Lanka, all the books on the Boston Tea Party for a term paper, the mechanics of glass blowing, why mollusks abdicate their shells, the Spanish word for pigeon, or a plea to be placed on the waiting list for the new Stephen King.

As the quest for Byron proved futile her confidence diminished markedly. It's heartbreaking to see somebody fail when you sense, as I do about Karen, that professional skill is all she can lay claim to. She is unmarried, unkempt and probably uninterested in everything that happens outside the library. I'm not proud that I've stumped her, but after some fifteen hours in her company I figure that if she unearths the merest morsel about John Byron her own euphoria may exceed even my own.

Evidently that is what has happened.

"Have you eaten yet?" she asks, patting her stomach.

Have I or haven't I? The freebies at the Cattleman constitute my regular Tuesday night dinner.

"I'm starved, Mr. Miller. I came directly from the library."

So I'm to be held hostage with some meat loaf. The woman's earned it. "There's a coffee shop around the corner," I say. I head that way and she follows me. "Do you live around here?"

No, she lives about ten miles north of here. The news must be pretty important to take her so far out of her way. I'm bursting to hear about John Byron and my eagerness, compounded by the five beers at the Cattleman, makes the three blocks to Leo's seem miles.

At Leo's Karen indeed orders the meat loaf and two vegetables. I settle for coffee only, though Karen and the waitress try to cajole me into sampling the cherry pie. The coffee shop's fried fragrances also arouse my appetite, but it's clearly my place to pick up the tab and I barely have enough to cover it.

Karen chronicles the series of events that inspired her vocation and brought her to the outskirts of Kansas City. She always loved books, they were friends who offered exciting escape from her stultifying hometown of Chanute, Kansas. As a girl, her nose was always in a book, always dreaming of a better life.

The meat loaf arrives. Karen inhales her plate and reaches for the ketchup bottle. She lavishes ketchup directly on the slab, rather than pouring a heap in the corner of her plate and dipping the slices. Where was I? she asks. I have no idea, but she quickly resumes her story. She lived at home and worked her way through college. Her younger sisters had both married and divorced. She worked in various humdrum offices, getting her library degree at night. Her dream is to eventually work at the large downtown branch in Kansas City. The profession enthralls her, even though "they cut my budget to the bone." You meet lots of people, some of them very interesting. (Is she batting her eyes at me or are they tussling with a mote?) Every day provides gratification in finding some elusive bit of information, directing a patron toward his goal, helping a child. The pay sucks, but her needs are simple. She's never been what you'd call a material girl.

I'm itching for Karen's scoop on John Byron, but she deserves a little slack. "I never spent much time in the library, but after a few days and all the help you've given me, and all your other, uh, customers, I realize why, when the government tries to close down a neighborhood branch the people are up in arms."

I don't add that my own quest is a transitory one. I'll either get an answer, get a job, or whatever, but I'll stop coming.

My praise clearly excites Karen, but in a self-deprecating tone she relates her difficulty in handling this old widower who hovers over her desk every day—"You've seen him, long white hair, pink tinted glasses and brown corduroy jacket"—and harangues her about her resemblance to his late wife. She fears he plans to abduct her or worse. I tell her he's harmless, though if she were my daughter—and she's practically young enough—I'd insist on police protection or some kind of restraining order on this guy.

She bombards me with questions about myself, tactfully avoiding my marital history. I've told her I hold a part-time job at the Hawkins Envelope factory. I plucked that one out of the air. She has no doubt guessed my age, so cruelly betrayed by a profusion of gray hairs. I share with her samples of tonight's repartee from the Cattleman, along with a few anecdotes about Goode, whose cantaloupey visage had shone at her through his windshield. She asks if my friend appreciated the copies of the article; I'm embarrassed that I neglected to thank her for her troubles, and I extend Skretch's gratitude along with my own. That pleases her sufficiently for me to deflect the conversation to John Byron.

So what has she found?

Her eyes swell as if engorged: Well, get ready for this Mr. Miller, hold on to your buggywhip. I have discovered, through sources at a county office, that the will of a Jack Byron was probated a few months ago. Jack as a real first name, not a nickname. Could John Byron have been a Jack?

I've heard of Johns who were Jacks but not Jacks who were Johns. With Byron, as I remember him, anything would be possible.

"I've never seen anyone so passionate as you before, Mr. Miller. It's very attractive. Do you mind my saying that?" I gulp, shake my head. In fact, I'm flattered to the gills. "People come into the library every day, and they are persistent but nothing like you. What does this man mean to you? If you don't mind my prying," she pries.

"I knew John Byron many years ago, over thirty years ago. I believe I did him a great wrong, maybe even ruined his life, for all I know. I was just a teenager. From what you've told me it's very possible that he's died and left something to me as a legacy."

"You mean like a fortune?" She spanks the ketchup bottle with startling violence. Don't ever cross this woman.

"It has nothing to do with money. I haven't seen the man or thought of him in over thirty years. I have no idea what his motives were."

She probes for more, but I don't feel like getting into the story. I don't intend to tell anyone about John Byron, especially now that he's gone, never to resurface again. When the waitress slips the check in between the napkin dispenser and the salt shaker, Karen lowers her eyes into her glass of pop and drinks deep. So I must ante up. I hold my breath and let it out when Karen says she won't need dessert or coffee. I can handle the bill, though the tip will be scanty.

Karen's meal reduces my immediate net worth to a few coins, which jingle in my pocket as we stroll to her car. She takes my hand. A wavelet of lust rushes up my arm like a pain.

I say goodnight but she clings.

"I feel I've come to know a lot about you in a short time, Jared," she whispers, this time definitely batting those lusterless eyes.

So I've totally misread this librarian, unwittingly taken advantage of her, though she came to my place on her own initiative, on the pretext of a professional obligation. It's so rare and downright flattering when a woman makes the first move that till now I've never said no. But I intend to this time, and the only reason I can think of is that the search for John Byron has become so intense that it boxes out any other passions, to the point where I only see Karen as a vessel of information. If I had no Fridays with Joanne, or such freshly painful memories of Sheila...then perhaps.

Still, there's no getting around it: here we stand, a middle–aged bachelor bobbing away from a mildly dowdy temptress whose lips, in this light, ripened with lipstick, loom full, beautiful, primed for passion. Romance hangs in the air, or at least something—probably honeysuckle—hangs in the air, which enchants me like romance. I feel young again, a perilous delusion for a guy on the far side of forty–five. I wish we could neck till our faces grew numb and then never see each other again. I ask my addled mind what day it is. Tuesday. Joanne is four nights behind me and three nights ahead of me.

"I really like you, Karen. You're a special person. You're terrific at what you do. But, I'm engaged to a wonderful woman. It's a deeply committed relationship. If my fiancee even saw us talking here she'd take out a shotgun. She's macho." Several grains of truth, albeit extracted from different wheat fields.

"Does she know how lucky she is?"

"She knows exactly."

I slouch a little to brush her cheek, my consolation prize to her, but mostly my own compensation for the lure of her lips. The supreme kiss–off and Karen knows it. She ducks and I peck the soft evening air.

"Bad timing, the story of my life. Timing is everything," she adds, scooting into her car and slamming the door.

No, my dear, convenience is everything. Convenience is God.

She lowers the window just enough to shoot through an envelope which sails to the ground. Stooping for it I hear the engine rev. Some kind of love letter, some outpouring of the heart that I have callously, needlessly broken.

But no. It's a print out from the county clerk's office, on green shaded paper with that computerized sooty gray type. The will of Jack Enderly Byron was probated two months ago. Mr. Byron died at the age of fifty–two, leaving a wife and two sons, who inherited his rather meager estate. Race, African–American.

Not my John Byron in any way, shape or color. I watch Karen's tail lights vanish like red stars into the silvery midsummer sky. Her left turn signal throbs a farewell. I ball up the file on Jack Enderly Byron and peg him Karen's way, composing in my mind a final image of our relationship: the two of us chortling together that day in the outback of the stacks as Karen with a mischievous glimmer in her dull eyes points to the obituary headed "Leroy G. Bevins, Plumber's Helper."

CHAPTER 2

The summer I turned sixteen I worked as a carryout boy at the Chicken Coop supermarket. I wasn't thrilled to be working in a place called the Chicken Coop, but it was the only job I could get. In February my father had died in a traffic accident at rush hour on the way home from the shoe store he managed. Thanks to his life insurance my mother did not have to get a job, something my father had vowed she would never have to do. I told myself I needed spending money, although baseball came to me via radio and television, and movies I got into free courtesy of my friend Artie Goode, who was working as an usher at his dad's movie theater. I bowled and played pool on occasion. But since most guys my age had found employment I really needed a job for the sake of self–esteem. I could sure use one now.

My father's death left his brother Jake as the only surviving sibling of their large family. Uncle Jake had always been partial to me and he had a lot of money. At my father's funeral, presided over by a rabbi in a bewildering rush of Hebrew, Uncle Jake assured me that if I ever needed anything to come to him. Several people told me that, but only Uncle Jake sounded convincing.

Uncle Jake held an executive position at the Chicken Coop, at that time a fairly prosperous chain with stores all over the Kansas City area. One phone call got me a job.

That first morning my mother stood hovering over the stove in one of my father's dress shirts making breakfast for me. She fried up bacon and then dropped two eggs in the bacon grease, which produced two blackened eggs. She learned to cook them that way growing up in Nebraska and would never change. Amid the crackling skillet and some chokey aromas I studied the box scores from yesterday's ballgames. Maris had hit another homer, Mantle two. Both were on a deadly pace to break Ruth's record, and thereby break my heart.

My mother talked incessantly over breakfast, mostly about current events. This was a new phase. After Dad died she went into a total funk, which disappointed me, because, after all, she'd already lost an earlier husband in the war, why couldn't she cope better this time around? Plus she had me to share her bereavement. But she looked constantly forlorn, dressed exclusively in black, every garment a widow's weed; disdained make–up, contorted her neck–length hair into a bun, wore my father's shirts to bed. Her life, such as it was, centered on TV. She started with Dave Garroway in the morning, lolled before the soaps and game shows by day, reached an emotional apex with Huntley–Brinkley, lounged through sitcoms all night, and bedded down with Jack Paar. Sometimes I'd look in on her before going to school and find her fast asleep, the pewtery illumination of the tube glossing over her like a haze. She devoured <u>TV Guide</u> and worried mightily over the crossword. She once had a crying jag because she couldn't get the first name—only four squares, first letter K—of an actor named Donovan. "He's somebody's husband, I've seen him a thousand times, I can see his long nose, hear his hoarse voice," she wailed.

I didn't mind too much when Mom summarily disowned my father's family and the friends they'd made together, since I figured she intended to devote her time and love to me. She'd never cottoned to Dad's family and vice versa. They wanted her to convert to Judaism. It annoyed me when one of her former friends would call and bitch to me about my mother, or try to wrangle from me her motives for dropping everyone, or get my projection on when she might emerge from this hibernation.

"Everybody's couples," Mom would tell me, "and I hate being a spare tire." Although to me she looked eternally fresh and youthful my mom was pushing fifty and may have been entering menopause. Her vivacity had vanished, without makeup she looked doughy and tired, and her slumping posture made her seem stunted. She never smiled anymore, which made me realize how electrifying her smile had been. It used to be that wherever we went, say, pushing through the revolving doors of a department store, people would beam at her and say hello. "Who was that guy?" I would ask. "I have no idea," my mom would reply. "Then why did he smile at you?" "He was just being pleasant." It took years for me to discover that people are not pleasant by nature. Even at her worst she was still more beautiful than anyone's mom, except Naomi Fischgrund's.

By the time I started working at the Chicken Coop she had become what they now call a news junkie. She soaked up every tidbit from the paper, television and <u>Newsweek</u> and jabbered about it non-stop. It didn't matter whether I responded or even listened. I couldn't know, of course, that the identical pattern would recur after the deaths of her next two husbands. When she had a husband she couldn't care less about America's brinksmanship with Russia, or the atrocities committed in third world countries, or the ups and downs of the nation's economy, or the latest medical breakthroughs. But without the burden of wifehood she readily assumed the burdens of the world, at least in her mind.

My first day Mom drove me to the Chicken Coop and offered to take me in, but I didn't want to seem like a baby. "Just go up to the manager and tell him who you are," she advised, and gave me a big proud kiss. Her eyes were droopy, not from crying, though she did cry often, but from staying up late to watch Jack Paar. As I scooched away she touched my shoulder. "Did I tell you there's a town in

Michigan named Hell? It's got two hundred people, is all, and they've been fighting for ten years to get their own postmark. The government I guess thought the word hell was profane or something. But on July 21, 1961 they'll get their own postmark. Imagine living in a place called Hell. No way of not making a joke about it."

The manager of the Chicken Coop, a nearly hairless man in a bow–tie, scowled down at me from his perch behind the row of checkout counters. I stammered a few sentences and Mr. Kuker jotted down something and then he tossed me a white apron and directed me to the Assistant Manager, Hickey, at that moment chewing out one of the stockboys. Hickey's black eyes, thick eyebrows and gargly sneer reminded me of Lash LaRue.

Hickey asked me my name and I said Jerry; Kuker peered down from the watchtower and shouted, "You told me Jared, J–a–r–e–d. So which is it, bub?" I answered Jerry, because really only my mother ever called me Jared, but then again, I wondered if I should use a more dignified name in the world of work.

Hickey showed me how to punch a time clock. He guffawed when I had trouble lacing the apron in back. A carryout boy whisked me over to the checkout counters to instruct me in the basics of sacking. He worked swiftly and my one good eye was continually obstructed by shoppers and workers. I couldn't tell what to do with things like three–packs of toilet paper or oblong cartons of cereal and it would be weeks before I would develop a system.

The bags were stuffed and heaped onto a metal shopping cart. At the cry of "sacker" my mentor arrowed off to another counter.

"Carryout," shouted the cashier at that station, a plump blond woman with a voice like an air raid. "Hop to it already."

The customer was a man in his thirties, with powerful arms and calf muscles bulging below cutoff jeans. He marched in front of me as I wheeled the cart out to the parking lot. He opened the trunk and waited. "So?" he growled, pointing to the trunk, wherein reposed a huge spare tire. Under his scornful eye I struggled to fit the heavy paper bags into the trunk; the laces of my apron got unstrung in the process and when I started to reach for them I nearly dropped a bag stuffed with sodas, frozen foods, canned goods. The man huffed at me disapprovingly. "Thanks for nothing," he said as he slammed the trunk shut.

I bounced from checkout counter to checkout counter as merchandise flew down the conveyor. I could see other carryout boys sacking rapidly, hands moving in feverish tandem; wherever I stationed myself the cashier had to pitch in with the sacking, which slowed down the lines and infuriated the cashiers. I kept shifting my identity—Jerry, Jared, Jerry, Jared—never telling any two people the same name. I tried to watch how the other guys did it but there wasn't time. In my haste I dented egg cartons and scrunched bread loaves all over the place, and I could envision tomorrow a long line of customers storming Kuker's watchtower, their outstretched arms holding mutilated egg cartons and battered fruit, demanding refunds and pointing their fingers at me.

"Don't they ever train you people?" asked one angry woman customer. "My god," "Jesus Christ." People hurled expletives at me all morning but I had no better chance of catching them than the groceries that kept coming.

During a momentary lull a fellow carryout boy took me on a tour of the store. There were no directories above the aisles so I tried some mnemonics—tomatoes in two, dried fruit in four, salad dressing in six—but it was a lost cause. Aisles were narrow and cramped. Produce men hovered over the vegetables, heaping armfuls onto pendulous scales. They were big stout guys, who looked like they should be slicing meat. I saw one of them pull out a plug of watermelon to be sampled by a customer, who shook her head vigorously. She went through at least three watermelons and I wondered if subsequent tasters, nice women like my mother, could get her germs. Behind the meat counter the butcher, a runt who looked better suited to weighing turnips, paced back and forth conking a cutting board with his fist. Up the aisles men rushed dollies groaning with boxes, which were promptly snatched up by stockboys who ripped the boxes open and heaved the stuff onto the shelves. There was a constant cacophony of shrieking voices, slamming boxes, squeaky carts. MUZAK had not yet been installed to muffle the clamor. In addition to my primary job of sacking and carryout I also had to assist customers or anybody else who needed a hand. I had seldom shopped with my mom and the supermarket chaos overwhelmed me. The floppy apron made me feel like a housewife. I got fleeting introductions to my co–workers, none of whose names registered.

As I hunched over a soft drink display, catching my breath, Hickey thumped my back and barked at me to take thirty minutes and not a minute more for lunch.

My mother had packed me a bag lunch consisting of a bologna sandwich, a box of raisins, two Hydrox cookies and a banana, all of which I figured I could polish off in five minutes and spend the remainder of lunchtime regaining some energy.

I bounded through the swinging door marked Employees Only into the back room. I searched the corner where that morning I'd set my bag on a pile of Birdseye boxes. The boxes had disappeared and so had my lunch. I went foraging. A black cat named Mango strutted in my path as if leading a parade. The frozen food compressor whistled, the back room smelled like mothballs. A covey of staff people sat around on boxes and crates, smoking and chatting. It sounded like the usual boring grown–up chatter, about spouses, money, friends, cars, home appliances. They fell silent a moment when they heard my heels clicking on the cold cement floor, but once they noticed me they resumed their gabfest without anyone inviting me to sit in. I couldn't find my lunch anywhere and I was beginning to suspect Mango. The air was gauzy from cigarette smoke. Profanities, from the women, too, pierced the room, the first time I had ever heard such speech from a woman. Hell and damn were wash–your–

mouth–out offenses in my household, and I conceived an instant dislike for these crude grocery folk.

A sneeze blustered from behind pillars of boxes. I slipped around a column and saw a slight man with dark hair and glasses, sitting cross–legged. He gave me a crinkly smile that vanished like a mirage. He held a sandwich in one hand and a book in the other; when I ventured a step toward him he inserted a finger in the book to mark his place and closed it.

"I'm allergic to that confounded cat," he said, in a smooth, elegant voice that sounded almost British. His expression was not hostile or sour like most of the others. He had a shock of black hair that he slicked back gangster style. A gray forelock gave that patch of his head a skunk–like look. "That cat is a secret, you know. Never tell anyone that the Chicken Coop harbors a ratcatcher in its catacombs."

"I can't find my lunch," I said. I grabbed a plywood apple crate and collapsed onto it. The apron caught on the splintered wood and I tugged at it angrily.

"Your maiden experience with an apron, eh?" he asked.

Unsure that I'd heard him correctly (I did feel like a girl, wearing an apron), I sputtered, "First time with everything. And probably the last."

"Don't let on to Kuker or Hickey that I told you this, but the trick with an apron is to double–knot it," he whispered. "Now, I trust your name was inscribed on it?"

"On my apron?"

"Your lunch. Did you not meticulously write your name, in large cursive in indelible ink, on your lunch bag? If not, you may be out of luck. It's catch as catch can around here. If Mango doesn't get it, one of these desperadoes will." He folded the front dust jacket cover into the book to keep his place. The book rested in his lap. He stroked the crisp paper cover absently.

No, the bag didn't have my name on it. <u>My mother forgot to</u>.

"You are welcome to the rest of my sandwich. I have to return to the salt mines." He offered me half a sandwich wrapped in a paper napkin, braunschweiger with mustard, not my favorite but I gobbled it up. Before I could thank him he said, "And here's a quarter for the pop machine. Kindly reimburse me tomorrow. Same time same station." As I muttered a thank you, he stashed his book on some shelving in a benighted cranny and swept through a side door which led I knew not where.

Hickey awaited me at the time clock. I had forgot to punch out when I went to lunch, thus throwing the entire operation into chaos. "Lots of young guys would kill for your job," he reminded me.

On the ride home I sulked and groaned as my mother peppered me with questions. By nightfall my body teemed with bruises, gashes, slashes, splotches, my hands and feet were laced with calluses. I had foolishly worn loafers, thinking they would look more businesslike. My father had always worn loafers to the shoestore and I had five pairs of them. Tomorrow I would wear tennis shoes. I would come in early and go up and down the aisles and memorize the shelves. I would write my name on my lunch bag and find a secure haven for it. I would bring a quarter for the pop machine.

Uncle Jake dropped into the Chicken Coop early next morning. Before I saw him I heard people chiming "Hi, Mr. Miller" and I had this startling sensation of my father returning to magically rescue me. Mr. Kuker threw on a sportcoat, clambered down from his loft and accompanied my uncle in a shuffle up and down the aisles.

Fortunately, I was in the midst of a simple task, just a few oranges and a cantaloupe with no carryout required. Which I dispatched with rare competence just as Uncle Jake approached. He tousled my hair and said, "Boychick, how's by you? Anyone asks you what you are, you tell them you're a general factotum. That'll show 'em." He chomped on his cigar, which always made me laugh. When I was little he used to put the burnt end in his mouth, roll the cigar between his lips and pull it out still aflame and his tongue unscathed. "By the way, you tell that mother of yours that Eichmann's gonna be sliced up like brisket of beef." Uncle Jake and Mom had quarreled over the Eichmann trial, which had started in Jerusalem a few months before. Mom felt Eichmann deserved to be acquitted.

Everyone at the Chicken Coop seemed to share my fondness for Uncle Jake. He rode a tide of good wishes out the automatic door, which whooshed with extra hospitality just for him. I grinned with pride and newfound confidence, which dissolved immediately under a cry of "Carryout!" from Hugo the cashier. I tried to load too many bags onto the cart, whose bottom rungs tilted under the weight of a ten–pound bag of charcoal briquettes, with the result that I wobbled toward the door with two full bags in my arms and a weak pinky guiding the cart. "Hunh," scoffed Mr. Kuker, who had just bade farewell to Uncle Jake and pumped into the store with his sportcoat dangling by his thumb. At ground level, Kuker was only an inch or two taller than I. His hair receded to the crown of his head; he looked like a half–peeled orange.

Once I'd hoisted this load into the car, a nice older woman thanked me profusely. "You're sweating buckets, young man. Now, you take this and get yourself a sody–pop." She handed me a quarter. "Oh, no, I can't, I said." One of the carryout boys had warned me I'd get canned if I accepted a tip. "But I tip all the boys, and I worked you to death today, young man. Please." She dipped the coin into the front pocket of my apron, which fit snugly, double–knotted. She asked me my name and I opted for Jerry. "Go ahead, you have one on me, Jerry," she said. I hoped she had some brawny soul at home to help her unload. I would have offered to ride home with her and do it myself, I was so grateful for this interlude of decency.

I made sure to punch out at lunchtime. In the back room the klatch was discoursing on <u>The Hustler</u>. No one could believe Jackie Gleason and Paul Newman performed their own trick shots. I'd seen the movie with Goode and his dad and we loved it so much we'd taken up pool at the bowling alley. Artie called me Deadeye. Pool was one sport where having only one eye gave me an advantage.

I found my lunch, got a bottle of pop from the machine and angled behind a produce man perched on a crate. I waited for an opening to voice my opinion of the movie, but people seemed to avert my gaze and each time I started to speak someone broke in. There was some debate about the woman character, whether she was a nympho or just lonely, or whether any woman in the world, lonely or not, could resist Paul Newman. A diminutive woman whom I'd never seen before said Newman could ride her from dusk till dawn, and a low voice—it was Hickey!—rejoined that it would be easy for Newman to ride Lily, seeing as how she was so well broken in. Indeed, Goode and I were mystified about why Fast Eddie's girlfriend killed herself, and what she wrote in lipstick on the mirror before she wolfed down the pills. Goode's dad was too embarrassed to explain it to us.

A stifled sneeze from yonder corner reminded me of the strange man I'd talked with yesterday. There he was again, reading with one hand, eating with the other. I crept back to his domain. Taking a swig of pop I remembered I owed him a quarter. Thanks to the kind old lady I was able to pay him back.

"Much obliged," he said, rising, "much obliged. It's reassuring to know there's one honest man left in the world. Diogenes would run out of kerosene if he hung out too long at the Chicken Coop."

"Whatchareading?" I asked.

"The Winter of Our Discontent. Steinbeck's latest. Heard of him? One of my favorites. Some of this takes place in a grocery. You old enough to read?"

I shrugged. My reading diet consisted of the sports pages, baseball histories and baseball magazines. My dad always read history, thick volumes with tiny print and intricate maps, and I had been making my way through them. My mother stuck to magazines. "I read history and whatever I have to during school," I finally answered. Junior year <u>David Copperfield</u> lay ahead of me, fat and ugly in its blue buckram binding.

"Reading, it is my one great pleasure, doing it to excess is my one great vice. Mind you, at your age, which I gather to be fifteen or sixteen, I read constantly. I would lend you one of Steinbeck's books—you might appreciate <u>Of Mice and Men</u>, but I don't lend books. Neither a borrower nor a lender be, that's my motto."

"You loaned me a quarter."

"Lent you. I bend the rules for those in dire distress."

We ate and gulped together a while. Boisterous laughter echoed throughout the room, the crates creaking under shifting haunches. My companion remained expressionless, but it was a lively blankness with a sly crinkle of a smile ever latent. "You're Miller's boy, aren't you?"

"His nephew. I mean, he's my uncle. Did you see him? He visited the store today."

"I didn't catch him, but I heard the commotion."

"He's popular," I said.

"Really?" The man's hands made a globe in front of his face.

"Well, everybody smiled at him and said hello. They made a fuss over him."

The man looked at me as if revolving in his mind whether to tell me something. He blinked, a sign that he had reached a decision. "I'd better get back to my reading. Only a few minutes left. I have a quota of pages I simply must meet." He opened the book and turned a page very carefully. His hands were small, hairless, delicate.

I twisted my head to see his watch. I had two minutes. Most of the crowd had filtered back to work. The room was silent, except for Mango darting around some boxes, and the compressor.

I wrapped my lunch bag around the pop bottle and tossed the trash into a bin. "Uh, what's your name? My name's"—Jared or Jerry, Jared or Jerry—"Jerry, Jared Miller."

"John Byron," said the man, reaching up to shake my hand, his gaze not straying from the book. "Wait, listen up, Jerry–Jared" and he read, *On Monday perfidious spring dodged back toward winter with cold rain and raw gusty wind that shredded the tender leaves of too trusting trees. The bold and concupiscent bull sparrows on the lawns, intent on lechery, got blown about like rags, off course and off target, and they chattered wrathfully against the inconstant weather.*

The lilting voice and the weird words made a sick music in my ears and I back–pedaled from this strange man, vowing never to spend lunchtime, any time, in his company again. He was just too weird for words.

🍁   🍁   🍁

Eventually I struck up a companionship with Pete, one of the stockboys, with whom I exchanged fleeting observations about baseball. He was a dunderhead. We mostly argued because unlike me he rooted for Mantle and Maris, even hoped both of them would break the record. He wanted to bet me a dollar Mantle would do it in one hundred fifty–four games, but I refused to bet. I had lost a quarter bet, a week's allowance, to my father over the second Floyd Patterson–Ingemar Johansson fight, and I promised Dad I'd never bet again. And I haven't.

I grew fond of talking with customers as I wheeled their provisions through the parking lot. It occurred to me how vulnerable people are at that point, because you're guiding their lives—at least that part of their lives dependent on hygiene and nutrition—in a wire cart across a paved path. I regarded this part of my work as a public trust, overlooking the fact that my incompetence at the checkout counter amounted to sabotage of a goodly portion of the contents of those brown paper bags. I recalled that my father considered small talk the only redeeming thing in a dull day around shoes.

People talked a lot about Jack Paar. Some feared his frequent threats to quit the show and render their late evenings desolate, while others considered his outrages petty, childish, and found great relief in his summer replacements like Jerry Lewis, Bob Newhart, Joey Bishop, Johnny Carson and Lord knows who else. Along with the weather, movies provided another staple of chitchat. Thanks to Goode and his dad, I could discourse on <u>The Guns of Navarone</u>, <u>Snow White and the Three Stooges</u>, <u>The Parent Trap</u> and <u>Tammy Tell Me True</u>. I could usually cajole the rare male customers into some discussion of baseball, and was pleased to find that a huge percentage pulled against Mantle and Maris.

They also complained to me about store items and products, as if I could do anything about it. Plastic pop containers had just been introduced; I appreciated them, from a sacker and carryout boy's viewpoint, but people said they made the pop go flat faster in the ice box. They thought it was a conspiracy on the part of Coke and Pepsi. I remember one fellow insisted that the new aluminum coating used in frozen food packaging would cause cancer. "Now you tell the manager what I say," they would tell me, as if I would have the gall to suggest anything to Hickey, or speak to Kuker if not spoken to first.

I had no time to dawdle. I would speed headlong pushing the cart back to the store, half expecting the evil Hickey to be posted at the door with a stopwatch.

One of my constant fears was that teachers or kids from school would show up and catch me in a fit of ineptitude, or that some cute girl would ask me to secure a gargantuan box of Modess from a high shelf. The very sight of that antiseptic blue box gave me the willies. I blushed every time I had to sack it; once I tried to mask my embarrassment with a grin and this hoity–toity woman dealt me a withering glance. The female menstrual cycle mystified me, along with most things sexual. Mom once gave me a cryptic lecture and later placed on my bed a thick black book, whose baffling illustrations included a penis in cross section with a profusion of colored lines and labels like a road atlas. She also gave me Pat Boone's <u>Twixt Twelve and Twenty</u>, a code of conduct book which said nothing about sex, though it temporarily added "twixt" to my vocabulary. I wondered why the folks who churned out those inspiring Made Simple books about history, geology, math and grammar couldn't come up with a Sex Made Simple.

Fortunately, a lot of the kids I knew had gone away for summer vacation, or, like me, they left the shopping to their mothers. The guys who came in tended to envy me for having a job; esteem rose grudgingly in their eyes. That was nice, that was status. The girls, who had steadfastly ignored me for the full nine months of the school year, took a sudden interest in me and expected me to talk at length, which only incurred the wrath of Hickey and the cashiers.

Worst of all were questions from customers in the store, who interpreted my apron as a tunic of priestly wisdom. Even a month into the job I still had only a vague awareness of where certain things were shelved. I knew the large easily classified items but anything out of the ordinary threw me off. Pete told me to just ignore their questions or direct them to one of the produce guys. Most of the time this worked, but some customers just wouldn't take "wait a minute" for an answer.

One old ogre grabbed me by my apron strap and mumbled what sounded like turkeys. I ushered her to the poultry section, her clinging all the while to my apron, but she shook her head, stamped her feet and hollered turkeys turkeys turkeys. Cashiers cried out for carryout and sacking, and I looked way up to see Kuker's pate rolling to and fro. The woman had hold of me and wouldn't let go. Customers passed by us laughing. Turkeys turkeys turkeys the woman screamed. She gripped my apron with one hand and flailed with her other arm, and I thought she was going to roundhouse me.

Finally Hickey joined us. "What's all this ruckus, you knothead," he said to me. "She wants turkeys, but I showed her the turkeys," I said. Hickey had rolled the sleeves of his white shirt up his arms and when he placed his hand on the woman's shoulder I could see the raw red elbows. "Now, m'am, what can I find for you?" he said gently. "Turkeys enagag," is what I heard. Hickey snapped his fingers. He led the woman back to her abandoned shopping cart and then two aisles down he plucked down a bag from its metal clips. The bag seemed to contain motley granules, like crushed bouillon cubes. Hickey shoved the bag into my face, tapping an angry finger at the Durkees label. The woman smiled a toothless smile. "Now go sack," Hickey said with a wrathful flourish of his arm, like an ump giving a manager the old heave–ho.

By now two of the registers were backed up. I chose Howard's, one of the more tolerant cashiers, and worked as rapidly as I could. Pushing a cart on the sidewalk I swerved to avoid a freshly laid pile of dog–do. As I returned from the parking lot I saw Kuker standing over the heap, bodily fencing it off from customers. He signaled to me and clapped his hands, "Hey you, clean up this mess. Pronto."

I cornered Pete, who told me, "You don't have to do it, Jerry. The union says we don't have to do that kind of thing." I didn't think that would wash with Kuker, who was eyeing us from his perch. I sailed into the back room in search of a shovel or something. A man was putting sticker prices on M&M's. The store had big sales on M&M's that summer, because of an ad promotion tying in the candy with Mantle and Maris, the M&M boys.

When I told the man I had to clean up dog–do on the sidewalk he just smiled. I asked two other guys what to do and ran around in a dither until I discovered John Byron in a distant corner with his nose pressed close to a clipboard. He must have heard my pleading voice, because he looked up and offered his crinkly smile. "Is there some emergency?" he asked. His voice was so soothing.

"I have to clean up some dog–do on the sidewalk. Mr. Kuker said I have to."

"Ah, the canine detail. Messy work, Jerry–Jared." He took my arm and led me to a scrub closet, where a dustpan hung by a nail on the wall.

"Is it a mountain of dog turds, or just a molehill?" he asked.

"Kind of in between," I said.

He reached into a paper towel dispenser and snatched about ten towels. "Now, into the trenches with you," he said.

The dog–do had attracted moans of disgust, gleeful cries from kids, and hundreds of flies. Sidewalk traffic had become like an obstacle course, with folks slanting this way and that. The mound looked larger than before, as if in my absence the hound had returned to make another deposit. The sun had baked it and the fumes rose sickeningly. I knelt, almost toppled over, and broke the fall with my hand, which landed just inches from the dungheap. I tucked my apron under my knees, put my knees to the sidewalk and began scooping up the mess into the dustpan with the paper towels. It seemed like hundreds of people skirted to avoid me, and there was lots of razzing.

"Why, it's Jared Miller," I heard a voice, the dreadfully recognizable voice of Naomi Fischgrund, the Black Widow. We called her the Black Widow because she was so hideous her kiss could kill. When we biked past her street we would hold our breath in disgust, so as not to inhale any of her toxic ether. "How can that be, her mother is so attractive?" my mom wondered. Obviously Naomi took after her father.

And now to have this homely girl hovering over me at this degrading moment. She giggled. A light green chameleon reposed on her shoulder blade. She saw my gaze go there and said, "Isn't this cool? All the girls are doing it. This is Boris and he'll sit there for hours and hours. Say hi to Jared, Boris." Yeah, cool, I said. I swaddled the dogshit in paper towels and raced with the dustpan through the store and into the back room, where I shoveled the mess into the toilet. I lingered there long enough to allow Naomi to shop and be gone.

It was doubly mortifying to see Naomi Fischgrund because I had dreamed about her only a few weeks before. A dream that haunted me, bewildered me.

In the dream, which retains its fulsomeness after thirty years, I'm proceeding on and on down a pitchblack alleyway silent but for the shuffle of my hush puppies and the faint rattle of a trashcan, utterly alone, till a weaving silhouette smacks into me, revealed by a ribbon of moonshine to be the emaciated, titless, speckled, septic–tank–haired Naomi Fischgrund, the Black Widow. I start to run then stop, because by some miracle I'm excited out of my mind by her, ready to flout death to taste her lips. Which I do. When we at last come up for air the Black Widow clamps her claws on my shoulders and twirls me round and round and when the spinning ceases I see her freckles have turned a sickening green, to match her eyes; she's tweaking her chestnut breasts with her fingertips just like the girls in <u>Playboy</u>; and when she peals like a cowbell into the sultry night air on rush the mad pulsations like sap being chugged out of me and I'm jolted awake, damp on forehead and crotch, horrified that I've wasted myself on this girl, and frightened that if anyone ever found out—but how could they?—I would be ruined.

❦   ❦   ❦

Biking home from work gave me a nice interlude to brace myself for my mother. She was sullen and dejected most of the time, and had cut herself off from any sympathizers. That whole summer I measured my life by my mother's moods. Her eyes would well up at odd moments, such as dishing me up green beans with fried onions and mushrooms, one of my father's favorites, and nothing I could say or do gave her any consolation.

Although I earned under a dollar an hour minus union dues and social security, I reigned as the man of the house, if not exactly a breadwinner at least not merely a bread consumer. I intended to blow my first paycheck at Joe Sprung's bowling alley and pool parlor but, as happened so often that summer, my mother's needs got in the way. Father's Day was coming up, the first one without my dad. Mom talked about it for weeks and I desperately sought some way to help her through it. <u>Gone With the Wind</u> was revived that summer and my mother sighed the morning she saw it advertised in the morning paper. She mentioned wistfully that her first husband had taken her to that movie when it premiered in Kansas City back in 1939, twenty–two years ago. I volunteered to take her, all expenses paid, that coming Saturday, Father's Day weekend. As she hugged me the sleeve of my father's gingham shirt dipped into the blackened egg yolk and dragged across my plate.

She picked out my wardrobe: light gray khakis, a blue rayon short–sleeved shirt, and, instead of the hush puppies I wanted to wear, a snug pair of black loafers. She herself eschewed her usual black for a bright yellow scooped–neck dress. She said we would run into all sorts of people we knew; in her eyes, the occasion may have represented her first baby step back into society. I bought her popcorn and a Coke, and some Milk Duds for myself.

She cried all through the film, maybe harder than she cried at Dad's funeral. Her tear ducts operated at full tilt that whole summer, but <u>Gone With the Wind</u> marked a kind of pinnacle. Women were weeping all around us, so she didn't embarrass me too much and I figured she really was crying over the dead little girl and Ashley Wilkes, and not over her own miserable life. Then again, I recall that she downright squalled at that moment before intermission where Scarlett claws the earth for tubers and vows never to be hungry again. Perhaps Mom was secretly vowing that she would never again starve for companionship, that she would marry repeatedly if necessary.

I worried about Mom too much to enjoy the movie, not that I would have enjoyed it under the best of circumstances. Goode, of course, worships <u>Gone With the Wind</u>. He's read books about how they made the movie and he's even got the soundtrack on record and CD. He may own every soundtrack ever recorded.

<u>Gone With the Wind</u> has returned umpteen times, and of course now you can get it on videotape, but my mother has refused ever to

see it again. Seeing the movie when it and her life were both fresh, and later seeing it with her dear son, consummated the experience for her. She still mentions that date sometimes, in her current miasma.

I escorted my mom through much of that summer and into the fall. We would go to musicals at the Starlight Theater in Kansas City, an open–air theater that I hated because it was invariably muggy, rife with mosquitoes, the pop was watery, and the shows were terrible. We saw <u>Oklahoma</u>, <u>Annie Get Your Gun</u> and the one I remember best, <u>Gypsy</u>, because the male lead was clearly looped and kept forgetting his lines, which provided me some amusement and fodder for gossip with my customers at the store. Mom imposed certain movies on me, like <u>Fanny</u>, which I was embarrassed to admit seeing. The films I really wanted to see were the ones with racy ads in the paper, usually portraying a couple in a feverish embrace or a disheveled woman in her underthings. <u>Claudelle English</u>. <u>Parrish</u>. <u>By Love Possessed</u>. <u>A Summer Place</u>. And most of all <u>Return to Peyton Place</u>. I had squirreled away a paperback of <u>Peyton Place</u> with select pages dog–eared for erectile reference.

It was a week or so after <u>Gone With the Wind</u> that the first of a strange series of events took place at the Chicken Coop. The Fourth of July was coming up and the new fifty star flag was to be inaugurated. The store was planning all sorts of festivities, including an appearance by the mayor and one–day sale prices on items stickered red, white, or blue. The employees all thought this was a crock and during their lunchtime caucus they traded puns and off–color jokes. As usual I strolled the perimeter, sandwich in hand. Someone remarked that the stupid gimmick had been dreamed up by Jake Miller, and sidelong glances came my way amid titters. At that point Herbie, one of the stockboys, pranced into the room with his hands behind his back.

"You won't believe what I found behind a can of Crisco," he said.

"A hundred dollar bill?"

"Jackie Kennedy?" piped up another voice.

"A dead mouse? Here, Mango, here Mango."

"A douche bag?"

Herbie frowned. "Damn, you're awful warm," he said, somewhat discouraged. But his smile returned when he pulled his hands forward, to a chorus of stupefaction.

"How in God's name?"

"Who would have done that?"

"Never in all my twenty–two years!"

"Judgment Day is upon us!"

"It's a communist conspiracy."

Looped around Herbie's index finger was a pair of pink panties, and decidedly not a new pair either. Everyone rose to get a better look. I remember my own mixture of alarm and erotic frenzy. A lovely maiden sprang to mind, probably Miss June, stripping off her underpants and placing them lovingly behind a can of Crisco, then…well, I didn't know exactly where to take it from there. Herbie snapped the elastic, a produce guy snatched them away and the chase was on. I felt a hand on my shoulder.

"Mind you, it is deeds such as these that mark an epoch," laughed John Byron, and I realized why he opened his mouth so reluctantly—the lower front teeth that seemed to collapse on top of each other.

CHAPTER 3

❀

I can tell Malcolm is surprised to hear from me, from the pause when I say it's me calling. Except for Goode, I seldom communicate with our group members beyond our Tuesday sessions.

First I make him promise to keep this in confidence. Goode is the only other person in the world who knows about Byron, not counting Karen, who doesn't count. My desire for secrecy is not as strong as my desire to find Byron.

Malcolm at his office adopts a clipped, businesslike tone, which suits me fine. I can be businesslike, too. I tell Malcolm how I received an old baseball from a man I haven't seen for over thirty years, how I've tried to track the man down, he's not listed anywhere, and I wonder if Malcolm in his capacity as a realtor has any bright ideas, such as a title search or any county records, or anything. Malcolm sounds annoyed, but he agrees to do some delving.

He may feel he owes me one, because it was I who recruited him for our Tuesday night group. Every week we used to see Malcolm stationed on one of the Cattleman's red vinyl barstools, alone. He had the air of a man expecting someone, but no one ever joined him and he would toddle off after a while. He seemed comfortable with waiting. I admired that. I started greeting him with "Hello there," and so did Goode and the other guys. We never asked his name. We referred to him as "The Hello There Guy."

Skretch and Caspary balked when I proposed inviting him to join our table. Malcolm is black, and on occasion those two like to disparage minorities, especially "the nigras." "It's going to mess up the integrity of the group, it's like asking a woman to join," Skretch protested. "It will make us too inhibited. We won't be able to joke as freely," added Caspary.

But Goode sided with me and we held sway as charter members of the group. It started when Goode and I would just get together for a drink at the Tuesday happy hour, the only time he could work me in. Gloria and the baby were locked in breastfeeding's bond, and it was she who suggested that Goode and I institute a weekly boys' night out. Goode met Caspary when Caspary sold him disinfectant for the theater's washrooms; he enjoyed Caspary's sense of humor and I okayed letting Caspary join us. Caspary brought along his best friend Skretch, and though Goode and I found Skretch a bit abrasive he did add diversity to the group.

So that night I waved to Malcolm, who strode over with a "thought you'd never ask" grin. I had violated one of the sacred rules of the group, namely that we should never expand our number to five. But I couldn't resist the opportunity to stir up Skretch and Caspary. The group was growing stale and I thought Malcolm would add a new flavor, not to mention color. He turned out to be such a pleasant fellow that we formally installed him as a member a week later.

I don't know if Malcolm really feels obligated to me or is just being neighborly, but he asks me the precise neighborhood where this John Byron lived. That I can do. I only visited the house one time, thirty plus years ago, but I do know the general neighborhood.

Talking to Malcolm inspires me. On a whim, and with time to burn, I decide to venture there myself, on the hunch that Byron might still inhabit the old house I visited over thirty years ago. Not all old folks migrate to Florida or sit desiccating in nursing homes. Yes, I can picture John Byron in that stately two–story house, a bachelor, slumped in that cushioned cane rocker and surrounded by Louis the Something furniture and doodads in the living room where we had our last talk, his scalp now overrun with silver (thus camouflaging the skunkish forelock), squinting at his precious books through thick lenses, bereft of his few friends and kin, all dead or offended, Byron himself now idle and addled—when a notion hits him like a thunderbolt forcing the Hemingway to drop to his feet: the Chicken Coop…what was the name, Jeff? Johnny? Jimmy? Minor? Mueller? Miller, Miller. His frail heart thumps in his chest, his temples pulse as he marshals his ebbing faculties. All the frustrations of his life literally roll up into one ball, which he'd like to heave through the window of that despicable boy who must now be middle-aged. Now, where in God's name have I stashed that old thing? he asks himself. He stomps his cane, rests both palms on its curved handle and boosts himself up. He inches up the stairs. He has not been to the third floor attic in decades. He's not sure he can make it.

    I'd love to trap the old coot in his lair and put it to him: "What possessed you?" But what I hope and what I can expect are two different things. I have no memory for locations. Goode says it stems from my never learning to drive. If you drive somewhere you tend to remember how you got there. But I did once bike to Byron's house, which stood about a mile from the Chicken Coop. I remember his street had a name like Elm or Oak or Chestnut or Maple. The phone book has a street guide and I circle the general area, where a cluster of streets bear tree names.

    When my bus gets to the vicinity I get off at the first street with a tree name. I stop everyone and pose my burning question. I ask the mothers and nannies and househusbands who hunker down on the stoops, corner-of-the-eye watchful. I intrude on a group of girls jumping rope to those convoluted rhymes that only prepubescent girls can master. I even stop a small boy costumed as Batman who has sailed toward me with his arms outstretched and so enraptured that I don't have the heart to inform him that his hero, despite the cape, cannot fly.

Everyone young and old is cheerful, friendly, unable to help. Several wish me a nice day, and a sparkling June day it is. Huge continent-shaped clouds cruise overhead, so that the sky mimics a flat map of the world. Blossoms float in the air like pastel snowflakes. Forsythia and dense green hedges front many of the houses, including this one, where a man rocking in a porch swing waves and calls, "Hi, neighbor." His house is of weathered white clapboard with limegreen shutters. From the sidewalk I holler that I'm looking for a man I knew many years ago, name of John Byron, and he nods and says the name sounds familiar. I follow the winding sidewalk and skip up four stone steps.

"Sit a while," says the man, pointing to a white wicker chair. He pushes back his Royals baseball cap to reveal a high sunburned forehead whose black freckles look like swatted flies. "Name's Walter Kempton," he says, flicking his fingers. "Jerry Miller," I say.

"It's John Byron you're looking for? Well, I'll place him, but while I search my memory would you care to see my collection?" Before I can reply a gray-haired woman flounces onto the porch. Walter introduces her as his wife Edna, and she pours me a glass of homemade lemonade from a sweating pitcher.

Walter tells her that I have come to see his collection and they hook arms to lead me into their home. As we trod through the dining room an opalescent chandelier jangles and a grandfather clock dongs four times. The rugs and furniture are frayed but dying with dignity. At the top of the carpeted staircase the Kemptons veer left into a room bursting with sunlight. It faces onto a spacious back yard whose colorful garden is in bloom. My pride and joy, Edna says. John Byron, John Byron, it'll come to me, Walter keeps muttering.

At the center of the room are two twin beds pushed together, each with a tightly tucked white chenille bedspread. The walls are bare except for a poster of Kansas City's 1970 Super Bowl champions and something else in a small wooden frame. The surface of an oaken dresser is strewn with framed pictures. Against the long left wall stand two sheds, each over six feet high, one all shingles of gray wood with a sloping roof, the other a flat–top of gleaming mahogany. Each shed is cordoned off by a thick velvet rope slung between brass stanchions.

"You see before you, young man," Walter announces, "the finest collection this side of Tennessee." I assume Walter refers to a display case resting upon the window seat and, over the beds and extending the width of both of them, a shelf mounted on hardware holding what looks like doll house furniture.

Mrs. Kempton drops her head to one side and smiles, "Walter, don't boast. For all we know, this Jerry here has a collection of his own, completer than yours."

I explain to her that I'm looking for John Byron, a man who used to live in this neighborhood. The street had a tree name, like Walnut or Maple.

"You're on Chestnut," says Edna. "Walter, I thought you said this young man had come to see your collection." Her husband shrugs. Mr. Byron does not ring a bell with Edna but she has always been a homebody and Walter knows hundreds of people even in this very neighborhood she has never met. He retired five years ago, after forty years with Kansas City Power and Light. Her chin ruts into her neck and she eyes me suspiciously. "People come from all around to see Walter's collection. He's been written up. You a dealer, Jerry?"

"Edna, don't talk like this man's here under false pretenses. He stated his business plainly before you even came on the scene. Jerry, if a John Byron ever lived around here we'd know him for sure. I'm just trying to place him exactly." Mrs. Kempton offers to get me another lemonade and I accept, figuring I might have a better shot with Walter with her out of the room.

"Edna's not been so neighborly lately." He pronounces it Ed–i–na. "We were broken into a few months ago. Two colored men with Lone

Ranger type masks. Held guns to our heads, stole Edna's jewelry. She's fearful."

"I don't blame her." Edna returns in a trice, as if to rescue her husband. I ask her about the pictures on the bureau.

"This used to be our sons' room," she says. She shows me several double framed pictures of the boys at various ages. Dicky died in Vietnam. Walt Junior lives in Overland Park, Kansas, and owns a chain of very successful photocopy centers. Lickety–Split Copy. I compliment Walt Junior's family, though his wife looks terminally frumpy and one of his boys is cross–eyed.

Walter stamps his foot. He has unlatched the velvet rope that guards the shingled shed, whose door he now raps three times. "Edna, my dove, Jerry didn't come to hear about the saga of the Kempton family." He flings open the door to reveal a wooden platform with two large holes, its walls hung all around with a ball peen hammer, monkey wrench, scythe, shears and assorted garden tools. A narrow shelf juts from the wall to the left, on which rests a thick Sears catalog dated 1947, and two artificial corn cobs, one reddish brown and one yellow.

"That's really something," I say.

"I take it you didn't grow up on a farm." I shake my head. "Even better. You can appreciate an outhouse like this as a piece of history, not just a fancy crapper."

"Walter," scolds his wife.

Walter clucks at her. He tugs the chain. A cataract echoes in the chamber. Walter chortles when I jump.

"What is that star for?" I ask, pointing to a cut–out at the top of the door.

"Means it's for men, though ladies could use it in a pinch. The lady's john usually has a crescent moon on the door. The opening also provides your ventilation," says Walter.

I ask Walter to open the mahogany companion, but he takes my arm and leads me to a cabinet on the window seat, which holds a village of outhouses of all sizes, maybe twenty of them. Walter proudly points out the richness of detail, the carving artistry, and I am duly impressed. Not all are made from wood. One was carved from a black lump of coal, another from a red brick that evidently used to be part of a brick outhouse. Another twenty or so specimens grace the shelves above the beds. Three of them play music when you open the door or pull the chain: "Jingle Bells," "Go Tell Aunt Rhody," and a third tune I don't recognize. There is even a tiny outhouse swimming in a bottle, complete with a Sears catalogue.

Edna, reading my thoughts, says, "Now, we didn't have Walter's collection in here when the boys were growing up. We used to store it in the cellar. And then, Walter didn't go the whole hog with this till maybe twenty years ago, after Walt Junior moved out. We pushed the beds together to make room for Walter's collection."

"This I bought at a auction in Chillicothe, Kansas," says Walter, referring to a framed poem on the wall. "The Passing of the Outhouse," by James Whitcomb Riley. It is handwritten, autographed by one of Riley's descendants. "The interesting part is the frame. It was made from the seat of an old outhouse behind a church in Riley's hometown in Indiana."

"We read some Riley poems in grade school, I think."

"The poem's okay, I guess. It's the frame that's special." "Another?" asks Edna. I have downed my second tumbler of lemonade, using gulps to disguise my lack of astute observation. Still, my mouth feels as if I've inhaled sawdust. I request one more, praising the lemonade as the best I've ever tasted.

"Grew up on a farm outside Hays, didn't see an indoor toilet till I was sixteen," Walter confides. "There was nothing glamorous about crapping outdoors," he adds, as if I had suggested there was. "It stank to high heaven, was colder than a witch's tit in wintertime, and summer it swarmed with water bugs, mud daubers, snakes, ticks. Got seven ticks on my balls once when I was little and my older sister lanced them off."

Edna steps into the room with my third dose of lemonade.

She glowers when I ask how much this collection might be worth. Does she suspect me of casing the place? Walter just scratches his chin and says it's somewhere in six figures.

"So, do you collect anything, Jerry?" asks Edna.

"Not since baseball cards, when I was a kid."

"Now get a load of this," says Walter, who has unlatched the velvet cord and climbed the steps to the mahogany outhouse. When the door swings open it trips on a small jukebox in a cranny behind the commode. Walter explains each detail as Al Jolson croons "April Showers," then "California Here I Come." Ornate likenesses of ducks are carved throughout the woodwork like motifs in wallpaper. There are three toilets with brass hinged mahogany covers. The pull chains are silver plated, the base of each commode bears a woman's face with tresses streaming down over a thrusting bosom, like the prow of a ship. An oval stained glass window hangs just above the middle toilet. A side bench groans under the ubiquitous Sears Catalog, this one bound in resplendent red leather. The floor is covered with an Oriental runner.

At Walter's insistence I step carefully over the velvet rope and take the steps one at a time. When I lift a wooden cover to gaze down into its deep well Walter hollers, "You gotta switch on the light," pointing to a switch where a modern–day flush handle would be. The inside of the vault lights up and I see blue, yellow, orange, all colors of fish swimming in a turquoise sea. Aquatic sounds gurgle from some invisible speaker.

"That does it. That's my coopdegrass," chirps Walter, who offers me a hand as I emerge glassy–eyed from the hallowed chamber.

As I follow the Kemptons downstairs my bladder expands to a watermelon in diameter, from all the lemonade.

"Now, what would you say this John Byron looked like?" asks Walter over his shoulder.

His question startles me. The John Byron of 1961 had black hair with a white streaked forelock, stood two inches higher than I and had the sonorous voice of a late–night deejay. That doesn't give Walter much to go on. The man may be dead or have moved away. He has no listed number. Early on I thought of calling the police and asking for missing persons, but Byron isn't missing just because I can't find him.

Walter slaps the newel post just as he had done before we climbed the stairs. Perhaps it's a private superstition. "You write down your name and address, you hear? So I can let you know when it comes back to me. Edna, get that pad over there and a pencil."

Edna smiles at me. "You playing hooky from work, Jerry?"

"I've got flexible work hours." The grandfather clock chimes, drowning out the end of my sentence. I am seized with a double ache, to urinate and to get away from here.

"You got much experience in gardening? I could use a helping hand." We're now on the porch and she gestures toward the backyard garden we had viewed through the upstairs window. "You've got the knuckles of a horticulturist."

"Thank you, no. My knuckles may be okay, but I have the opposite of a green thumb. I don't know a peony from a piano."

She squints as if she intuits there's an unemployment check in my wallet. "You don't need to know anything, except how to dig and how to take orders from an old lady."

"You've seen nowhere near my whole collection," says Walter. "I got a passel of life–size specimens in storage with my cousin Ray, near Osceola. There's a honey of a one, made of white brick and a louvered door I'd put on the second floor here, if we could get rid of those beds." He leans toward Edna, accusing her with a thrust of his shoulder.

"Walt Junior's kids spend the weekends here sometimes," Edna informs me.

"Not any more, those kids are grown up. We could move the beds to the cellar, for guests."

I shift weight from foot to foot. "I've got to run, folks. Thanks so much for a fascinating afternoon." As I head off Walter calls out, "John Byron, John Byron."

I stride briskly up the street toward my bus stop. Employed people are returning home and children are getting in their last licks before dinnertime. The cloud continents have merged into one huge gray nimbus, blotting the sky. I sprint toward a shoulder–high hedge that leans against a chain–link fence. The coast seems clear so I let fly, but in midstream comes a growl then fierce barking and a boxer charges the fence and hurtles itself against the wire mesh. The impact jolts me sideways. When I hear the sharp cry of a woman I scamper away and pass three bus stops before I consider myself safe. I've just begun to catch my breath when a bus arrives, and I board it with my hands clasped to shield my lap.

❦   ❦   ❦

You might think, upon learning that I'm on the far side of forty–five, never married, and that I've lived with my mother periodically during my adult life, that I am a classic mama's boy. Or a closet homosexual—the conclusion of a shrink I saw once, at the behest of a woman who couldn't accept my refusal to commit myself to her and thought I needed to have my head examined. My lunacy consisted in dating her at all: she had a snide way about her, she smoked, wore a faint mustache she refused to depilate, and insisted on playing Vic Damone records during sex. Marie was Catholic, the eldest of eleven children and I remember while making love to her I would try to filter out the Damone by conjuring the names of her ten brothers and sisters in chronological order.

The women I've cared for were opposites of my mother. My mother has light hair and eyebrows so faint they look sketched in by chalk. My girlfriends have always had bushy eyebrows. They've also been busty, ample of hip and thick of thigh, whereas my mother, were she a wrestler, would occupy the same weight class as Nancy Reagan. Sheila was the only woman I ever proposed to, and our break–up had nothing to do with my mother. The seeds of destruction were sowed the night we met.

Which was a Tuesday night at the Cattleman back when my men's club comprised just four of us, pre–Malcolm. We had drunk well beyond our capacity when Caspary took out a bright orange ballpoint inscribed with the name of the company he sells for, Chem-Find. Holding the pen aloft, Caspary filled us in on an old salesman's trick: you "mistakenly" leave the pen behind and the prospect nabs it, thinking he's gotten something for nothing, and that you must be scatter–brained, easy to get the better of in a price negotiation. Oh, it's very subliminal, Caspary protested, when we all moaned. Caspary said, "I mean it, it works. The potential customer finds this free pen and he's happy as a clam."

Skretch, just to be contrary, said, "Now, just how happy is a clam, anyway?"

Caspary piped up, "For that matter, how cute is a button?"

"How sharp is a tack?" I contributed, and we were launched on a trail of one–upsmanship.

How hot is a two–dollar pistol? How much do bunnies fuck? How cold is a witch's tit? How tight is a drum? How sober is a judge? How flat is a pancake? We might have gone on indefinitely, if a woman with a purposeful look on her face had not suddenly materialized between Skretch and Caspary. I assumed a penitential frown, thinking we had disturbed a party at a nearby table and the woman had marched over to shush us up.

"I'm in a jam and one of you guys has got to help me out," she said. She stood erect, resolute, her voice deeper than mine or Caspary's; she hardly suggested a damsel in distress. She nonetheless plaintively told us that she had to go to a big dinner party and her date, the lousy fuckhead, had stood her up. She had come to the Cattleman expressly to find a suitable replacement, and she had zoomed in on our table because we were all cute, presentable guys with terrific senses of humor. So which of us would volunteer to escort her to the party tonight?

Goode, happily married with an infant son, instantly disqualified himself. Skretch also had a wife and Caspary was living with someone, though both men held themselves open to new sexual horizons. They shuddered with temptation, then after a quick glance counted themselves out. Skretch pointed to me.

"Jerry here's your man. The rest of us are spoken for."

Caspary chimed in, "Yeah, Jerry was picked as one of the Kansas City area's most eligible bachelors, in a recent straw poll."

"And that ain't hay," added Skretch.

The woman ignored them. She swaggered toward me, sizing me up, this winner by default, till she suddenly arrived on my left, my blind side, and I had to shift my seat to get a better look. Then her hand touched my thigh, sending erogenous shock waves through my body. My thigh is my Achilles heel where sex is concerned. Although a bit tipsy I was sober enough to know my judgment was cloudy, so I looked to Goode for guidance. He squinted, as he does when he's weighing options. He had his hands folded in front of his face, and when he wagged his thumbs at me I knew I had the go signal.

I plunked a ten on the table, roughly my share of the bill, and rose. In fact I wobbled. My cohorts bade me a boisterous farewell. The woman grabbed my shoulder to steady me; the steely grip startled me—that should have been my warning right there. She asked about my car. When I confessed I didn't drive she looked at me as if I were a leper and nibbled her upper lip. Oh, God, I've picked a loser, I could hear her thinking. As we climbed into her yellow pick–up she introduced herself as Sheila. She tightened my tie, brushed some debris from my lapel and patted my face. We swerved past the payment booth. Sheila waved at the attendant, informing me that she owned this lot. In fact, I own lots of lots all over town, she added.

The party was held at a large downtown Kansas City hotel in a lavish ballroom that felt terribly overheated, although my semi–inebriated state might have influenced my body temperature. A glitzy placard heralded the occasion as a banquet to honor area businesswomen. I downed two bourbons as Sheila tugged me pillar to post. A few men wore tuxedos, but most wore simple business suits like my own, though of a better make and more recent year. It mattered little, because no one took any interest in me, beyond wondering what I did for a living. I slurred in response that I was an actuary, not bothering to add that I was the last of the one–eyed actuaries.

We feasted on what Sheila later described as latex chicken and peat moss broccoli. We endured several droning speeches. A man across the table from me inadvertently blotted his mouth with the tail of his tie. To my amazement, this clumsy fellow later stepped to the podium and recounted the poignant tale of a twenty–five–year–old woman who spent a desperate winter living in the freezing back room of a parking garage, shivering under a musty army blanket, with an antiquated kerosene heater as her sole source of warmth. That young woman came from a working–class family, had never finished college, and lived utterly alone, yet never forsook her dream of success, and after ten years of unremitting hard work she's become a business force to reckon with, in an industry that eats strong men for breakfast, not to mention a young woman. Ladies and gentlemen, we are proud tonight to honor Miss Sheila Crenshaw.

My date rose to thunderous applause. An extremely tall fellow with gold cufflinks the size of golf balls pinned a purple ribbon on her blouse. All eyes were on us, so I kissed Sheila on the cheek and tried to look proud. She touched my thigh several times under the table, but otherwise ignored me during the meal. I tried to make conversation with an elderly woman to my left, who had a teal blue hearing aid in each ear, like earrings that had migrated. She either ignored me or couldn't hear me, but I knew she could talk because she bawled out the waiter over two lemon seeds swimming in her gin and tonic.

While I was scarfing down a slice of strawberry cheesecake a band began to play loudly. People stampeded the dance floor. I explained to Sheila that I was an atrocious dancer. "I love to dance, but most guys just won't. Except gays." She glanced at me sideways. "But you're not gay, are you?"

I couldn't tell which response she would have preferred. It momentarily stung me that she could question my sexuality. Then again, I felt no particular attraction to her, beyond the titillation of her picking me up in a bar; as she enlisted me for company, not sex, I hadn't flirted with her or engaged in the repartee two people perform when sex is in the offing. I regarded myself as her retinue of one, here only to bask in her moment of fame. She said, what the fuck we had to dance once just for appearance's sake, then we could split. She had to be up at six in the morning anyway. We danced at a distance of a yard to "You Really Got a Hold On Me," which Sheila later designated as <u>our</u> song.

The parking lot attendant smiled at Sheila and asked her to give her regards to someone named Jimmy. I gave Sheila directions to my apartment and the yellow pick–up growled into the night. Sheila manhandled the stick shift with an intensity that made the car lurch like a beestung mule. Hillbilly music blared from the radio, partially drowned out by the rumble of the engine. I shut my eyes against the clamor, fell into a snooze, and awoke to find the back of Sheila's head deadweighted in my lap, her legs slightly raised and her bare toes curled around the base of the window on the driver's side. I had a foul taste in my mouth, my left foot had fallen asleep, my insides roiled. "You have one noisy stomach there," she giggled.

"Not compared to this truck. Please get up," I said. My arms were pinned under her body, and I could not have moved them without copping an inadvertent feel. Sheila stretched a hand to the steering wheel to hoist herself up. She slipped on her shoes, exited the driver's side and hurried around. Only at that point, as I staggered up out of the car, did I realize something. "This is not my street." Sheila said of course it's not, dickhead.

I breathed in her perfume, which carbureted with the evening's beers and bourbon to produce a heady essence. Her body ground into me, dirty dancing style. I bruised my buttocks on the door handle.

Next morning an alarm buzzed at six. Sheila sprang to the bathroom. I fell back to sleep to the sound of a shower. I believe I had told Sheila I had to get up by seven but she did not reset the alarm and I slept till almost noon. By then Sheila was long gone. I called work to tell them I'd be in in one hour. I showered, shaved and deodorized myself with male–brand products strewn about the bathroom. Sheila's cupboards and ice box were even barer than my own. I found a box of Special K, which I doused with sour milk. The house presented a maze of fast food packaging, splintered chopsticks, a bottle of Tabu (whose cap I replaced), pop bottles, a People and months of TV Guides, vases whose expired flowers reeked like overcooked collards, unisex underclothes, and cassette tape boxes of Reba McEntire, Garth Brooks and their twangy ilk. For all the clutter the place seemed not so much lived–in as neglected. Might as well still live in a parking garage, I muttered to myself.

I discovered my own clothes in a neat pile on top of the enormous television that dominated the living room—evidence that I must have had some wits about me the night before. Under my jacket, lying flat on the TV was a picture of Sheila shaking hands with President George Bush.

In our three years together we mostly slept at my place. I like to wake up amid tidiness, the one thing I inherited from my mother. Sheila and I enjoyed a simple relationship. She simply got everything she wanted. Sheila must have been born with a special wanting gene, she incessantly wanted things, any thing, much more than I didn't want them. She bullied perhaps, but I preferred not having to make any decisions. Finally she slapped me with the ultimate ultimatum, propose within two weeks or go fuck yourself, and on the fourteenth day I succumbed.

I did not hanker to get married, but I could find no rational reason to deny her. We had fun, she didn't try to change me in any material way, sex maintained a satisfying plateau. Goode, who had held out till age thirty-eight, was forever extolling marriage, and I figured if he could be happy then I could. Goode did not particularly like Sheila; she was too brazen for his taste, and of course his first impression of her was as a cheeky broad ransacking the Cattleman in search of single males. But he agreed to serve as my best man.

My mother may have liked Sheila, but I never knew for sure. The craziness had started. Mom never got Sheila's name right and may have confused her with any number of former acquaintances. Sheila's parents and four sisters generally approved of me, though I believe they had reached the point where any white male with no prison record would have sufficed.

So over dinner at a posh restaurant I whipped out the engagement ring—the one Sheila hand-picked during a tryst at the jewelry store. Mom still had the rings from her four deceased husbands, including my dad's, but I knew Sheila would only appreciate the one she had selected. She certainly wouldn't want an heirloom for which I paid nothing.

Soon Sheila decreed that she would dispense with birth control starting on our wedding night. That sent me emotionally sprawling. We had never talked about children. We had no use for them: I was too old and she was too busy. Now she revealed an obsession about giving birth before her thirty-fifth birthday. She invoked that tiresome image of the biological clock—no doubt in her case a souped-up digital one. We would name our child Paul, after her father; or Paulette, but she intended to have a boy. When I resisted she used every possible ploy to change my mind, including a trial period for us as caretakers for her favorite nephew. That experiment backfired in the tumultuous incident that ended it all.

Joanne tells me that I'm passive–aggressive, that I manipulated the relationship all along by giving in on minor matters, then ended it by unleashing my latent aggression.

I say, talk about passive, get back to your thesis, honey.

❋ ❋ ❋

Malcolm and I meet early at the Cattleman bar, where I buy him a beer to reward him for his efforts, though I learn these have proved futile. My Walter and Edna adventure greatly amuses him, and he agrees with Goode that I should share it with Skretch and Caspary. There could be value in "creative brainstorming."

I mull over his suggestion as we all gather at our table, but the question turns out to be moot. Caspary has broken up with his live–in girlfriend Barbara, which is to say, he moved out. He is morose, as deeply hurt as his shallowness will allow. He wears his baseball cap backwards, which gives his forehead a sawed–off, cave man appearance. He refuses to disclose any details beyond "certain considerations were not met." We're all surprised, because Caspary and Barbara have lived together for five years, and though they had their quarrels he had grown quite attached to Margo, Barbara's little girl, and we all envisioned a wedding. He never said a harsh word about Barbara, while the rest of us, even Goode, have used the group to vent our frustrations with the women in our lives.

Skretch presses him to elaborate, without success. I figure Caspary will supply details in due time, much as I did following my rift with Sheila. You need time to assimilate what happened before you go whining to your friends. Caspary and Barbara had lived in the same apartment building, and they met when somehow their telephone wires got crossed and they were getting each other's calls. From this they reckoned that a relationship was predestined and after a few years bought a house together. Caspary spent a good deal of time on the road, which he and Barbara both considered healthy. We are all fond of Barbara, who is frumpy, quiet and much brighter than Caspary. No one dares bring up Margo, who has come to regard Caspary as her stepfather. Malcolm asks about the possibility of a reconciliation, to which Caspary delivers a somber "Never." He's now holed up at a motel off the interstate called the Welcome Inn.

"What serendipity has brought together, let something, God knows what, tear asunder," says Skretch, miffed that his supposedly close friend refuses to confide in him. Skretch has a tiny cleft in his chin, which retracts when he clenches his teeth.

"She told me I'm not in touch with my feelings," says Caspary. Ah, but Warren, you are in touch with your lack of feelings, I'd love to say.

I scan the women at the bar. Slim pickin's for single guys tonight, excepting one luscious broad bottom encased in tight denim. "Nice ass," I mutter, inaudibly. I'd like to think I'm better than the out–loud insulters of women, but am I? Something drives me to lip synch the words, a pleasurable way of giving my thoughts flesh. It's harmless, unclean fun. My sex life is as laid off as I am, with Joanne serving as my sexual unemployment insurance. I only fantasize about strange women in my immediate line of vision. Two good eyes would probably make me a sex maniac. I tried to picture Karen the librarian nude yesterday, and drew a blank.

I excuse myself to take a leak. I call my mother's room and get Lionel. He says Mom has been asking for me, probably true, for she's apt to wail "Oh, where is my Little Humming Bear?" even when I'm standing right in front of her. Lionel informs me that he has joined a support group for families of those stricken with Alzheimer's and it has done him a world of good. Will I come along with him next time? I promise to consider it. I sound apologetic, which gratifies Lionel.

I return to find my friends huddled together. They fall silent when they see me. Nobody will tell me what they were talking about so intimately. I look angrily at Malcolm, for I suspect he has spilled the beans about John Byron. He has cued me repeatedly. Perhaps he told my story in an attempt to lift the gloom Caspary has cast over us.

"I have to see myself as a kind of widower," says Caspary.

"How come?" I ask, and while he explains I think what a peculiar word "widower" is. Shouldn't a widower be someone who kills husbands? A maker of widows?

I share that observation with the group, but it fails to ignite any discussion. Glumly, we break up early. In the car, Goode wonders what considerations were not met and whose considerations were they? I say it's none of our business. He could at least have told Skretch, Skretch was really pissed, said Goode. I reply that sometimes the measure of how much you care about somebody is the secrets you keep from them. I'm not sure what I mean, it just came out, but it irks Goode into a lengthy silence. Finally, Goode says he sees Caspary's breakup as one more harbinger of our group's demise.

"What were you guys talking about behind my back?" I ask him. "Baseball. The pennant races." Goode predicts that by the dog days of August the group will disintegrate and his theater will go belly up. I tune him out, trying futilely to conjure that gorgeous ass at the bar; my inattention leads Goode to switch on the radio, which happens to play a song popular during our senior year, which in turn reminds him of the class reunion only a few weeks away. For some reason Goode brightens up. He pleads with me to come, though I've insisted I have no interest in going. "Do you really want to see Nikki Feeley again, or Peter Elliott? Or Allison Kunreuther?" I ask. "I don't want to see or not see anybody in particular. I just want to be there. Come on, we skipped the tenth, fifteenth, twentieth and twenty–fifth. Aren't you the least bit curious to see how everyone turned out?"

No, I'm not. And I'm not so thrilled for them to see how I turned out, either. I find it hard to understand Goode's interest in revisiting the scene of our adolescent humiliations. We met when we took gym together freshman year. My single–sightedness exempted me from many activities, like tumbling; my mother had written the principal some note. I spent most of the period doing odd–jobs for Coach Steinhoff, one of which was to go locker to locker to make sure every boy took a shower. Goode at this age was nearly obese, and thus a laughingstock. He pleaded with me not to make him shower and expose his corpulence to ridicule and, at the risk of flunking gym, I let him furtively slip away. That made us friends. Somebody got wind of this one day and a group of guys stripped Goode and dragged him into the shower. He screamed like a pig being massacred. He was all blubber, and his tiny weenie crept upward in an arousal of terror. The coach stood by shaking his head. "It's the law, Miller. Every guy's got to take a shower."

Goode tells me that next week he's showing <u>The Ox–Bow Incident</u> and <u>Madame Curie</u> and will I come. I believe I'm due. Unbeknownst to Goode, each member of the men's group has agreed to patronize Theater 50 at least once a month.

At my apartment building the Kapinski twins huddle together at the elevator, their childsized arms trembling with sacks of groceries. As I live only two flights up I usually take the stairs, but when I greet them the dwarfs ask me to dinner, which they do about once a month. Terence cooks ultrasimple fare like beans and franks or canned beef stew. Nothing from scratch. When I offer to bring a six–pack Randy goes up on his toes, tilts the brown paper bag toward me so that it reaches my navel, and I peer down at the aluminum wrapped top of a champagne bottle.

"What's the occasion?" I ask.

"Randy got a promotion," replies Terence. "Ten per cent increase in salary, plus more health benefits." The elevator door whines open at the fourth floor. I pat Randy on the back, genuinely happy for him. He works as a word processor for the phone company, and he jokes about how his first week there he sat on two volumes of the Yellow Pages until Terence bought him a cushion.

The Kapinski's apartment is like a child's playhouse. Everything not built in is built low, with even the pictures hanging just above the chair–rail. Stepstools hug the walls in every room. In the living room Terence brings out an adult–sized folding chair while Randy perches on the little couch. It has been a smoldering day and the air conditioning feels luxurious. My own place is not air conditioned.

Terence pours the champagne and we toast Randy, who excitedly tells us that the best thing about the promotion is his new responsibilities: there are none, he's just getting paid more for doing the same job. After the third or fourth toast the twins look at each other, frown simultaneously and put their glasses down.

"Amid all this celebrating...we want to know, how is your job search going?" asks Terence.

"Going nowhere, but hey this is a day to celebrate." They still look rueful. "Listen, you guys, I get almost two hundred dollars a week for doing nothing. And I've got three or four months left to collect, and possibly an extension after that. After twenty–five years at that lousy job it's nice to have some time off. You know?" They think I'm protesting too much. And it's true, unemployment does go against my work ethic.

Terence says, "I like the way the newspapers say, when a top executive resigns or is fired, that he has left to pursue new challenges and opportunities. When thousands of the rank–in–file get laid off their only opportunity is unemployment insurance."

"So how do you fill up your days?" asks Randy.

I tell them I spend a great deal of time at my mother's bedside, which elicits an overlong discussion of Alzheimer's. Terence, who reads up on these things, claps his hands when I mention that Lionel goes to a support group. Then he brings out the tuna salad and creamed corn. He subscribes to the dictum, if you haven't got it, flaunt it. You have to admire his spunk, if not his cookery.

"I wonder, have you seen anyone suspicious hanging around the building?" I ask. When they respond with puzzlement I mention that a mysterious package—an old baseball, actually—was deposited at my door a few weeks ago and I've been unable to find the culprit.

"Are you sure it was for you?" asks Terence.

"My name and address were handwritten on the outside of the package." Because they're such good listeners I give them a recap of everything, including most of what I can remember about John Byron. I catch Randy yawning a few times, but Terence is fascinated. He happens to know a private detective, a fellow midget. Barney would be intrigued by my story, might even offer to do some sleuthing for a modest fee. I have no money to spare, but I suppose I could cut out a few necessities, like lunch. I could save on toilet paper by using public rest rooms.

I ask Terence, "I thought detectives were supposed to be invisible, you know, kind of fade into the woodwork. Doesn't it hamper Barney's job being so physically, conspicuous?"

Terence gulps some champagne and sloshes it like Listerine. He holds up one finger, a signal to wait till he swallows. "Evidently it's like reverse psychology. Nobody expects one of the little people to be a private eye. So they notice Barney, sure, but they never realize he's spying on them."

"New fields are opening up for all other minorities, so why not us?" asks Randy. He tends to be the more political of the two. He has a scar above his forehead, from the time he was heaved headfirst against a dartboard in a saloon. It was part of a contest. He also can hardly bend his left arm, which broke in two places when he tried to break his fall.

Terence races into the bedroom to get me some information on Barney. "Barney's a fraud and a liar, don't get near him," whispers Randy.

Terence hands me a vivid yellow sheet. The agency insignia shows a silhouette profile of Sherlock Holmes with pipe, enclosed in a serrated border. Barney Robinson is listed as an investigative associate. A florid italic script ticks off the agency's expertise in handwriting analysis, research on insurance claims, bodyguard services, surveillance, investigations into suspicious deaths and missing person searches and delving into public records. "Any idea what these folks charge?" I ask.

Terence shakes his head. Randy flashes me a surreptitious thumbs–down. "I saw that, you little bastard," snarls Terence. "Barney's an ex–con," says Randy. Terence clenches his fists. I brace myself to break up a fight. I can't help being amused at the image of me restraining them with a headlock on each, the way Superman used to do. He would always conk together the criminals' skulls, one of which was invariably bald, as if baldness itself constituted a felony.

Terence is seething, "Barney did two weeks for shoplifting. That hardly reflects a criminal nature." Randy points his finger at me like Uncle Sam, "The guy was caught stealing two cassettes of Johnny Mathis. I'd have given him life without parole just for bad musical taste."

I'm piqued because I like Johnny Mathis. An ancient album of his, "Open Fire, Two Guitars," is one of my prized possessions, though my record player broke years ago and I've not had it repaired. Maybe if Marie liked Johnny Mathis as much as she liked Vic Damone we'd still be together. Hear Johnny Mathis sing "What'll I Do?" and "In the Still of the Night" and see if that doesn't alter your opinion of him forever. Not that it ever changed Sheila's mind. Nothing short of dismantling the medulla oblongata could change Sheila's mind.

The twins finally simmer down for dessert, a store–bought cherry pie lifted from the quick sale rack, as the stale crust attests. Terence brings in two mugs of coffee, muttering, "Decaf left regular right, decaf left regular right." He hands the decaf to me. I'm seated on a small pillow with my legs crossed, so that the table top hits me just above the waist. Suddenly I hear a whoosh like air escaping from a balloon, and a chair crashes to the floor. Randy has disappeared. Terence now bends over him, gently patting him on the head and loosening his twin brother's clothes. Adrenalin pumps through me.

Leaping up I spill my coffee. "Can I help? What can I do?" I holler, swabbing the table with a paper napkin. "Just go, please go, I can handle it," Terence grunts, as Randy's arms and legs twitch and the gasping sounds continue. Standing over Terence I notice how his hair has thinned out at the top of his head, and through the wiry strands I can see his scalp reddening. He looks up at me and murmurs, "It was too much excitement. He's not supposed to get too excited. Please go."

   I cling to the banister as I walk down the two flights to my floor. I feel as if I've just witnessed a violent death, though I realize it was probably some kind of occasional fit and Terence has everything under control. It's just as well that there's nothing for me to do, for I go all to pieces in these situations. Horrible shivers so rippled my body when Mom had her first minor stroke that I had to squeeze my right wrist with my left hand just to dial 911. I will never be a father, but had I taken that leap I never could have stood in a delivery room entwining fingers with my agonized wife, plying her with ice chips as her yelps resounded above the hum of fetal monitors—unlike Goode, who recounts his delivery room heroics with manly pride. Lord knows what Caspary and Skretch saw in Vietnam, and I'm thankful they've chosen to keep the lid on it. There is too much grief in the world: the gravity of that thought arrests me between stairsteps. I decide to give it twenty minutes and then call Terence to see if I can be of any help. My feet move more resolutely but at my own floor I come to an abrupt halt when I spy a squarish bundle wrapped in a brown Safeway sack at the threshold of my apartment. I know instantly who it's from. I rush over but lift the package gingerly and press it to my ear. One deep breath later I look up and down the hall and slip furtively inside. It is a book. An old battered book, impacted with dust. The innards fall to the floor as I hone my single working eye on the barely intelligible words etched into the spine.

   <u>Byron's Works</u>.

CHAPTER 4

❈

When a fourth a pair of panties surfaced at the Chicken Coop, this time scrunched between two plump pouches of flour, Hickey called an emergency meeting in the back room. He announced that the jig was up. He branded every one of us a suspect, women and men alike, and if you got caught you'd be fired and possibly imprisoned. Kuker had hired a floor detective. We would never meet the man, never know who he was, but he would be watching us. If we tried to plant any panties we would be seized and handled none too gently. Hickey's eyes surveyed all of us, but his gaze rested on me. As I considered myself the last person to get his hands on a pair of panties, much less stash them on grocery shelves, I figured he just hated me. At any rate his stare felt like crushed ice down my back.

I avoided John Byron, whom I'd written off as a nut, but we were thrown together one afternoon when I got deputized to help Byron deliver groceries to the home of a Mrs. Rosenberg. Byron did not belong to the delivery fleet, but he had served once in a pinch and had somehow charmed this woman. She was a prized customer and insisted on Byron as her delivery boy. Kuker didn't like it and neither did Byron, but the woman rang up a huge bill plus the surcharge for delivery. So she could call the shots.

"You're riding shotgun," Hickey advised me, "and don't screw it up."

Mrs. Rosenberg had ordered one hundred fifty dollars worth of groceries—a lofty sum in 1961, comprising about twelve full paper sacks and unsackable cargo like cases of pop, charcoal briquettes, tons of kitty litter and so forth. As we loaded up Byron's Buick Roadmaster he joked that we needed a trailer. We chugged along, slipping in and out of lanes like a drunk trying to toe a straight line. People on all sides honked at us. Byron rarely eyed the road; his neck swiveled, his eyes roved as if he were the passenger, not the driver. His hands hung parallel on the sides of the steering wheel, like ears on a face. His lax approach to driving should have frightened me, but I realized that even if we hit something it wouldn't make much impact. Even the eggs might go unbroken.

Byron informed me that Mrs. Rosenberg was the wife of a rich real estate developer, a Jew. Did I know the family?

So Byron took me for a Jew because of my uncle, which meant everyone else at the store probably shared that assumption. I had heard incidental remarks about Jews at the Coop, and on several occasions people in quiet conversation would abruptly hush up when I appeared. This I had to clear up right away.

"I'm not Jewish," I told John Byron.

He turned his gaze from the road. "But your uncle…"

"My father, he practiced Judaism, too. But my mom is a Christian and I'm a Christian."

"You go to church?"

"No, we don't belong to any. I was just brought up that the important thing is not to be Jewish," I blurted.

Byron chuckled. "That was nicely put, Jerry–Jared. It poleaxes the whole dialectic of faith and reason."

Before I could ask Byron to clarify, he had scraped the curb on a sharp right turn and we momentarily cruised along a sidewalk, nearly striking two terrified pedestrians. Byron piloted on, unfazed, as if tootling along a sequestered dirt road. Byron pointed out how ugly the front of some government building was, how another used to be a hideout for runaway slaves. The car had a radio but Byron—did he intuitively know I hated the sound of car radios?—did not turn it on. A chorus of beeps accompanied Byron's every move; I could hear the grocery bags heaped in the back seat and trunk lurching, for his every turn was a hairpin. It was, paradoxically, breathtaking to plod at such a pokey pace. Derring–do in Byron's lack of daring.

Byron pointed to two women crossing before us when we waited at a red light. "You know what the difference is between men and women?"

I paused. "Well, yes, of course I do."

"The difference is in how they walk. Men put one foot in front of the other. Women put one thigh in front of the other."

"Oh."

"So what do you make of the Pantyman? Who is at the top of your list of suspects?" he asked.

"Hickey," I said.

"A wit. Mind you, I don't take your suspicions lightly. Hickey is a bitter man. Every assistant manager thinks he should be manager. Hickey will never make manager, though, and he knows it. It's not impossible that he'd devise such a scheme, just to drive Kuker crazy. He despises Kuker."

I had figured Kuker and Hickey for bosom friends, if only allied in their hatred of me. "But I was only joking."

"Jerry–Jared, some of the greatest wisdom is expressed as jest. Alexander Pope. Or Shakespeare's fool in <u>King Lear</u>."

"I hate Shakespeare. We had to read <u>Hamlet</u> and <u>Othello</u> sophomore year. Yecch."

"I suppose there's more to life than literacy. Or religion. So what's your enthusiasm? Elvis Presley? Girls? Baseball?"

"Baseball," I said, and then, to amend my earlier statement, "in fact, baseball is more my religion than Christianity. Babe Ruth, Lou

Gehrig, Ty Cobb, Tris Speaker, Honus Wagner, they're like gods to me."

"I know little about baseball, but I believe not one of those gentlemen is still active. They all hung up their spikes before you were even born. Are you a baseball paleontologist, who restricts his admiration to the extinct?"

"I like some of today's players. Kaline, Aaron, Mays, Mantle."

"I see. Well, what's your learned opinion of Dizzy Dean and the 1934 Cardinals?"

I couldn't resist. I rattled off the complete line–up of that team, plus relevant statistics.

"Very impressive. I don't care a fig for any of that, of course. But...but, remind me about the Gashouse Gang sometime. I have something that may interest you."

The Rosenberg house was not a house but a mansion, broad as a city block with grounds that spanned acres. Four skyhigh ladders leaned against the house, manned by painters touching up the windowpanes on the second story. I thought of Santa Ana's men storming the Alamo. Byron followed a meandering driveway to the rear of the house, then eased onto a patch of pea gravel encircling a fountain that looked like a gigantic, chalk–white champagne glass. The waters danced and purled in the midday sun; a breeze blew a soft spray on us as we began to unload our freight.

I should say, as *I* began to unload. Without a word John Byron disappeared through a rear entry into the house. A black man in servant's livery pushed some lever in the door to prop it open and motioned to me to lug in the groceries. I must have made a dozen trips. A black woman uniformed in white directed me to set each bag on a blond wood table, where I had to divvy up the groceries into plastic bins labeled Vegetables, Fruits, Bread, Condiments, Dairy, as she checked off each item in a ledger. I could hear the faint buzz of Byron and a woman in conversation, accompanied by classical music. When I finally finished the maid handed me a tall glass of cherry Kool–Aid and led me down a narrow hallway into what she called the sitting room, though neither Byron nor the woman sat, but stood beside a floor–to–ceiling bookcase that contained more volumes than my high school library. Byron pointed to a shelf just out of reach of the woman, a shortish, plump, very attractive blonde in one of those shapeless silky get–ups that used to be called a mou–mou. (Is it a coincidence that something that makes the slimmest woman look bovine is called a mou–mou?) He plucked the book from the shelf and handed it to her, and she pressed it to her chest. "I've always meant to read this some day, but you've now convinced me that that day has come," she said, in a voice that seemed to echo the purling eddies of the fountain out back.

She looked so much younger than Byron that I took her for a daughter of the house and was startled when he introduced her as Esther Rosenberg. She extended a small hand with brilliantly lacquered nails. I had never shaken hands with a woman before and, between shifting the Kool–Aid glass to my left hand and wiping the grimy right one on my apron, I doubt I managed it very well. Her black hair was teased Jackie Kennedy style and frosted with hairspray.

"Jerry, or Jared, is the nephew of Jake Miller, whom I believe you know," said Byron.

Her small lovely hand tapped her cheek. "We know Jake well. We were so sorry about your father, Jerry. It has been what, five or six months since he passed away? My husband knew him much better than I did, from committees they served on together at the shul. We would have come to the funeral, but we spend so much of the winter in Florida. I think I went to your bar mitzvah, about three years ago?"

I shook my head. Byron came to my rescue. "My dear, I'm afraid Jerry–Jared and I must drag our carcasses back to the salt mines."

On our return trip to the Chicken Coop Byron informed me that Alvin Rosenberg was a heavy drinker and a philanderer par excellence, who publicly belittled his wife as a culture vulture. Esther was his third wife, approximately half his age. "He trades for a new model every ten years." Byron found amusement in this, which led me to wonder about the gallantry he had showed Mrs. Rosenberg.

In the beginning, it was sound. I was six that summer afternoon when I was twiddling the radio knob and a voice arrested my hand. It was a mildly gruff twang, punctuated from time to time with song, and in the background an intermittent pop followed by swells of human voices. At first I took it for a story with sound effects, maybe about the Apaches, because the lingo was so peculiar. "He's a wipin' the prespiration from off'n his brow," "They aina gonna git him, he done slud inter second," "Now he's a takin' his pummonary warm-up pitches." Podna this and Podna that. What was a Podna? The voice drawled through commercials not for cereals or candy but Falstaff beer, which lent an air of naughtiness. When my mother entered the room I reached for my erector set. I expected her to angrily turn off the radio and scold me for listening to such trash, but she flicked some dust from the top of the console and said, "My big boy, I didn't know you liked baseball." "Sure do," I said.

I listened on into the afternoon and continued to listen the rest of that summer. It seemed every time I turned on the radio to that particular number the voice would be there, narrating adventures that roused multitudes. Eventually it dawned on me that those multitudes were not responding to the voice but were in fact watching a game, whose terminology and rules I mastered quickly. My father, who took only a passing interest in baseball, explained the rudiments to me; he normally read one of his fat history books while the broadcast wafted by. What's a podna? I asked him. He thought it might be a gardening term.

Mom and Dad did not encourage my passion for baseball, because they feared that I'd dream of playing for the Cardinals, only to be thwarted on account of my impaired vision. They both tried to protect me, more my mother than my father, who seldom meddled in my upbringing. They diverted me from certain playthings, like cars or military paraphernalia; it was understood that I would never drive a car or fight for my country.

This created no conflict whatsoever in me. Being half blind has only been half frustrating, really. It has liberated me from a host of burdens and responsibilities—car insurance and military service among the most notable. I enjoy passengerhood. I suppose I am the type who never wants what he cannot have. (Lionel once accused me of deceiving myself. He suggested that I attend a support group for "low vision" sufferers. I figured I would end up giving support rather than receiving any.)

The fact is, I never had any desire to play baseball, or to watch other kids play, or even to see a big league game. We lived on the outskirts of Kansas City, which only had a minor league team in those days, peopled with future Yankees. Most people rooted for the St. Louis teams, the Cardinals and Browns, whose broadcasts I'd latched onto. But my love of the game was auditory, linked to a man's voice, which belonged to Dizzy Dean; more akin to a love of music than the fantasy of fame that grips most American boys. To this day I never daydream about a future. Sheila hated that about me; she could spend hours dreaming about our future together, replete with kids and money, but I refused to go along. I am aware there is a future, of course. I spent over twenty years of my life predicting the future in the name of premiums. Don't tell anyone, but the future is death.

As my knowledge of math expanded I was swept away by baseball's numerology. The purity of numbers mated with the purity of sound. I studied statistics, memorized volumes of them, chiefly of players long past. I cut my actuarial teeth on batting averages, earned run averages, slugging percentages. I plowed through record books doing calculations and then checked my answer in the printed column, exhilarated that there had to be a right answer, and—ecstasy!—sometimes I had the right answer and the book didn't. The men who embodied these numbers were superhuman in their skill and valor. I never collected baseball cards. I cherished numbers, not faces.

When major league baseball came to television and then to town my father became an enthusiast. He dragged me to A's games where, unless a Ted Williams or Al Kaline were featured, I busied myself with the mechanics of scorekeeping, or closed my eyes and imagined I was in Yankee Stadium for the 1927 World Series. For TV we had to rely on broadcasts from Channel 2 KFEQ in St. Joseph; the picture was snowy no matter how much Dad wrestled with the rabbit ears. To my delight, Dizzy Dean was the announcer for the televised game each Saturday.

Because my passion for baseball was only constrained by my imagination, it was a year–round occupation for me. For my seventh birthday I received a board game called All–Star Baseball, which consisted of a cardboard baseball diamond bearing two metal propellers, one for the home team and one for the visitors. On the game board you would mount thin cardboard disks imprinted with a great player's name and coded with numbers to indicate strike, ball, single, home run, and so forth, give the spinner a plink and by a kind of roulette put the ball in play. What fascinated me was the coding on each disk, which reflected that player's lifetime statistics: the Babe Ruth disk had a huge home run and strikeout space, Ty Cobb singles, Tris Speaker doubles. It was the law of averages that I loved about baseball.

I would play the game for hours. "Just imagine, if all those great players could be on the field at the same time," my father used to say, and I would huff, "They are." The games were palpably real to me. I would bellow the proceedings in the mock–heroic style of Harry Caray, and more than once my mother barged into my room to see if I had injured myself. Mom worried that I would be a recluse. My right index finger, my spinner trigger, formed calluses until my mother, fearing permanent damage, persuaded me to wrap the finger in adhesive tape.

Dad, a history buff and private Jew, understood that a man has to have interests that exclude the rest of the world. He fed my addiction by continually renewing baseball books from the library, alternating his card with mine. His greatest gift was countless requisition pads he swiped from the shoestore. By coincidence, these contained sufficient lines and boxes to simulate a scorecard, which I used to document every inning of my imaginary games. I used the pink sheets for American League games, white for the National, and canary for All–Star games and World Series. My fingers were constantly stained royal blue from ripping out the shiny carbon paper that separated the sheets.

I pored over statistics to create additional players with scientifically calibrated disks, made from cut outs of the cardboard used to stiffen Dad's shirts from the laundry, and painstakingly printed with the player's name. I recorded every play of every game, kept strict averages on every player, standings of every team, and ran my year–round pennant race. By my grace the 1919 Chicago Black Sox were reinstated, only to be blasted by the 1927 Yanks and Dizzy Dean's 1934 Cardinals. I could invent history and record it at will. I was God.

I did follow current baseball events, though they were ancillary to the evergreen season waging in my mind. I read all the literature and the daily box scores, and kept up a continuing dialogue with Dad and a few friends. But by the summer of 1961 my passion for baseball started to ebb. I had outgrown All–Star Baseball several years before. And then my libido kicked in, so that kissing and breasts, and kissing breasts, increasingly supplanted reveries about the number of two–baggers Rogers Hornsby stroked in 1923. My statistical passion diverted to women's measurements. Just reading the measurements in a <u>Playboy</u> caption could spawn an erection; I didn't even need to see the picture. Only the bust size really mattered. You couldn't always tell where the waist and hips began and ended, but registering a 34B was like batting .350.

The fact is, baseball let me down. Its heroes shrunk in stature, while the game itself suffered elephantiasis, franchises metastasizing to the West Coast, the schedule expanding to one hundred–sixty–two games, and even adding a second All–Star game, thus debasing a grand tradition beyond recognition. I bemoaned the move of the Dodgers and Giants to California as much as any Brooklyn boy.

Experts consider the 1961 season one of the grandest in the game's history. The Mantle and Maris race to break Ruth's record riveted the nation, franchises were cropping up all over the place, which expanded the season to feed the addiction. But for me it was a season of hell. My father died the week before the start of spring training. (It was also the day after Valentine's Day, for which my mother never forgave him.) Having outgrown All–Star Baseball I was left at the mercy of reading and reality. The fact that Roger Maris lived only a few miles from me exacerbated the agony of the Mantle–Maris slugfest. Kids I knew would make journeys there, to beg for autographs or deck the landscape with streamers of toilet paper. They were merciless to the man. I did bike to his house and aim hexes at his front door. I despised him for his mediocrity, his frailty (he missed half a season due to appendicitis), his drabness, and above all his gall in challenging the Babe. Even his bat weighed ten ounces less than the Babe's.

I also rooted against Mantle, whom I regarded as vastly over–rated. I saw Ruth's record as sacrosanct; beating it was like razing an ancient temple and replacing it with a shopping mall. I clung to Dizzy Dean's television broadcasts and to the radio antics of Harry Caray (whom people tell me is still around). But each day of the season tolled a death for me. I missed my dad. Watching and talking baseball was the only thing we did together, the only thing we had in common besides adoring my mother. It was also the only thing we did together separate from her. Mom didn't know Minnie Minoso from Minnie Mouse.

My break with baseball was not a sudden thing, like my rift with my Ex–Fiancee, or my father's death. The Maris travesty was just the Fort Sumter in this quiet campaign. I went though a long period of apathy, my mind turned to other things—my mother, math, girls—then moved to outrage as the game drifted into such inanities as the designated hitter, astroturf, pine tar, batting gloves, outlandish salaries, Canada for God's sake. The old greats had no more to say than their plaques in Cooperstown, where Dad had planned to take me some summer.

Ultimately, everything associated with baseball so irritated me that I could only cope by pretending the game was "gone," rhyming with "zone," as Ol' Diz used to pronounce it. Goode is wrong to call it a phobia. Isn't he?

※　　　　　※　　　　　※

The summer after my father died I often spent my Sunday afternoons reading history. History had always been my father's domain. He never talked about these endless tomes he was reading, though he loved poking fun at anachronisms in movies like <u>Demetrius and the Gladiators</u> and <u>Ivanhoe</u>. He amassed a large history library and shortly after his death I determined to wade through it in chronological order. By my second week at the Chicken Coop I had reached the Elizabethan period, which fascinated me, despite Shakespeare. We had been forced to read <u>Hamlet</u> and <u>Othello</u> sophomore year, neither of which I could get through.

I remember one Sunday afternoon I paused in my reading about the Spanish Armada—feeling some guilty sympathy for the Spaniards—to press my palms together as hard as possible and hold it for ten seconds. Exercise for young people was all the rage as part of President Kennedy's Council on Youth Fitness. I was supposed to be able to do at least fifty sit–ups and engage in some kind of physical exertion fifteen minutes every day. I rode my bike constantly, which I figured took care of the lower half of my body. Push–ups were out of the question, especially after Coach Steinhoff told us you could do isometrics and get the same improved arm strength.

I had reached five or six in the count when Mom knocked on my door and peeked in. She looked startled at first to see her son trembling with tension and red in the face, mashing his hands as if impassioned with prayer. She probably thought she had caught me masturbating—though for that pastime I always locked my door and gaped at <u>Playboy</u> rather than at photos of two monster galleons locking mainmasts. The book lay in my lap with its spine arched upward. She turned away.

"Come in, Mom," I gasped. "Just doing isometrics, to build up my biceps."

"Well, am I bothering you, Jared?"

As usual that summer, my mind said yes and my voice said of course not.

"I was over at the Ramsey's today," she said, striding toward me. "Dottie has been cleaning out the basement, just like you and I did a few weeks back, and you won't believe what she found." I realized why her posture had seemed odd: she had been concealing some object behind her back.

"Do you remember this?" she asked, handing me a rumpled sheet.

I ironed it on my chest with the flat of my hand before I looked at it. "I did this?"

"You must have been in second or third grade. You used to play with Sally Ramsey all the time then. I'd forgotten all this till today. You must have had the urge to write Sally a love letter and you didn't know how to go about it, so you kept listening to the record. It was an old 45."

"<u>Love is a Many Splendored Thing</u>."

"You must have listened to that record a hundred times and copied down the lyrics, word for word. And you gave it to Sally. Of course, she showed it to her mother and Dottie showed it to me. I remember being proud of you, for being such a romantic."

"I didn't spell too well. The Aprul roz that onely groz."

"You were always so determined once you decided to do a thing."

The letter was printed in pencil on pages from a Big Chief tablet, shredded at the perforation. The sharp point had pricked holes in the paper every five words or so, an indication of my intensity, or perhaps I had resharpened the pencil that often. I used to love sharpening pencils; it had the gratification of completing a task and I loved the aroma of the shavings.

I did not recall writing this, but there was the tell–tale lopsided "Love Jared" at the foot of the page. Sally Ramsey had been a cute girl with blond hair, blue eyes and little hoop skirts. We were thrown together as little kids, but by the time we reached puberty she had cast her lot with the older boys, sixteen year–olds who could drive and, presumably, kiss.

"Well, you get back to your exercising or your reading, or whatever. But I had to show you this. I really thought you'd get a kick out of it."

"I did get a kick out of it."

"Give it to me and I'll throw it away," she said, backpedaling toward the door. With her hair twisted into a bun her widow's peak streamed like a white arrow toward her enchanting blue eyes. She ratcheted her engagement and wedding rings up and down the joints of her fingers. If she had a mood ring it would have shone black constantly.

"Wait, Mom. Can you tell me what Secretary Freeman did today?" This was a game I had created, to get her interested in something. I latched onto the members of Kennedy's cabinet and beseeched her each day for an account of their activities. Excitedly she would recount whatever the paper or TV had to say about the travels and doings of Robert McNamara, Douglas Dillon, Dean Rusk, Orville Freeman—but under no circumstances Arthur Goldberg and Abraham Ribicoff. She didn't see why Kennedy had to appoint so many Jews to his cabinet.

Mom insisted she was not an anti–Semite, but what else could you call it? My father's Jewish faith repelled her; it was the only thing she disliked about him, and converting was the only thing she ever denied him. They had a prenuptial covenant that my father could keep his Jewish ways but had to keep them to himself. He could attend services on Friday nights and Saturday mornings, observe the high holidays, eat matzo instead of bread during Passover. (He had to buy the matzo himself. Mom would not allow it in her shopping cart.) He would also light a candle to mark the anniversary of his parents' deaths. The candle burned in an open jar the diameter of a juice glass and I remember mounting a kitchen chair to peer at the flame, trying to imagine in the warm radiance the faces of these shabby, sullen, heavy–set immigrants known to me only through dim sepia photos.

Eight days into my life I underwent the ceremonial circumcision, a grudging concession from my mother, who had prayed for a daughter so she wouldn't have to make good on her promise. At my Uncle Jake's the three Miller brothers, my two Miller aunts and a gaggle of Jews rejoiced at the nipping of my foreskin. Mom did not attend, but my father vested much in this occasion, as if he secretly felt that some day as a delayed reaction to the surgery I would miraculously enter the Jewish fold. My mother considered it all disgusting, though her third husband told me in drunken confidence that she preferred her men circumcised. Mom once hinted that the loss of sight in my left eye may have stemmed from a trauma related to the lopping of my penis, although we all knew that semi–blindness struck me in the womb, courtesy of my mother's genes. But it consoled her to put the blame on my father's barbaric ritual.

She smiled. "Jared, I told you this morning. Secretary Freeman spoke to a group of farmers in Iowa and said that the government would begin a food stamp program in eight areas, to see if that would help the needy. Somebody asked him if food stamps would be like Green Stamps and Secretary Freeman said don't make fun of the poor. I think he's my favorite member of the cabinet. I don't suppose any of your customers at the Chicken Coop will need these food stamps. What are you reading?" Her fingers ticked the spine of my book, whose title evoked my father and made her sigh.

Mom frowned. "Why don't you read the Britannica like I suggested?" One of her TV heroes, Dave Garroway, claimed that he had read the whole Britannica cover to cover. My mother considered him the most brilliant man in the world.

We don't own the Britannica," I reminded her.

"The Wilson's have it. We can borrow theirs, one volume at a time. They're always borrowing things from us. Like the lawn mower." At this her eyes teared, no doubt remembering how my father used to push the mower—an old manual reel job that spit up grass like green sparks—as his lean body crouched over his adult push toy. I did the mowing now but it wasn't the same.

I'd had enough of my mother. "I'm going out," I said, brushing past her.

I had no destination in mind, but when I saw the sweep of the eagle's wings I pumped my green Schwinn into a grove of maple and pine, whose limbs stretched toward the bronze figure. As a small boy I would jump up and down in the back seat whenever we passed it, for it always meant we were close to home. My father dubbed it "Jared's Eagle," as if its whole reason for being was my celebration of it. Oddly enough I'd never gone near the statue, as if it were as physically remote as a real eagle, to be celebrated and not touched.

But this day out of nowhere sprang the urge to see it up close. From the road the bird looked frozen in midair, but actually it perched on a granite pedestal scarred by graffiti and valentines scrawled with bits of rock. A bronze plaque credited the sculpture to Cornelius Van Dyck, dated 1928 and titled "Argus." The huge spreading wings dwarfed the head and torso, the eyes bore deep red stains. The wingtips and talons had eroded. Standing there with my arms folded, I wondered if the authorities, the parks department or whoever, knew about the condition of the statue. Or cared. I knew I wouldn't call the parks department or anyone else. The eagle would have to fend for itself.

Then I burst into tears. My father had died six months ago and I hadn't yet wept for him. At the funeral I was too distracted by the bewildering Hebrew, the flurry of strange faces, the silky beanie topping my head and the ill–fitting black suit I had borrowed from a cousin, to cry. Also, the sun went into total eclipse that day, as if God had erred in taking my father so soon and thus had shrouded His grandest star in shame—though even God couldn't bring my father back, couldn't reverse the slick trafficway or the swerve into the embankment. The eclipse was all people could talk about.

Suddenly I missed my father desperately and wanted him back. I stared at the besieged pedestal as if it were a tombstone, and

decided that my father's spirit indeed rested here, though the official grave lay in a Jewish cemetery a distant bus ride away. Placing one hand over my heart and the other against the bird's cool plumage, I vowed that I would visit this site every year on the anniversary of my father's death. I lost himself in that wintry tableau, until jarred by the rustling sound of one squirrel chasing another across a red pebbled path, then the scratch of claws as they spiraled up the bark of a maple.

I have kept that vow. It's invariably a chilly but intensely sunny mid–February day, with clumps of snow dropping like wounded doves from the naked maple and pine branches. Today the eagle is in fine fettle. It may be the only thing under the sun that looks better than it did thirty years ago. The park area was refurbished and some affluent citizens—including Esther Rosenberg, of Chicken Coop delivery fame—donated funds to give the statue a thorough makeover and restore some details.

I've never told a soul about my little ritual, for I doubt there's a soul who wouldn't laugh at me, and that includes my mother who, several marriages later, says she never forgave my father for dying the day after the most glorious Valentine's Day they had ever spent together.

CHAPTER 5

❦

It's not what Lionel says so much as the sound of his voice that drives me to the far side of distraction. Maybe to compensate for my poor vision God endowed me with hypersensitive hearing that renders most music and many voices painful to me. Lionel has a gravelly voice, not the outright gravel of, say, Jimmy Durante, but rather a pea gravel, the way Jimmy Durante might sound after a gulp of herbal tea. A disastrous hospital voice, because you can hear Lionel no matter how softly he speaks, and so much of what one says at the hospital must either be confidential, or quiet enough to allow inmates to sleep.

Today is a good case in point. Both Mom and her roommate Mrs. Western have slept most of the day. Mom has grown increasingly sluggish and Lionel furrows his brow as he mutters, too resonantly, "It's out of our hands now." This is his moral equivalent of faith, but Lionel doesn't have a religious bone in his skeleton; he prefers strong opinions to God. For years he tried to get me to read books by Eric Hoffer, a philosophical dockworker from San Francisco and one of Lionel's heroes. Now Lionel listens avidly to Rush Limbaugh, whose family he knows personally. Evidently Limbaugh did a show on serial murderers the other day.

"If Rush ever does a show on serial matrimony, he could feature your mom," he says, chortling.

Lionel's ring finger sports what must be the largest ruby in captivity, barring Elizabeth Taylor's vault. "Only six hundred dollars," he had informed me, waving it in my face first thing after he and Mom disembarked from their trip to Turkey. I believe they visited every continent but Antarctica and Greenland their first ten years of marriage, always returning with the gaudiest merchandise imaginable. Blessedly, Lionel was not the slide or picture taking type, so I was spared any detailed account. Mostly there was just a display of all the new possessions on the coffee table for me to gape at on cue.

Lionel's first wife had been a recluse, so he was making up for lost time. Lionel is the type who just up and goes, and they up and went constantly. Mom always hated to fly but for Lionel's sake she conquered her distaste for it. There is no question Lionel has made her happy and, as with her previous husbands, she employs some form of alchemy to transform all his flaws into virtues at best, foibles at worst. "He wants to kill all black people, for God's sake," I told her, the time I tried to persuade them to get rid of that black jockey statue in front of the house. "Oh, he just says that to impress," Mom replied.

I wouldn't want to travel with Lionel. "He will never change his watch," Mom told me once, "and it drives me crazy. I mean, here we are in Bangkok and his watch is nine hours off. It's very confusing. But he won't change it. He says Missouri is the center of America, which is the center of the universe and he won't change the time." Lionel once almost got into a fight with a man on an airplane when Lionel shushed the man's wife for talking during the stewardess's lecture on emergency procedures. I never got in the habit of liking Lionel, in all the twenty years he and Mom and have been married—thus surpassing my father's term of office, though the last year or two should only count half, because Mom hasn't been all there.

The first memory lapses we could joke about. Mom always had a permeable memory, and the fact that her forgetfulness escalated did not disturb us. She still had an ironclad grip on people's names and suchlike. She suffered two ministrokes, which sapped her strength, disrupted her bowels and slurred her speech; she gave up driving and travel but remained as vivacious as ever. We knew something had seriously gone wrong when Sheila and I dropped in for coffee and ice cream and Mom forgot not just the coffee but how to brew the coffee. As I loaded the machine she watched in rapt fascination, as if witnessing some arcane ritual.

Then came the hunger strikes, the public outbursts, accusing her cleaning lady of theft, the order of two thousand mangoes from a mail order outfit. I must admit Lionel handled all this well. He had tended to his sick wife years ago and knew the routine. I couldn't cope with it at all. I just got angry, and I got angry at Lionel for flaunting his cool while I was losing mine. They tried nurses at home but the women kept quitting.

I've steeled myself. This woman is not my mother but some demented spirit that has infiltrated her beautiful form. Her mind now is naked to us. The thought processes are on constant display and it's embarrassing. But Lionel presses on as if nothing had changed but her residence.

How would I rate Lionel among my mother's husbands?

Darryl Park, husband number one, was a handsome fellow, but most guys look good on their wedding day and in an army uniform, the only two pictures I've seen of him. He died early in World War II and Mom seldom mentioned him around me, perhaps in deference to his successor, my father.

I'd like to think Dad was the love of her life. She must have loved him to marry a Jew. Yet just two years after Dad died she married Victor, a retired insurance salesman in his sixties. He courted Mom for months and they honeymooned in Haiti. I told people they were in Hades. Mom brought me back a machete, whose smooth wooden blade I'd have loved to use on Victor's cervical vertebrae. I shuddered every time he put his arm around Mom, or manhandled her: she constantly slapped his roving hands from her rear end or her bosom, and if she had protested with any seriousness I'd have belted the man.

When we moved into Victor's ranch style house I holed up in the cellar, which happened to be under their bedroom. Victor walked heavily, even barefoot he thumped like a hippo. I cringed at the groaning bedsprings, which I convinced myself was tossing and turning and not the sexual intercourse I prayed they were refraining from. I had a TV in my room and stayed up through Johnny Carson's monologue, a habit that endured as long as Johnny did. (God! How I miss him.) Victor's heavy trod would awaken me at dawn on Saturday mornings, when he got up to play golf. He would take a lengthy spattering leak in the hall toilet as he boomed "Everything's Coming Up Roses."

Victor offered to pay my college tuition, preferably for a college far away. He wanted Mom all to himself. And I couldn't wait to start life over, far from home. Everyone I knew who went away to college came back different—not necessarily wiser or better, just different—while those who stayed home stagnated. In the distant reaches of a college campus I would wear an eye patch over my non–working eye and become a figure of mystery. I would let my hair grow. I would join a fraternity, attract girls, maybe learn to dance. With minions of other horny males, I would storm the barricades of the female dormitories in search of silky underthings, like my cousin Natie, Uncle Jake's son, whose freshman year at the University of Wisconsin was highlighted by a panty raid so tumultuous the Governor notified the National Guard, though local police managed to quell it with tear gas, according to Natie a small price to pay for a sliver of silk, possibly from the crotch, that had been lobbed at him from the twentieth floor of a high–rise dorm.

I daydreamed about going away to college. Unfortunately, much of the daydreaming took place during my classes at the junior college, where my grades were so awful I could only get probationary acceptance to Southeast Missouri State in Cape Girardeau. I flunked out in one semester: I missed my mother, and my friend Goode, who was at a local college. About all I can remember from that grim period is this gigantic turd in the men's room at our dormitory. It literally filled the toilet bowl and we stood in line to view it, trying to imagine what mortal rectum could have deposited it.

My lack of an eye spared me from the draft. As Goode and I used to say, we avoided Vietnam because I was half-blind and he was half a ton.

Victor bluntly called my father a loser, on purely financial grounds, and he chided me for majoring in math, which had no earning potential. He tried to get me to change my major to business administration; he also tried to get me to shave with an electric razor, let my flat-top grow out and part my hair on the left. He hollered at me for pouring too much Wishbone on my salad. Finally I moved into my own apartment, and after I got my B.A. and was at my loosest of loose ends Victor persuaded his company to enroll me in an actuarial trainee program. It agreed with me and I stayed with the company for twenty-five years, hardly noticing it, until I got laid off.

Victor was such a stark contrast to Dad, it seemed like a repudiation; I learned later that this was not the case, my mother simply never married the same type of man twice. Unlike Uncle Jake, his younger brother, my father was taciturn; only Jackie Gleason could make him laugh out loud. I got the sense that he never wanted children but acceded to my mother's wishes, perhaps as part of the quid pro quo that allowed him to play Jew on weekends. He always looked weary. I remember asking him about the bags under his eyes and he told me that's where he stored his dreams, the good dreams under the left eye and the bad dreams under the right. Dreams were tiny; thousands of them fit into a little pouch under the eyes and the dreams that came true instantly dissolved, making more room for future dreams. To this day I'll give a panhandler a quarter if he has bags under his eyes.

Victor's laugh was the kind of overpowering ha! you hear on TV laugh–tracks where one guy rises above the crowd. When seated, Victor often laughed so hard he had to stand up to quell his shaking body. Victor did everything noisily, from the way he rattled his keys opening the door to battering a newspaper as he turned the pages, to his megaton farts, which themselves produced hailstones of laughter. When seated he liked to raise his left haunch and shout bombs away, and it amazed me that my mother, who used to consider audible gas mortifying, now frequently exploded farts of her own and rejoiced at her digestive vapors.

Everything about Victor was exaggerated, from his overhanging belly to his shaggy eyebrows to his enormous wallet, which bulged like a huge tumor on his right buttock. He whipped it out for me once to show me pictures of various children and grandchildren, all of whom wisely lived far away, countless credit cards, a suppository, at least four driver's licenses, which he kept because he considered the photos excellent and liked having pictures of himself at various stages of his life, a folded up article that appeared about him in the paper years ago, the obituary column on his mother, his birth certificate, an autographed picture of Heddy Lamar, ticket stubs from a Broadway play, a due–bill from a department store and, as they say in the ads, much much more—all secured by a rubber band wound twice. He kept a box of rubber bands on his dresser and, my mother proudly informed me, strapped on a new one every Monday morning. Such fastidiousness. They went out dancing every Saturday night, which Mom loved. Victor was Mom's Dancing Husband, just as Lionel would be her Traveling Husband. My father never took her dancing or traveling. He worked late. He was tired.

Victor and Mom lasted nine years, until Victor died of a brain tumor. They found it late and the end came swiftly. No funeral this time around: Victor left his organs to science, in homage to his brother–in–law from his first marriage, a transplant specialist who cajoled all the family into recycling their vital organs. I don't envy the poor soul that inherited Victor's intestines, and those who live around him.

Victor left Mom well-fixed, but she nevertheless lapsed into a despondent widowhood. She was still beautiful, but she was nearly sixty and figured her marital string had run out. I ate dinner with her every night and stayed over about half the time, in my old cellar room. I had nothing going on in my personal life, though I did manage to get out most weekends. At that point I hoped my mother would settle in for a comfortable widowhood. She got hooked on <u>The Love Boat</u>, <u>Fantasy Island</u> and a host of other TV shows that featured washed-up stars. "It makes a nice evening for me," she would say dolefully. At least she didn't wear Victor's shirts to bed.

Perhaps it was <u>The Love Boat</u> that prompted Mom to take a Caribbean cruise. There she met husband number four, Alfred Lizenby. I hardly remember Alfred. He died of a heart attack only two months into the marriage, at a shriner's convention where they wear those thimble-shaped red hats with the tassels. It was almost like Pippin IV, or that Pope who died right after his installation some years back. All that to-do and then poof! he's gone before he can make any impact.

That didn't lessen Mom's grief, it only added insult to injury. I had never been so worried for her. People always praise Mom's resilience, but she's not really strong, she completely disintegrates in the face of sorrow—but I have always been there. I rescued each time from the jaws of grief—like America rescuing England, the Mother Country, from Germany war after war. Mom has been extraordinarily lucky at finding eligible men, not that her standards are terribly discriminating. Instead of resilient I rather think she is elastic. Or chameleon-like, the way she takes on the properties of her current spouse. Perhaps she went mad in order to leave Lionel before he could die on her. She told me after Alfred kicked the bucket that her husbands died intentionally just to spite her.

The other day she told me something about Alfred I'd never heard before. They had been married about three weeks, and one night she felt something sticking her in the ribs in bed. She thought it might be the TV remote, or a pen she used for the TV Guide crosswords, or Alfred seducing her from a strange angle. But no, Alfred lay sleeping, facing in the other direction. She almost screamed when she reached behind her and came up with an upper set of dentures. She put the teeth near his hand so he could find them easily when he woke up.

It shook her up, not that he wore dentures, for the guy was in his sixties, but that he had kept it a secret. Soon he woke up and she could hear him feeling around for something. Then he got up and went to the bathroom. She never let on that she knew, directly, but she did tell him about an old Hawaiian custom, where it was grounds for divorce if you discovered that your husband wore a toupee, or that a woman wore falsies. He didn't bite, so to speak. She never did ask him directly and then one day he slugged his chest, toppled over and deserted her forever. I never thought she would rebound. But along came Lionel. Mom's husbands got progressively richer. Lionel, a real estate developer, may own whole towns. Malcolm says Lionel was a pioneer in middle–income housing projects, often through bribing zoning officials.

Dr. Bratz pussyfoots into Mom's room, his shoulders hunched like Atlas. Dr. Bratz is in his sixties and has been Mom's doctor since she married Lionel. Mom always appropriates her husband's physician, except my father's, the hopelessly Jewish Dr. Feingold.

Dr. Bratz pats my mother's forehead like a faith healer and chitchats with her. More chit than chat at this point, for Mom has faded rapidly in recent weeks. It takes her three guesses to distinguish Dr. Bratz, and even then she starts talking about some ailments of yesteryear, a touch of lumbago, a kidney stone, a bout of dysentery.

Dr. Bratz diagnosed Alzheimer's early on. He could barely disguise his glee at the rare certainty with which he ventured an opinion. I tried posing some hardboiled questions about the course of the illness, medicines and their side effects, and assorted other queries, to which he responded with his patented shoulder shrug. "He even shrugs over the phone, I can hear his neck muscles creak," I told Mom. But the man has served as a comfort to Lionel, for which my mother treats him with extra deference, and like most men the doc fawns on my mother.

Lionel and I quit the room to allow Dr. Bratz some wasted time with my mother.

"Aren't those the same socks you had on yesterday?" asks Lionel as he escorts me to the elevator.

I look down at my feet. He's got me dead to rights.

At least I've got a ready answer when people ask, So why didn't you ever get married? My mother got married often enough for the both of us. She probably had feelings for Victor, but I'd say her last two marriages were marriages of convenience. Maybe Skretch is right when he says that convenience is the driving force in life. I suppose my own life has been driven by convenience, mine or someone else's.

It would have been convenient to marry Sheila.

※　　※　　※

Once Sheila and I were betrothed she began planning the rest of our lives. She exploded one immediate bombshell: she intended to get pregnant as soon as possible. She patted her abdomen, evidently wherein her biological clock ticked frenetically. A total shock, worse than discovering your spouse wears dentures. Sheila expected me to cave in, as usual. Her agenda was my agenda, her needs my needs. We would farm out the kid to day care as soon as possible while Sheila continued her quest for entrepreneurial nirvana. Meanwhile, Jerry would work another five years, take early retirement, and then tend to parental and housekeeping chores. I had the makings of an exemplary househusband. I kept such a tidy house, and I was bored with my job so why shouldn't I just pack it in?

Then suddenly I got laid off, so that the company could "better manage its resources and enhance its bottom line and exert prudent management controls to streamline the operation by downsizing." I felt very important. Just my departure would transform the profit picture. I'd never felt so integral before, what with bosses constantly pressuring me to take classes, pass exams, master computers.

Not that this cataclysmic change in my life had any effect on Sheila's scenario. She just factored it in. She figured I'd get another job, probably one that I would like a lot better than the one I lost. Even if I proved unemployable (which turned out to be the case), I'd get unemployment insurance, scheduled to expire right around our wedding date.

Sheila didn't count on my abhorrence of children. She had never tracked her periods and her cavalier attitude amazed me; if I were a woman I'd want to pin the time down to the nearest hour. I emotionally held my breath each month until the blessed flow occurred. Even if I had experienced parental quivers they would have been squelched by all I've heard from Goode. I made this clear to Sheila. I uttered a definitive no. Definitive to me but not to Sheila. We're not getting married for six months, let's see if I can change your mind, she said.

Sheila's wiles were many and unsubtle. Each time she got her period, with its moratorium on lovemaking, she reminded me that no periods would be one of the blessings of pregnancy, and that she would fuck my brains out every night for the whole nine months. Even assuming I could physically withstand such rigors, I'd learned from Goode that sex during pregnancy is sporadic at best, unwieldy at worst; plus sex disappeared entirely for months post–partum and waned for years, until your wife hungers for another child.

Sheila didn't take my back–talk easily. Once she flung a telephone directory at me, crying, "Look, every fucking person in this book had to be born. It's not such a big fucking deal!"

It was her mother's suggestion that we adopt Sheila's nephew Everett for a couple of days, on the supposition that I would glimpse the fun and fulfillment of parenthood, telescoped into forty-eight hours of bliss with Everett. The boy was cute, with huge brown eyes, a creepy little sneer reminiscent of the early Elvis, and unremitting gusto. He was a fanatic about baseball, which hardly endeared him to me, but he would also do handsprings over a Hardy Boys mystery, a fudgsicle, or a pair of argyle socks.

On the pretext of checking up at the lots Sheila left me alone with Everett one afternoon. As part of the experiment, and to avoid confusing Everett, we stayed at Sheila's for the whole three days. Everett had watched a tape of E.T. and now he sat on the floor flipping through several ring binders of baseball cards packed into cellophane pockets. He hummed to himself the theme music from E.T. I lay nearby on the sofabed, which was serving as Everett's bed. I had tucked in the sheets and pushed it in.

I was reading a People magazine and had my leg slung over the back of the couch.

"Did you ever collect baseball cards, Jerry?" asked Everett. He slurped a can of pop through a straw.

"No, never did."

"But you liked baseball?"

"At one time. When I was your age."

"But you don't, still?"

"No."

"Why not?" Everett had sucked the straw to a flat head.

"People's interests change. I went on to other things."

"Like what? So what are you interested in?" He looked at the cover of People, which featured Madonna in some lewd pose.

I hesitated.

"You're interested in Aunt Sheila?" Aunt Sheila and Uncle Jerry.

I nodded in accord. Everett, feeling he had scored a coup, took his attention elsewhere. Sheila had mentioned she had a few baseball cards from the Seventies stashed somewhere and if he could ferret them out they were his.

"She said there might be a Pete Rose. Do you know what a Pete Rose is worth?" and before I could answer he asked if I had any baseball cards from my time. "A Mickey Mantle from 1951 is worth thousands and thousand of dollars," he announced. Lord, I thought, Mickey Mantle himself was only worth about forty thousand in his career year, 1956.

After a bit more discussion I realized that Everett, who had only seen one or two baseball games in his life, rarely watched a whole game on television, and expressed little desire to actually play the game, could quote the going rates for baseball cards with all the precision of a stockbroker. So this was fandom, reduced, as the game itself had been reduced, to financial strategy. Baseball had fostered this. It would live by the dollar and die by the dollar.

As Everett plowed through the debris, taking the run of the house at a full gallop, I immersed myself in the magazine and tried to tune out the sound of an upended house being re–upended. I had fallen into a doze when Everett slugged me in the right arm. "Are these old baseball cards, or what?" He dumped on my chest a small narrow box, the kind that might house jumbo paper clips. "These are slides," I said, somewhat surprised, because Sheila never took pictures, didn't even own a camera. She also doesn't photograph well. In the photo with George Bush she looks older than he does.

"You mean like sliding into second base?"

"No, they're pictures you take with a camera and then a photo shop converts them into these little squares that you then project on a screen." None of this registered with Everett. He knew video. "People use them for their vacations. When you show them on the screen they're larger than photos and much more impressive." The boy still looked dumbfounded. Another indication of my unsuitability for parenthood: an inability to explain simply the things of this world.

"See, I bet these are from a vacation, a long time ago." I held one of the little squares up to the light and Everett looked at it. I showed him several. "Okay," he said and resumed his search.

When I studied a few slides I thought my one good eye might be playing tricks on me. What I could make out was Sheila in a two–piece bathing suit standing beside a paunchy bearded guy who had his arm around her. It was not her father. I went through the whole series. Sheila and the guy seemed to be operating a kissing clinic. Other people cropped up in the pictures; it was evidently a time of great semi–nude conviviality. I felt sharp pangs of jealously and a woozy stomach. I would ask Sheila to destroy them. I knew she'd had considerable experience ("I've slept with twenty odd men, but you're the oddest of them all, Jerry") but I figured it was my prerogative as the husband–elect to obliterate all trace of her previous beaux.

Then I noted the date on the back of a slide.

"She's at lot forty–one," said Ward. "Is this some kind of emergency?"

"I'd say so."

"Has there been some kind of accident?" he screeched.

"Just page her, Ward. Now."

"Is Everett all right?" Sheila cried, first thing.

"He's fine," I said.

There was a pause, and when I didn't go on she asked, "You okay, Jerry?"

"I saw the slides."

"What slides?"

"You and this fat guy posing for a Harlequin romance cover."

She could only muster a subdued "Oh. Those."

"You swore to me you hadn't been with anyone, from the time you met me."

"It was, it was a relationship that was ending. When I met you. I broke it off when I found you."

"You found me in a bar. Where did you pick up this guy? The zoo? I thought you hated body hair on men." If I could have strangled her with my voice, I would have.

"Jerry, you're being so fucking childish."

Suddenly Everett was at my side, looking terribly upset. He had only heard my side of the conversation. I could tell he felt somehow he was to blame for this quarrel. I rubbed his soft brown hair and forced myself to smile. He smiled back. I put my hand over the phone and whispered, "Remember, this has nothing to do with you, okay?"

"Sheila, I have to get out of here. Come right now or I'm putting Everett into a cab and getting him out of this disaster area you call home. Got it?" I hung up.

Sheila materialized in about ten minutes. That gave me time to reassure poor Everett and even try to help him find the baseball cards. He was still upset, and I considered giving him the consolation of knowing I would never be his Uncle Jerry and that I hated baseball and probably would be a lousy uncle anyway. I gathered my clothes and toiletries and any other traces of myself into a duffle bag. Sheila arrived ready to fight. She had pumped herself up driving over and had clearly determined to take the offensive.

"This is all because you're fucking unemployed," she shouted. "You're taking it out on me." I just glared at her. I wanted my ring back, but at this point I feared I'd get her fist with it. Sheila is very strong. She wanted to arm wrestle once. I declined. I said nothing. I pointed to the slides. Then I grabbed my duffle bag and headed through the door, which she had left open. She yelled after me a dozen names that I hope Everett never has the occasion to hear again.

I jogged several blocks to a bus stop. I had to wait forever for a bus, but Sheila didn't come after me. On the bus I sat beside a woman who slept restfully with her fingers twined around the handles of a red canvas bag inscribed "The Family that Prays Together,

Stays Together." As our driver negotiated a sweeping right turn he waved to an oncoming bus driver with that camaraderie all bus drivers everywhere seem to share.

🍁   🍁   🍁

There's a knock at my door. I approach warily. Byron could strike at any time. Resting my hand on the doorknob I squint through the peephole. I see nothing but there's another rap at the door. Then "It's me, Barney," and two little fingers blot the aperture.

Barney is shorter and squatter than Terence and Randy, an altogether different breed of midget. He wears a bright purple t–shirt, green iridescent sportcoat and dark glasses. His feet are so tiny his white bucks look sawed–off at the instep. He meanders through my living room, palpates my sofa, toes the legs of the coffee table. Then he roams my kitchen and bedroom and peers into my bathroom, all the while taking notes. Standard operating procedure but I can't forget he's an ex–con with a streak of kleptomania. Is he drooling over my Johnny Mathis album? Thank God there's nothing of value. I'd love to direct him to Lionel's house, chockfull of jewelry and knick-knacks brought back from journeys to foreign lands. When Barney completes his tour I offer him a seat in the living room. He prefers to pace. I sit, which makes us eye to eye.

"You don't believe in air conditioning?" he says, mopping his forehead with a red polka dot kerchief.

"I prefer fans. I like breezes," I explain. I've got a window fan in the living room, a standing fan in the bedroom and a little round portable in the kitchen. Normally I get through the summers fairly comfortably, except for the most sweltering days. In the old days I'd spend most of the day in an air–conditioned office and nights at Mom and Lionel's, or Sheila's. "Why don't you take off your jacket?"

"Terence says you might be needing help tracking somebody down."

"I might," I say.

And I proceed to spill everything to him, everything from my experience with Byron at the Chicken Coop right down to my latest vain effort to get information from Tom Hickey, the Coop's old assistant manager. He notates everything on this spiral memo pad, his little fingers working so rapidly it must be some kind of shorthand (Ha Ha). He scrutinizes the baseball carefully, claws at the stitching with his fingernails, squeezes it and drops it into his coat pocket.

"Hey, you can't have that," I say, rising.

"Okay." He places it back on the table, propped against an ashtray so it won't roll. He sighs, as if amazed at how naive I am. He skims the volume of Lord Byron's poems, stopping at pages that are dog-eared or scribbled on.

"You say you got laid off in February, Jer?"

"Yes."

"You were there how long?"

"Twenty-five years."

"Tough. Now, is there anyone at your previous place of work that might have cooked up this joke on you?"

I repeat that only John Byron had possession of this particular baseball. Only he could be the culprit. The task is to find Byron. I mention all the avenues I'd tried, that I had exhausted all possibilities.

"You've only scratched the surface," he says. "The library is the last place to go in a case like this. This is no term paper you're talking about here."

"So what do I do, sign some contract with your agency?"

"I'm freelancing."

"I have very little money. I am unemployed."

"I can sympathize. I been there a time or two. But this won't cost you much. Terence is my good buddy, I'd almost do this as a freebie excepting I need the bread. Anyway, I won't gouge you like my agency would, on account of they have to factor in overhead and expenses that I don't have, working solo." He points his Bic pen in my face in a way that gouge takes on both its meanings. "Like, with our computer we could track down the guy's Social Security number, credit records. State–of–the–art stuff, you know, but I'm not authorized to use it on my own."

He charges a flat one hundred dollars for his time and expenses. When and if he finds Byron, he gets another five hundred. If he doesn't find Byron, or at least evidence of Byron's death, then no more charges. He summarizes this arrangement briskly. He gives the impression that money is not as important to him as the thrill of the chase.

I offer him something to drink.

"I never drink on duty. I'm the child of three alcoholics."

"Three?"

"A stepmother makes three."

"Not even ice water?"

"Nothing. I will need to see your mother."

I'm assessing whether this guy is possibly worth one hundred dollars—I can't even remember if it's Franklin or U.S. Grant on the bill, it's been so long since I've seen one—and he comes out with a ludicrous request like this. "Why in God's name do you need to see her? I told you she was batso."

"Just five minutes. I have to examine every minute particular of your life. Now, do you think this Byron character may have been stalking you?"

"He knows where I live. He's left two packages for me."

"Do you consume pornography?"

"I don't see..."

"By which I mean girlie mags, X–rated videos etcetera."

I have a slew of magazines in a drawer in my bedside table. I swear he didn't look in the drawer.

"I'll take that for a yes. Jer, there are forces operating here you may not be aware of. And you don't have to worry about them, you're hiring me to do that. But you got to realize, if somebody's invading your life it could be anything."

"It's revenge, Barney, pure and simple. A vendetta. Granted, after thirty years it's a time–release vendetta."

"Let me finish, Jer. You have to be more paranoid. We can't rule out anything. The U.S. Government could be after you. Byron could be a code name for some top–secret operation."

"It is?"

"No, but it could be. Maybe this Byron was a CIA agent. Maybe this baseball, that you for some reason refuse to entrust me with, maybe it has stuck inside it some top–secret information that Byron has dumped on you for safekeeping. Maybe one of them poems in that book is in code. You got to believe anything is possible. You might even be in great personal danger. Not that I want to frighten you. Now, how much do you know about this Lionel who's married to your mother?"

"Lionel!"

"You tell me he's a developer, that means he's crooked all ten fingers and toes. Developers blow up whole townships, they're capable of anything. I told you, we haven't even scratched the surface."

"I don't think the surface is as itchy as you make out, Barney."

"Jer, there are only two principles I live by in this business. One: nothing is what it seems. And two: most of what you're looking for is right under your nose. This is all happening to you, so you don't know what's real and what isn't. Even if it's right under your nose. You can't be objective, even if you happen to be intelligent, which I can't really tell yet. And isn't it worth a hundred dollars to find out?" Barney's face caves in like the rippled paper wrapping of a blueberry muffin, after you've removed the muffin.

"You being a friend of Terence, plus out of work and all, you can pay the hundred in installments. Say, twenty now as a down payment, and twenty a week for the next four weeks. Does that sound fair to you?"

I pull two tens from my wallet and shake hands with Barney. Terence will get me my money back if it comes to that.

"You know, Jer, if this pans out you can sell the damn baseball and pay my fee ten times over. Some of those things are valuable. Very important, Jerry. Tell absolutely no one, not even Terence, that I am working for you. I must be completely under cover."

"How do you expect to see my mother, without me there to get you in?"

"Leave that to me. That might be the simplest thing on my whole laundry list of things to do."

"So can I expect to see you lurking about everywhere I go?"

"Jer, if you spot me, I am not doing my job. Tell you what, any time you see me—not counting when we set up a meeting and it's intentional—but any time you spot me I will refund twenty dollars payable on demand."

"When will I hear from you again?"

"Maybe in fifteen minutes, maybe a week. Depends. You're sure I can't take that baseball with me? We have a lab with all the latest techniques."

"No way, Barney."

Inching toward the door, whose knob abuts his Adam's apple, Barney pans my apartment one more time. "Oh, one other thing, Jerry. You got two window screens in your bedroom that need to be replaced. And a faucet in the bathroom that's dripping money away. I do a little contracting on the side and I'd be proud to give you an estimate."

"One job at a time, Barney."

I don't trust Barney any farther than I can throw him—which is relatively far—but my conversation with him leaves my heart palpitating and I look at the baseball and the volume of poetry on my coffee table and I think, Okay, you guys, your days are numbered. Talking to Barney has made me realize how desperate I am to solve this mystery, and how alone I've been in trying to solve it. Barney is the first person I've told the whole story to, the only one with a vested interest in it. It felt good to spew out to him every aspect of my life—my crazy mother, Sheila, Joanne, the men's club, the unemployment office, my thirtieth reunion. It gives me perspective. I even kind of like the idea of my life being in danger.

My phone rings and I fully expect it to be Barney with some great revelation. But no, it's Joanne, begging off for tonight, which is Friday. Truth to tell, I forgot today is Friday. At first I'm relieved. I've begun to wonder if we should switch our arrangement to every other Friday night. I don't think I'm really satisfying her, and I find myself growing restless in her company. Joanne sounds distressed, her voice has that quaver in it that usually follows a meeting or conversation with Edward. Her thesis has got her down, she must dedicate every free moment to finishing it, even if it means sacrificing our Friday nights. I feign disappointment.

I'm due to drop in on Goode, but he's playing <u>Lassie Come Home</u> and <u>Song of Bernadette.</u>

Joanne calls back ten minutes later and says please come over now. She needs to talk to me. I get a bus to her place, where she greets me empty-handed, no Jack Daniels, and restrains my wrist when I start to disrobe. She's sabotaging our custom and it makes me uncomfortable. I had put on the bikini briefs, which I hate wearing; they get more snug with every washing and I can never tell the front from the rear. Just hold me, Joanne says, and I sit on the couch cradling her head against my belly. She closes her eyes and we listen to the radio, like an old married couple.

My stomach is gurgling from hunger and I wonder if the sounds annoy her or, better still, if she's getting the message that it's time to fix me dinner. She sits up and with tears in her eyes tells me that she is blowing her adviser. I feel a twinge of jealousy mingled with a jolt of arousal. Women are so much easier to deal with if you're not in love with them. I lock my face into a sympathetic frown and listen intently until she says she did it to get an extension. When I burst out laughing at the inadvertent pun her tears turn to laughter and we seem to have our Friday night back again.

But after we eat a delivered Chinese dinner she relapses into depression about Edward, her thesis, the general chaos that is her life. In bed she just wants to be held, so I put my libido in storage for a week. This chastity is chastening. Perhaps we should still see each other every Friday but make love only every other week. As she snuggles in my arms I tell her how much she has going for her: she's bright, attractive, a wonderful lover, dynamite cook, and as I rattle off her assets I ask myself why I haven't fallen in love with her.

"Then why hasn't anyone fallen in love with me?" she asks. "Because you're so tied to Edward," I reply, parroting what Sheila told me time and again. "In your mind you belong to Edward, and you project, well, a kind of unavailability."

I hate snuggling. Women can lie this way for hours, even sleep this way, it must be something hormonal. I feel pinned and desperate for escape. Joanne's hair itches my neck and chin. I keep having to reach up and scratch, but Joanne just coos. My mind replays the whole scene with Barney. He's got me feeling excited and hopeful again.

"I'm giving head to get ahead," Joanne says. "And I'm not even sleeping my way to the top. More like the top of the bottom. I bet Sheila never had to suck off anybody."

"How do you know?" I ask.

"Are you telling me she did?" asks Joanne eagerly, at last lifting her head from my shoulder.

"No, not that I know of. But nothing is what it seems. And most of what you're looking for is right under your nose."

She looks up at me perplexedly, pats my cheek, turns over and is asleep within minutes. I quietly unplug her digital clock. I like Joanne and wish I could help her. Perhaps she should threaten this adviser with a sexual harassment charge. Either he okays her thesis or she goes public about the coercive fellatio. She could get a pile of money, except Edward would dump her and she wouldn't want to risk that. I wish, just once, someone had sexually harassed me at the insurance company, promised me a promotion—hell, just promised to keep me on—in return for a small sexual favor. Of course, I mean a woman. Not that there were any woman bosses at the company. But how nice to imagine some stately fortyish woman with a modicum of sexual attractiveness ducking her head into my carrel and lightly tapping my shoulder and murmuring into my ear, Miller, you just step into my office for a minute and we'll get real comfortable and you can give me one good reason to let you keep that lousy job you've hated for twenty–five years.

CHAPTER 6

❀

The mayor, flanked by a Boy Scout and two Girl Scouts, looked down on us from a pavilion of knotty pine erected the night before in front of the Chicken Coop. The Boy Scout had yanked the American flag from its quiver near the doorway, slid it off the pole and folded it down to napkin size. He flicked a lighter and set the flag aflame—evidently what you do to a flag freshly obsolete because Alaska and Hawaii had joined the Union, though many of us gasped at what smacked of an act of treason—and then trampled on the charred remains.

The Girl Scouts unfurled the new fifty-star flag. One of them hailed from Alaska; she was visiting the area as part of a national Girl Scout convention in Lawrence, Kansas that summer. Goode and I had joked that we should crash the convention and find ourselves some girlfriends. Without such drastic measures, we feared we'd go through high school without ever having a date. This girl did not look like an Eskimo, which back then I assumed all Alaskans to be.

The parking lot was jampacked and Kuker had delayed the morning's opening for the fifteen-minute ceremony. All of us employees stood together toward the front, as Kuker ordered. A minister intoned a benediction and as the Girl Scouts hoisted the flag we recited the Pledge of Allegiance, with a jumble at "under God," perhaps because of atheists and communists in our midst. For whatever reason some people skipped the phrase and went right into "indivisible." Which promptly divided us. Through a whistling microphone the mayor read a proclamation from President Kennedy and then his own proclamation, which took longer than the president's. The Chicken Coop sponsored a Little League team and they tramped up to the platform all suited up with bats and gloves to lead us in the National Anthem. Then the mayor called for all Americans to unite to fight communism, deftly inserting a few plugs for the school levy and a bond measure to rebuild the civic center. There were TV cameras and I saw a reporter interviewing customers and some store employees. Uncle Jake greeted me brusquely; Mom had been snubbing him, or maybe he'd heard about my ineptitude from Kuker and was ashamed of me. He conceived the whole ceremony, so maybe he was just preoccupied with how it was going. Dark clouds drifted overhead and the Boy Scout told us we'd have to shelter the new flag if it rained.

The mayor concluded with an admonition about the dangers of fireworks. One of the owners of the Chicken Coop gave a little speech about this once in a lifetime opportunity to honor America and how proud he was that the Chicken Coop chain throughout the Kansas City area was conducting these ceremonies on this historic Monday, July 3. By this time nobody was listening. It was a hot humid morning and the crowd had grown restless.

"So I guess we're all present and accounted for," said the produce man in front of me.

"All but one. That bastard Byron," snarled Hickey. I pricked up my ears at the mention of the man whom I considered a friend since our excursion to Mrs. Rosenberg. I knew Byron was bitterly opposed to adding Alaska and Hawaii, which he thought would destroy the symmetry of our country. He thought we were getting too big for our britches and he didn't see how Eskimos and Polynesians fit into the picture. "The melting pot is already boiling over as it is," he said one day. "I detest this rickety bridge we're trying to build to alien cultures. Like we're latter day conquistadors, but with annexation rather than conquest in mind."

I disagreed, since I worshiped President Kennedy. We needed to be as big as we could, to fight Russia. Byron also pooh poohed the Alan Shepard space flight as unadulterated imperial greed. So I wondered if he might be boycotting this ceremony in protest.

"I've had about all I can take from that Byron," said Hickey. "I'm tired of his lip, and he's been dogging it for years."

"But maybe the guy is really sick today."

"He's probably getting drunk," scowled Hickey. "He thinks he's better than the rest of us because he went to college. Kuker says we can't outright fire him, because of the union, otherwise I'd have canned him years ago. And now he picks the busiest day of the summer to take a sick day. We'll have guys working here all night, and that's overtime, doing his job."

I didn't know if I should tell Byron what I'd heard. I'm sure he knew he was in Hickey's doghouse. I was in Hickey's doghouse, too. Hickey caught me taking a tip from one of the customers and he bawled me out, said it was grounds to fire me if he caught me at it again.

But I had little leisure to think of John Byron that day, a day of unremitting tumult. The store had labeled a variety of merchandise with red, white and blue stickers, meaning the item was half price today only from opening till midnight. I overheard Hickey saying that it was a flimflam, most of the stuff was to be on sale anyway and the extra discount only amounted to a dime or so off each item. But the customers stampeded the store as if looking to stock their fallout shelters. We had a couple of extra sackers to help out, but even so it was too much. I was run ragged. Mothers ditched their children in the frenzy of grabbing oleo at half price and I saw scads of little kids darting from aisle to aisle with terror on their faces. One kid was just crying and sucking his thumb and I took him by the hand and led him to Kuker's perch.

Kuker was furious. "It's a mother's job to control her children," he spat at me. "I don't pay you to babysit." As I turned to go I bumped into a woman who shoved me aside. She had something wadded up in her fist. "I found these behind the Charmin. Filth! Filth!" She threw the object at Kuker and I knew the Pantyman had struck again. The customers all seemed to have gone berserk. Stockboys ran helter–skelter to return displaced merchandise that had been dumped aisles away, and to restock the sale items. One customer was incensed that we had run out of Metrocal and I heard Hickey again cursing John Byron for not having requisitioned a sufficient supply.

Customers were rude to each other. I heard one man tell a woman, "If you think we're all in your way, why don't you just annihilate us with your breath?" I had a knack for being in the wrong place at the wrong time. I was loading groceries into a trunk when I saw a white Chevy Impala pull quickly out of a parking space and ram the fender of an oncoming station wagon. The Chevy sped away. The driver of the station wagon sprang from her car and grabbed my wrist.

"What was the license number?" I had not seen the license number or much of anything else, beyond the fact that it was a woman with one of those bouffant hairdos driving the car. There are times when one eye is not enough, mostly times involving cars.

The driver of the station wagon was a steady customer. She wore shorts which showcased the webs of dark red veins on her thighs, which led Peter, my fellow carryout boy, to dub her the Delta Queen. She had always been nice to me and in fact she was the one whose illicit tip had been spotted by Hickey. She probably figured I owed her something; she also assumed any teenaged boy witnessing an accident would have the presence of mind to note the driver's license on a hit–and–run vehicle. When I couldn't help her she towed me to Kuker's watchtower, where we waited in a long line of customers complaining about the depletion of sale merchandise, or needing to get their checks approved. The Delta Queen clung so tightly to my wrist I could feel the throb of my own pulse. The cashiers yelled for carryout help and here I was tethered to this she–devil.

Kuker took my side, grudgingly. "Jared's not the brightest kid, Mrs. Bonner, but he was doing his job by concentrating on loading groceries." The woman hissed, but Kuker appeased her. "You give me a good description of the car and we'll nab her next time she comes into the store. I'll hold Jared here personally responsible." I could see the woman's jaw relax a bit, though she retained her hold on my wrist. "Plus, Mrs. Bonner, here's a voucher for ten dollars worth of merchandise, redeemable at any Chicken Coop store. I can't tell you how sorry we are that this accident occurred on our premises." At that she released me and I dove back into the fray.

My mom laughed at my account of a day I regarded as catastrophic. She said it sounded like a Keystone Kops, everybody in fast–motion on a collision course. She had laughed so rarely all summer that I didn't mind her getting her jollies at my expense. At the mention of Uncle Jake's aloofness she just said he's always been a screwball and he always will be. I didn't learn till years later that he had asked her to make a contribution to the synagogue in my father's memory and when she refused he swore he would never speak to her again. Evidently the vow also included me.

Given Mom's mirthful reaction, I figured John Byron would enjoy hearing about the Fourth. He always spoke so cynically about the Chicken Coop, especially Kuker and Hickey, that I figured he would be thrilled. I could hear him say, "Well, I suppose they'll be burning this flag too, once we add Puerto Rico and Guam." At the same time, Hickey's remarks about Byron had made an impression on me. Was Byron really was so incompetent and condescending? I remembered his cavalier comments about Esther Rosenberg.

We had off July 4, so I didn't see Byron till two days later. I approached him in his lunchtime lair, but as I drew closer I noticed he had no book or sandwich but sat stooped over, staring into the mouth of a Coke bottle that he held between his knees. He sniffled—nothing abnormal about that, what with his allergy to Mango, and the likelihood that he was getting over the flu— but I saw his eyes moist with tears and the sniffles came in rapid gasps. I hesitated. I started to slip away but he saw me. He just shook his head.

"What's the matter?" I asked, pulling up a crate. It dawned on me that he had been fired, and my immediate thought was how lonely I'd be without him.

"Dead," said Byron.

"Your father?" I asked.

The crinkly smile, which vanished in a split second. No, his father died years ago.

"Then what? Who?"

"Hemingway. My Hemingway."

Mom had read me the headline about Hemingway's death, amid a torrential update on the Eichmann trial, troubles in Berlin, a stripper appearing in Kansas City named Mickey Maris, Kodak's introduction of Kodachrome II, and a new movie about Jesus that dared to show the Savior's face. I knew Byron revered Hemingway, but I never would have expected anyone to cry over some writer, unless you knew him personally. I asked Byron if he knew Hemingway, or were they related in some way.

"In some way," he said. He removed his glasses and ran a forearm across his eyes. Not even a blow–by–blow of the Fourth would have cheered him.

A short time later Ty Cobb, the greatest baseball player of all time, died at age seventy–five. He and Babe Ruth were the closest I came to a godhead. With a fundamentalist's zeal I had devoured every scrap written about Cobb and committed every available statistic to memory. Not the least of Cobb's achievements was his reign as the five–time batting champion in my private major league board game, which in many ways I considered more authentic than historical reality. The man's brutal competitiveness, reclusiveness and egotism were legion but to me his heroic numbers reduced matters of character to rubble. His feats on the diamond had been preternatural, incomparable, the outer limits of greatness and everyone but the Babe seemed puny in comparison.

Yet his death left me absolutely cold. I read the obituary carefully, checking for factual errors. I was far more impressed with a misbegotten headline, "Angles Trounce White Sox, 12–3," than I was by a sportswriter's windy appreciation of Tyrus Raymond Cobb. That morning Byron looked at me dolefully. He closed his book and set it gingerly on the cement floor. For a moment I thought Steinbeck had died. But he said, "I read about Ty Cobb. I know he was your idol." He patted me on the shoulder, only to pull away quickly when I snorted.

"He was an old man," I explained. "He has been out of baseball for thirty years." He looked at me with dismay, the way Eddie Felson's old partner looks at him when Eddie dumps him, tells him to roll over and die, and the old man says, "So this is how it ends. Just like that." I resented Byron's disapproval, his failure to grasp that the Cobb who mattered could never die.

He would forever live in my mind's eye—which unlike my physical eyes had perfect vision. Cobb the man had died the day he quit playing.

My emotions were far stronger about the second All–Star game, to be held in two weeks, a pointless charade that I would refuse to watch on television or even read about. And Maris was on a pace to break the Babe's record. That depressed me no end. My dad would have rooted for Maris. Dad always pulled for the underdog, maybe because Jews were kind of underdogs. I, on the other hand, always supported the indubitably great, which usually meant the indubitably dead.

"You may recall, Jerry–Jared, that I once mentioned a baseball artifact of mine that I thought might be of interest to you. Why not drop by this weekend and I'll show it to you?"

I had never tried to imagine a life for John Byron outside the Chicken Coop. We had never strayed from the place together except for that one mission to Mrs. Rosenberg. His invitation took me off balance, but I saw no reason to refuse. Mom encouraged me to go: "He's in a nice part of town, one of those old houses. You should feel flattered that someone at work takes an interest in you."

Byron's house was about a three–mile jaunt but I was a lusty biker upon my Schwinn, colored a baseball diamond emerald. I gripped the chrome handlebars and gritted my teeth. Bikehood was in flower: they made bikes heavy in those days, like cars. I loved its solidity. I had always disdained the frilly gestures of other kids, the crepe paper streamers on the handlebars, playing cards flapping in the spokes, popping wheelies. I would no more pop a wheelie than the Lone Ranger would hiyo Silver through a giant garter.

I needed grit and stamina because my pathetic sense of direction often took me miles out of my way. Today was no exception. I was lathered with perspiration when I arrived at Byron's doorstep. My moist fingers smudged the black wrought iron door knocker, which presented the face of a scowling bearded man. The Byron who opened the door wore a short–sleeved yellow knit shirt and a pair of blue shorts. For some reason his bare arms and shins startled me. At work he always wore a blue long–sleeved oxford shirt and khakis. I once asked him why he wore a blue shirt every day and he said, "It goes with my eyes," which in fact were light brown. His legs were spindly and hairless like a girl's. I stepped into a foyer of green and white hexagonal tiles and followed Byron into a high–ceilinged room, which further disoriented me. I was not used to seeing Byron in such a vaulted expanse, but rather in the dim confines of the Chicken Coop's back room. In this large hall he seemed to have shrunk in stature.

He touched my brow with the back of his hand and fluttered his fingers in my face. "You're damp as Hercules after his labors," he said. He had touched me occasionally, little pats on the back, the shoulder, always to encourage me, but this time I flinched. For the first time I noticed how delicate and small his hands were, with fingers so slim and smooth they seemed to lack knuckles.

"I got lost," I explained. He offered me a Coke, smiling that he would not charge me a quarter for it, though the ice would cost a dollar. I followed him through an immense dining room past a dark wood sideboard studded with little diamond shaped mirrors. Two hutches flanked a large bay window and housed a display of china, the dishes standing on their gilded edges with the illustrated surface facing outward. You couldn't imagine eating on them. A smaller case held ornate cut glass animals, mostly hippos. Oriental rugs covered the floors. Most people I knew either had bare floors or wall-to-wall shag like we had.

I wondered why a man who lived in such a mansion had to work at the Chicken Coop. When Byron handed me the Coke I was relieved it was in a regular plastic glass, the kind they used to give away at gas stations. Byron himself held a tall fluted glass brimming with foam-crested beer. In the living room I sat in a brocaded easy chair with curved fat legs. Byron sank into a rocking chair, which he called the genuine article, a nineteenth-century specimen, unlike the junk everyone was buying nowadays, in imitation of President Kennedy.

There were two wall high dark paneled bookcases in the room, holding volumes in glossy bindings that shone like jewels. The walls were hung with paintings like the kind you see in a museum. One was a portrait of a dignified man, with his hair parted in the middle and wearing a vested suit from the Twenties.

"My father," said Byron. "He was a very handsome man with a law degree but he never practiced. My mother came from a wealthy family and my father mimed a series of professions, but really specialized in golf. She had married beneath her, but then, as one noble lady put it, all women do. My mother was exceedingly cultivated, and it was from her I inherited my taste for books and music." Only then did I realize the music emanating from a console in the dining room. Our conversations usually were accompanied by the whir of the compressor, or the rumblings of our fellow employees.

My every word seemed to ricochet against the walls and my every move felt calculated, unlike at the Coop, where our conversations were brief, disconnected, ad lib. I crossed and uncrossed my legs several times. The vivid colors of the Oriental rugs swirled like a maelstrom at my feet. Even Byron's voice lacked its usual soothing elegance. Perhaps it was the acoustics of the large room but he seemed more formal, almost stuffy. Words came slowly and there were long pauses, as if there were a third party in the conversation who was speaking but whom I couldn't hear. Yet Byron smiled frequently, not the old crinkly smile but a wide–lipped one, exhibiting the mangled teeth. He rocked steadily and I had the sense of talking to someone in motion, whereas at the Coop he normally sat still as a statue with a book and his lunch.

He rose from the rocker, took the glass from my hand and placed it on a coaster labeled St. Louis World's Fair. All tables had white lace doilies under the lamps. The wallpaper was a pale blue with yellowish flowers. I later told my mother it seemed like a granny house, though I'd only known one grandparent, my mother's mother in Nebraska, who lived in a farmhouse.

"Where's your television?" I asked.

Byron laughed. "Dear me, I don't own one. I suppose I should, just to be au courant. I've long been a radio man, but the radio is worthless now, except for Bob and Ray and the Metropolitan Opera broadcasts. You want to know something else? I don't own a telephone, either. I know that seems positively antediluvian but I hate the telephone. I had ours disconnected after my mother died five years ago. It's all either interruptions, like salesmen, or wrong numbers, or bad news. I find it a most inadequate compromise between seeing someone in person or having them write me. Nobody writes letters anymore. The only letters they write are the initials of the power and light company, when they pay their monthly bill."

Byron wiped the sweat from his beer glass. He started to ask, "What do you want..." To be when I grew up? To eat? To do now? when I heard a ping. Without a word Byron slapped his knees and marched off into the kitchen. He returned with a platter of brownies, which he held under my chin. The aroma was intoxicating. I took one. "And a napkin, please," Byron said. He placed the platter on a side table. He broke a brownie in half and cradled it on a napkin as he strode back to his rocker. Crumbs fell out of my mouth and I tried to flick them back in. I stared at a picture on the wall over Byron's head. Framed in dark, heavy wood, it was another portrait of a man, in the garb of another century.

Byron trailed my gaze. "There have been several great John Byrons in history and this fellow is one of them. He served as one of the Royalist commanders during the English civil war. That was in the seventeenth century..."

"I know," I said, through a mouthful of brownie. I had just finished one of my father's books on this period.

"Oh, I forget, you're a history buff."

"I haven't seen any mention of this John Byron," I said, with some satisfaction.

"I've read a couple of books about him. Mind you, one can never read enough about one's namesakes."

"Does that mean you're an ancestor of his?"

"I think you mean a descendant. I've never attempted to trace my lineage but my great grandfather, also a John, must have had some reason for buying this portrait. I'll bet there was a notable Jared Miller some time in history. At any rate, the John Byron posturing here was a celebrated Puritan killer. A real ruthless take–no–prisoners mentality. Quoth he: `I put them all to the sword, which I find to be the best way to deal with these kind of people.' Please help yourself to another brownie or two, Jerry–Jared."

The brownies were delicious, chewy and dense with a rich fudge. I'd never heard of a man who could bake brownies.

"I wish I could claim Lord Byron, whose father and grandfather, incidentally, were also named John." Brandishing his beer glass toward the overstuffed bookcases, "I have virtually every edition of Lord Byron's works, at least up to about nineteen–fifty, including some in paperback. Remind me, when your historical survey reaches the nineteenth century, to lend you <u>Don Juan</u>. I found it quite stirring when I was your age. Haven't felt much affinity for the old libertine ever since."

"I thought you didn't loan books. I mean, lend books. Didn't you tell me that once?"

"You shouldn't pay such heed to my gratuitous remarks."

"But didn't you say that?"

"So I contradict myself. All men do, the great and not so great."

My whole body ached from the arduous ride; my skin felt clammy against the rough texture of the upholstery. I concentrated on chewing my brownie, as Byron went on. "Lord Byron was a great English poet. The Babe Ruth of poetry, you might say. Lots of home runs, but an excessive zest for life. I doubt they'll let you graduate from high school without making his acquaintance."

The reference to Ruth at last provided an opening. "You told me you had a baseball thing to show me?"

Byron said of course, but first he had to change the record, which he removed from the turntable with extreme caution, resting it on his palm turned upwards with four fingers supporting the label and a thumb to the edge. "The third Brandenburg is buoyant enough to serve as baseball music."

Byron motioned for me to join him at the dining room table, on which reposed a shiny wood case the size of a cigar box. He unlatched the case and there, on a flesh–colored satin lining, lay a baseball. It was covered with autographs and looked no different from the autographed baseballs Dad had bought over the years, signed by the A's.

Yet Byron held the ball in his cupped hands as if it were the most fragile porcelain.

When I deciphered the signatures I shouted, "Holy Cow! Holy Christ!" Byron had seen me dithery and frantic, but never so emotional.

"I thought you'd be impressed, Jerry–Jared. Not to the point of euphoria, however."

"Do you know what you've got here?" I asked. I still felt too awed to touch the ball. I just pointed to it.

Byron handed me the ball. I held it over the table, in case my quivering mitts fumbled it. With my index finger I followed each line and loop, declaiming the hero's name. Dizzy Dean. Paul Dean. Frankie Frisch. Pepper Martin. Joe Medwick. Rip Collins. Leo Durocher. Ernie Orsatti. Spud Davis. Jesse Haines. Burleigh Grimes. Dazzy Vance. The Gashouse Gang, the 1934 Cardinals, one of the greatest teams ever assembled. Third best of all time, according to my All-Star Baseball league of yore. The signatures shone as a divine calligraphy, as if for one moment gods had deigned to put pen to horsehide. I was transported to 1934, to the shadows of Sportsmen's Park; my trembling hands melted in the manly grips of these great men. Some of the handwriting was illegible, some signatures were even superimposed on others, but I knew the roster by heart and could almost read by touch, like Braille.

"Where did you get this?" I stammered.

"Oh, that's a long story."

"Can I have it?" I blurted.

"The story?"

"The ball. I mean, could you sell it to me?"

Byron frowned. "Oh, it's not for sale. It's a memento. A keepsake. You see, it's tied in with…"

"I'll give you anything," I said.

I was determined to wrest it from him. I was never a covetous person, so this overweening lust was as unfamiliar as it was overpowering.

Byron seemed to ponder just what he might extort from me, the way a man reacts when a girl he desires purrs, Oh I'd do just about anything in the world if…My insides churned. Byron reached for the ball but I clutched it to my chest.

"You don't even care about baseball. Baseball is everything to me. It means more to me than any human being." As my passion for baseball was just beginning to wane I suppose I was clinging to a love that was dying, and the ball stirred my moribund passion. I don't think I really coveted it so much as I wanted to feel the passion again.

Byron turned red. He had been so smug here in his castle, with its elegant decor and resonant walls, I enjoyed seeing him squirm. But I was also determined to get that baseball.

"I can perhaps make one offer," he said. "You can have it after, or when I die. I have no one else to leave it to."

He stroked the green felt carpet on which the ball had rested. "If you don't give it to me I'll never speak to you again," I said.

"I hope not. I have grown fond of you."

"So can I have it?"

"No, you cannot."

I wrung the ball in my hands like a pitcher rubbing the gloss from a new ball. I would throw it through one of the mullioned windows if Byron proved adamant.

"Why? I just want to know why."

"Give it back right now and leave my house," said Byron. He extended his hand. With my fist squeezing the ball I slugged Byron in the stomach. I had never hit anyone in my life, nor was I particularly strong, despite my isometrics, and Byron's stomach was surprisingly firm; yet I must have hit a vulnerable place because the air went out of him and he dropped to his knees. His glasses fell off.

"Hickey hates you. He wants to fire you," I said. I raised Dizzy Dean's scrawl to my lips. Byron grabbed a chair and pulled himself up. He again extended his hand. This time I put the ball in the case and slammed down the lid. I fled through the foyer, my heels clapping the immaculate tiles, and out the front door, full of anger, hate and righteous indignation. I found the way home easily, pumping furiously.

※　　　　※　　　　※

Hickey summoned us one by one. He had posted himself in a small office I didn't even know existed. You could only enter it from outdoors, on the south side of the store, through an unmarked grey door. Steve, my fellow carryout boy, came back looking distraught and told me I was next. I didn't know what I was in for except I knew it would be harsh. I had never had a pleasant exchange with Hickey.

The office was tiny, dusty and cluttered, with dingy stucco walls and a dirty maroon acoustical tile ceiling. Hickey sat with his feet up on a small desk. The soles of his shoes were splotched with gum, the heels worn almost flat. Behind him on retired aluminum shelving stood some ledger books and magazines. The supports tilted precariously. There were no windows and the overhead light had no covering for the one working bulb in the three available sockets. Hickey instructed me to sit down in a folding chair. A tall man in wheat jeans and shirt sleeves leaned against a wall. Hickey introduced him as Detective Huff. I had seen him moseying around the store but had never pegged him for our floorwalker. Both Hickey and Detective Huff were smoking.

"Miller, I won't beat around the bush," Hickey said. "Some bastard has been stashing ladies underpants in this store. It's been going on for months. But Detective Huff and I have found our man. I mean we have narrowed it down to two guys. Now, they could be in cahoots. First, what I want to ask you is, do you have any knowledge who this might be?"

I said no.

"I have now talked to every employee in this store and several of them say they think it's two people. One of those people is you. What do you have to say for yourself?"

Words caught in my throat. I began to tremble.

"I wouldn't put it past you, Miller. I've already got so many demerits against you I could can you in a minute, no matter what your uncle says. Even if you're not the pervert who's been doing this. In my twenty years in this business I've never seen such a total incompetent. Dishonest, too. You haven't been taking any more tips have you?"

I shook my head.

"Now, you confess to this and we won't press any criminal charges. We'll fire you, of course. We'll have to tell your parents. And it might go on your record somewhere, if you ever try to work for the government. You'll never get elected to the Supreme Court." He looked over at Huff smiling. "So what'll it be?"

"I didn't do it."

"Can't hear you."

"I didn't do it."

"Then who did?" He rose and leaned across the desk as if he were coming to get me. "I have a feeling you know, but you're not telling. Well, I told you we've narrowed it down to two. You were one. The other is that fairy, John Byron. Now, let me make it simple for you. Maybe Byron made you do this. We always see you guys off plotting together, avoiding the rest of us. Maybe you and that fairy have been hatching this together. Maybe Byron hatched it and got you to do it. It might go easier on you if he forced you to do it. Played you for a sucker."

I rubbed my eyes, inflamed from the smoke. "Byron."

Hickey sat down, put his feet back on the desk and blew a smoke ring. He grinned at me. "Have you seen him actually doing it? No? Well, did he mention it to you?"

"Well, sort of. He's always telling me how he has put one over on you and Mr. Kuker." This was true, although it referred to Byron's quirky requisitioning of merchandise he liked rather than those selected by the store's management.

"That sounds pretty persuasive to me," said Hickey.

"Next best thing to red–handed," said Huff.

Hickey handed me a ballpoint pen and a clipboard with a single printed sheet on it. "Now this is just between us guys. Don't tell anyone about this, ever, especially not that uncle of yours. You sign this and you can keep your job. Otherwise I would fire you anyway. I got grounds galore. But this store is going to pot over this scandal. All we need is for it to get into the papers and that would be curtains for all of us. I have worked twenty years in this business and I'm not going to throw it away because some dumb fairy is littering the aisles with underwear."

At this long range, I wonder what really gave me the willies at Byron's house, what made the atmosphere so sinister. Even if Hickey had used words like homo or queer, which I at least halfway understood, I doubt I would have imputed such perversities to Byron. All I knew was that I was off the hook. I had narrowly averted ruination. And a creature who had offended me would be removed.

I kept my pledge to Hickey and told no one, not even my mother. Any pangs of guilt centered on the act of lying rather than the consequences for the man who had himself betrayed me by denying me what I wanted. Any remorse was leavened with a sense of justice. Perhaps I even took pride in saving my own skin, putting myself first, after so many months of subordinating my own needs to those of my mother.

I missed Byron but not for long. A month later school began. I took a job in the cafeteria and a weekend paper route. The Eichmann trial ended, the Berlin Wall went up, the Commissioner ruled that Maris had to break the record in one–hundred fifty–four games or be forever diminished, Goode and I swung a double–date to <u>Gidget</u>

Goes Hawaiian, and my mother's spirits revived when some presentable suitors appeared, though she steadfastly refused them. For her forty–ninth birthday I bought her a bottle of crepe de chine, the perfume Dad always gave her. She hugged me and told me I was the number one guy in her life and wasn't she lucky. I never saw the inside of the Chicken Coop, or the face of John Byron, again.

CHAPTER 7

Skretch can't believe he was ever friends with a man like Warren Caspary, or that he could be a close friend yet know a man so poorly. We have given up trying to console him or change the subject. Now we talk amongst ourselves, while he sits staring at the dartboard. He hasn't spoken for a half hour.

Lila has avoided our table: she realizes types like us don't drown our sorrows, we hang them out to dry. Which means the tip will be smaller than usual. Or maybe she read about Caspary in the newspaper and wants nothing to do with us. Guilt by association.

But the Warren Caspary who captured today's headlines was not the man we had associated with. The newspaper account, and I suppose television (my tube goes unrepaired) home in on the sensational aspects, but there's always extenuating circumstances when something cold–blooded and senseless happens. Not that I intend to give Caspary the benefit of the doubt.

Skretch surprises me. I expected him to explode, wage a violent bout at the dart board or ram his fender into a neighbor's aluminum garbage can. But no. His broad face sags like a balloon whose helium has seeped out. Not only did we not know Caspary very well, perhaps we don't know Skretch either. Skretch sets a few bills on the table to cover a beer he hardly sipped and quietly takes his leave.

For a while we converse stiltedly about other matters. No one wants to go first with gossip about our best friends. It takes will power to avoid the topic. Goode, the embodiment of lack of will power, succumbs first.

"Do you think he was drunk when he did it?" he asks, not using Caspary's name, as if that purifies his curiosity. Caspary's lawyer claims Caspary was drunk out of his mind when he broke into Barbara's house (which he shared up to a few weeks ago), trashed the living room and microwaved Barbara's pet cockatiel.

"He hated Horatio," says Malcolm.

I say, "Something had to set him off. Maybe Barbara's seeing somebody else."

"But he dumped her, he was the one who moved out," says Goode. "And he adored Margo and the little girl loved the bird, didn't she? He wouldn't want to hurt Margo."

"Maybe Caspary was jealous of the cockatiel," I suggest.

"Jealous of a cockatiel?" says Malcolm.

"Well, it was an expensive bird," I say.

"I don't think he went there intending to cook the bird. I think he went there maybe looking for something, something he'd left behind, and then just got carried away," says Goode.

Skretch believed something snapped in Caspary after he left Barbara. None of us took Caspary for an alcoholic, even Skretch, though that fact seems as fundamental as my semi–blindness, Malcolm's dark skin, Goode's girth, and Skretch's dimpled chin. Caspary always drank his share but never to excess; yet Caspary's lawyer told the press that our friend drank himself to sleep every night, had an alcoholic father, and was prone to irrational behavior when inebriated.

Malcolm proposes a toast to Caspary and we all clink glasses. I'm not sure what it signifies. Although we are all disgusted with Caspary and have silently excommunicated him, this salute gratifies a need to reaffirm friendship in theory even as we banish this unworthy specimen. Goode has difficulty getting Lila's attention, but she finally sashays over and takes orders for another round. I'm not in the mood but I go along.

"The soundtrack to The Slender Thread is one of the best of its time," says Goode. "I found it at a flea market in Ruskin Heights on Sunday. That means I have every available soundtrack recorded in the decade of the 1960's."

"What did you pay for it?" asks Malcolm.

Goode comes out with a figure probably double the week's gate receipts at Theater 50.

"What's so great about movie soundtracks?" asks Malcolm, possibly irked that we didn't react more enthusiastically to his toast to Caspary.

"The music. The music is some of the best written."

"But isn't it supposed to go with the movie?" asks Malcolm. "What if you haven't seen the movie?"

"Never saw The Slender Thread. It's a Sidney Poitier, after Lilies of the Field."

I observe that collectors are irrational, no matter what they're collecting. "Look at Walter and his outhouses," I say.

"It's nothing to argue about," says Goode.

"I wasn't arguing. I was just trying to understand."

I say, "I've been getting all these offers of pornographic materials in the mail. Videos, dildos, lingerie, weird contraptions. I don't understand why I'm getting this stuff. I don't even have a video player."

Malcolm and Goode find this amusing. "You must be on somebody's list. Maybe the unemployment office sends it to all out of work males," says Malcolm.

"The stuff is expensive. The government wouldn't want me wasting my unearned money on porn, would they?"

"Maybe the government secretly peddles the stuff. If they can raise money from lotteries I guess they could raise it from porn," says Goode.

Malcolm asks me to save the stuff and bring it next week. He's not above a little adult entertainment. This ribaldry, and that extra round of beers, has raised our spirits.

I decline a ride from Goode, saying I just feel like walking awhile and then getting a bus. I don't want to hear Goode grumble about how the club is reeling toward dissolution. I don't want to talk about Caspary, whose madness seems unreal and too graspable to me. I would have strangled Sheila if I could.

I walk a few blocks and then call Joanne. Usually I can tamp down the longing till Friday. I try to be self-sufficient. Maybe a good night with the guys could have pulled me out of the doldrums but this session just pushed me down deeper.

Joanne is reluctant. She wants to keep it exclusively to Fridays. She's still smarting from my suggestion that we make it every other Friday. First she asked is there someone else, a weird question, because I am her someone else, apart from Edward; and strictly speaking, she is not my someone. When I assured her there was no other woman in my life she wondered if I have lost respect for her because of her affair with her adviser. We can call it an affair because it has happened several times now and Joanne thinks she is falling in love with him. He may even be replacing Edward, which she finds liberating and terrifying. Her adviser has a wife and kids, but at least he's local and generally nice to her, whereas Edward lives in Iowa and treats her like manure.

Neither of these guys is available on Friday night, which Joanne has consecrated as her do or die night. She's never explained to me why, beyond confessing that it's rooted in her adolescence. So what isn't? She also says it's something a man could never understand and I'm perfectly willing to grant that because women have been telling me that for so long it must be true. I insist that I don't respect her any less for her fling with her adviser. Of course, I didn't have a mountain of respect for her to begin with, because of her pointless, self-destructive relationship with Edward.

I don't know if Joanne looks forward to seeing me on Fridays anymore, much less on a Tuesday night. I tell her I'm really down and need some company, that one of my best friends has fried his ex–girlfriend's cockatiel. She bursts out laughing and says, you mean that guy they had on the six o'clock news is part of your men's club? Once you get Joanne to laugh you can have your way with her.

She will allow me to come for one hour, but there will be no dinner and no hanky–panky. She's already eaten dinner and she enjoyed a humdinger in her adviser's office this afternoon. She is sated. Plus she has a pile of M.A. theses to read, as a favor to her adviser. It must be part of their arrangement. Joanne never mentions her own dissertation any more.

I don't like going where I'm not really wanted. And I don't appreciate not being wanted. This makes me even more depressed. It takes forever for the number eight bus to arrive, and when it does the electric sign in front displays the wrong destination. The first of us to board, a woman, informs the driver.

"Lady, the sign is right. Look, I got it on my monitor," he yells, pointing to some little screen in the cockpit. "The sign is wrong," I say, dropping exact change in the slot. "Shut up," says the driver. "He won't listen," "He won't believe us," "We've been telling him since Braxton Avenue," chime in the other passengers.

I settle in between a mother with child and an attractive young woman who has fallen asleep with an economics textbook in her lap. A wisp of blond hair has fallen across her forehead and I have an irresistible urge—the kind one feels at a fogged up window—to sweep my hand across the surface. It's already a tight squeeze, but I inch my body against her in hopes of toppling her lolling head to my shoulder. The child next to me bounces on his mother's lap in rhythm to "Sing a Song of Sixpence."

Almost every disembarking passenger takes a parting shot at the driver. "Every person has a little mean in him," the mother tells the kid, referring either to the driver or the passengers. The sleeping woman's cushy hamhock feels so comforting I nearly miss my stop and swipe at the yellow strip just in time. I miss those dangling cords in the old buses that pinged when you tugged on them. These yellow strips you have to tap in just the right place, like erogenous zones, or they snuff you.

Joanne opens her door and stomps away, leaving me to close the door. "It's weird seeing you on a Tuesday," she says. "It's like when they change a favorite TV show to a totally different night." "This is an emergency."

"You look terrible."

"Everything is piling up," I say, checking my reflection in the mirror by the door. What does she mean, "terrible?"

"I'll get you a drink." I plop on the sofa, consider stripping then decide against it. "I'm afraid I have more bad news," says Joanne as she hands me my bourbon. "Sheila has a new boyfriend."

My heart thumps and butterflies (or are they moths?) shimmy in my abdomen. "I'm glad for her," I say truthfully. He is a lawyer, ten years younger than Sheila, which means about twenty years younger than I am. That does rankle a bit. They met when this lawyer represented a woman who tried to sue Sheila because her car was stolen in one of Sheila's lots. The lawyer lost the case but won the defendant.

"I hope he's not a neatness freak," I say.

"I've met him. He's totally different from you."

"Well, he's twenty years younger, highly educated and gainfully employed. That's good for starters. And he probably has perfect vision in both eyes."

"Wears glasses, actually. Not my type," adds Joanne which, whether she means it or not, is a kind thing to say.

Despite the admonition about dinner, Joanne does offer to warm up the leftover spinach souffle. I ate sparsely at the Cattleman and hearing about food reminds me how hungry I am. Perhaps the flutter of jealousy really signaled hunger. I can't imagine a foodless hour in Joanne's company.

Joanne reclines on the sofa with her feet on the coffee table while I sit across the room with a full plate in my lap. She ridicules the students and occasionally reads me sample passages. I titter on cue, but I don't really get the jokes. After an hour or so Joanne takes a dessert break. I haven't vented any of my myriad worries yet somehow the gloom is lifting in this very domestic scene, with two separate individuals bearing their separate burdens yet helping each other by their sheer presence. I can almost see why Mom was addicted to marriage.

Around nine Joanne puts down her work, stretches and yawns, and I fear she'll send me packing. After all, she has responsibilities tomorrow. Me, I might take a shower, see my mother, which really means seeing Lionel, and that's about it for an itinerary. I dread seeing Joanne's Saturday morning go–thither expression. Turns out she wants me to linger a while. Another cup of coffee? Maybe some brandy? We sit side by side on the sofa, the launching pad for our Friday funfests.

But this is Tuesday. I remove my shoes and slump down with my head resting on the roll of the sofa. Joanne mentions for the first time her older brother, a successful dermatologist in Wichita with a voluptuous second wife and an enormous country house backed by a sprawling horse farm. Charles is the apple of their father's eye, Joanne is more like a sty. Joanne's mother nags her incessantly about getting married and lately has insinuated that Joanne is a lesbian—and that it's perfectly all right to be that way, if it makes her happy.

I kiss her cheek fondly, not as an erotic ignition. She's already been through the sexual wringer with her adviser. "I think I should go. It's not too safe riding the bus any later than this time of night." Joanne knows I refuse to take a taxi. Too expensive, and I never know how to give them directions.

"I'll give you a ride, don't go just yet."

We exchange a few sweet kisses. The lights get doused. We are making out high school style—which I belatedly experienced some three years out of high school—slowly and in depth. It takes fifteen minutes for us to start breathing hard. We've never gone at this pace before. Tonight has all the trappings of bona fide love making. I don't even try to envision a climax. The word "mellow" comes to mind: my father's catch-all term for serenity, the height of comfort. Lately I have total recall for everything my dad ever said. He was seldom in my thoughts until this Byron thing; I was always too preoccupied with the series of pretenders to his throne.

Joanne and I remove each other's clothes to the tempo of strip poker. As I hike up my undershirt I hear a series of strange whirring sounds, like a yo-yo climbing its string. Joanne didn't hear it—but my hearing is so acute. I fumble with her bra. She laughs. "It's in front," she whispers, her lips clicking in a broad smile. Her teeth and the whites of her eyes glow in the dark. "Never seen one like this," I say. Her breasts tumble free. As I bob my head to bless them I hear the sound again and this time so does Joanne.

We both stop breathing and clutch each other. A floorboard creaks. I can feel her body pulsing. "He's, it's over there," I murmur, tilting my head. As I ponder what to do Joanne quickly switches on the light. Through my one squinting eye I see Joanne shielding her breasts behind folded arms. She calls out bravely, "Come out, you little bastard."

It is indeed a little bastard, Barney, with the lower half of his body swathed in one of Joanne's lush green velvet drapes. He holds a black object in his left hand I take for a gun, but Joanne mutters to me that it's a camera. She slips on her blouse and buttons it casually, her eyes fixed on the midget, who in turn gapes at her braless breasts.

"I am not here to rob you or anything, ma'am. I am a certified private detective, and I am here on behalf of my client, who's got to remain nameless." He drops the drape and yanks one of those yellow leaflets from his pocket. Dressed in black head to toe, except for glowing silver buttons on his shirt, he looks like a human clarinet. Barney's sidelong glance at me displays no recognition, which I interpret as a signal to keep my mouth shut.

Joanne's anger melts into deep concern. "Who hired you?" My heart stops. I am prepared to deny that I ever met this guy. I might as well never have met him, for all he's produced on John Byron. He called once to say he had visited my mother's room and she was very beautiful and Lionel was a dolt. He also took in a double feature at Goode's theater. Why is he here?

Joanne seems to know. "It was Edward Sellinger who hired you. Wasn't it?" she asks. She fidgets like an ex–smoker pining for a drag. "Please give me the film. I'll pay you for it."

Barney smiles amiably. I admire and despise him for his composure. "I am not supposed to get caught, you know. My client, who may or may not be the individual you mentioned, would probably report me to my agency. He already paid a bunch of money up front. My agency can't hack it, one of us getting caught. Still, these pictures are pretty, well, revealing. What say I give you the film and you pay me just the cost of the film and we call it even."

I can see Joanne calculating if there's a hidden trick here. "Are these the only pictures, is this all you have?"

"Just got the gig today. I never saw you before tonight."

Joanne has gone from wanting to mutilate him to equating his word with his bond. She takes a twenty from her purse. Barney extracts the film and hands it to her. Nobody has looked at me. I could be a tassel on the cushion on the sofa. Barney snorts, then struts to the door. When the door slams Joanne collapses onto the sofa, too distraught to cry, pale, disheveled. I touch her shoulder but she flings my hand away, rubs her eyes and yawns widely, not bothering to cover her mouth.

"I better go. I'm really sorry, Joanne."

"It's not you. My whole life's a shambles. I knew Edward was a madman but I never thought he'd go to this extreme. I mean, he's jealous, he checks every inch of my body for evidence every time we're together, but still…He must have detected something in my voice the last time we talked. I mentioned I had a new adviser. Maybe something crept into my voice without my knowing it. He is so acute, so brilliant."

"But Edward will never find out," I assure her.

"He doesn't need photos. He knows. It's a good thing Edward himself wasn't here. He might have killed both of us."

"I better go," I say again. Maybe Edward is lurking in the corridor with a pistol cocked.

"I told you I'd give you a ride." She tries to stand but falls back.

"That's okay."

"But I promised. Can I at least call a cab?"

I kiss her cheek. "I'll get home." At the door the brass knob round like a breast makes me want to stay. "Till Friday?"

"Sure," says Joanne.

Outside Barney leans against the fender of a small green car. I give him a dismissive wave and try to shoulder my way past him but he trots after me. "Wait, we got business."

"Not any more we don't."

Barney spits out a cigarette and tramples it on the sidewalk. "Great knockers on that woman."

"What were you trying to do?"

"That babe is a suspect. Everybody you come in contact with is a suspect. Even Douglas Curtis."

Douglas Curtis was my supervisor at the insurance company. He was only there two months before he fired me. He may have been hired expressly to fire me and thirty other people. I hate his guts but could hardly suspect him of planting Byron's baseball on my doorstep.

"Don't look so surprised, Jer. I cover the waterfront. And I work fast. Your mom, that movie theater guy. Your girlfriend. Even your old girlfriend. Your old girlfriend's got a new boyfriend, by the way."

He can't fool me here. He'd picked it up eavesdropping. "Tommy Lawson, a lawyer. U.C.L.A. law school. Makes fifty thou a year and he's only twenty–seven. They sleep at his place. A rehabbed loft in Westport. She seems real happy, Jer."

"I suppose you have photos of them, too."

"Video. Building's got a fire exscape and they're too eager to close the blinds. C'mon, I'll give you a lift home."

Barney's car is a Hyundai, specially equipped with raised pedals and an adjusted front bucket seat. I scoot into the back, where I assume a fetal position. "So why the pictures and the videos, Barney? You sell them to the porno underground or something?"

"Yeah." I slap Barney on the top of the head. "A guy's got to make a living," he says. I slap his head again. "Ow! Look, I was working for you all the time. I get evidence where I can."

"You're scum."

"Oh, you think I'm scum. I'm the cream of the crop in my profession. This Joanne's got dynamite boobs. The party I deal with would have probably air brushed you out except for your hands and your dick." Barney gropes in his pocket and slips me a twenty dollar bill. "Like I told you, you spot me, collect twenty dollars. Simple. Like Monopoly."

I pocket the twenty, the same twenty he extorted from Joanne. I'll return it to her, or maybe I should buy her a gift. "You know, Jer, your girlfriend made it easy for me. I could have been in deep shit. Like if she calls the police, or maybe has a gun tucked away somewheres. So we lucked out. But you know, most people are guilty of something. First rule if you get caught: assume the person who catches you has something terrible to hide and use it against 'em. It's sort of like judo, body leverage. Now, you could have blown it by confessing I was working for you. But you didn't have the balls to do that, did you, Jer?"

We have reached my neighborhood. Barney parks two blocks from my apartment. "I don't want the twins to see us," says Barney, opening his door and getting out. My back aches from the cramped quarters. I slither out of the car.

"You're fired," I say.

Barney shrugs his shoulders. The dull streetlight picks up the pewtery buttons on his shirt. "So, uh, you ordered anything yet? I mean, any of those adult materials? I thought a guy like you might have an interest. I get a commission if you order."

"I repeat, you're fired," I say, striding off to my apartment.

Joanne calls me the next day to announce that she doesn't want to see me again. Three lovers at a time is two too many. She wants to simplify her life. With her adviser's help she thinks she now has the strength to extricate herself from Edward. What about your Friday nights? I ask. She will handle it. I plead with her to reconsider. Last night had been so warm and loving. I contend that we need each other now more than ever. But she is tired of lying to Edward and she also doesn't want to risk a fight with Sheila, even if Sheila's now happily in love with a younger man.

I wish people would stop reminding me of that.

❦   ❦   ❦

I got my job at the Lickety–Split the old–fashioned way, through a family connection, but this time not my own family.

Once you honestly look for work and resign yourself to taking any job you can get, just for the sake of money and self–respect, you encounter a blizzard of Now Hiring signs. I might have signed on at McDonald's or Burger King, but I happened to pass a Lickety–Split copy center about a mile from my home and noticed a Help Wanted placard in the window. I recalled the chain was owned by the son of the old outhouse collector, Walter something.

I went into the shop and asked a young woman at the desk the name of the owner of the chain. The manager rushed to the counter to see if I had a complaint and if so, he'd be happy to handle it, there was no need to go all the way to the top. I assured him that I had simply met the owner's father socially and had said I would give the son a call. The manager gave me the name Walter Kempton, Junior, and his office number.

"So you met my old man. You want a medal?" asked Junior.

"I was looking for a man I thought used to live in your neighborhood. John Byron."

"Never heard of him. You ever find him?"

"No. Your dad showed me his collection."

"Can you believe it? He got on this kick some twenty years ago. I think it's just nostalgia for his childhood. He grew up on a farm, said he always hated it. Mom thinks he's out of his tree, but she goes along with it. He hasn't really been the same since...well, I guess he's retired and has nothing else to do with himself."

"Mr. Kempton, I passed by your shop on Lockton Street today and noticed you're looking for help."

"I got it. Your son is just out of college and he needs a job till he finds something permanent."

"I don't have a son. I thought the job might be for me."

Pause. "Don't take it personally, but you sound kind of old for this line of work. We mostly got kids, excepting for managers. I don't need any managers." He paused, I could hear him puff a cigarette. "Kids work cheap."

"I still might be interested."

"You don't have a family?"

"Not even a wife." It came out funny, like the Christmas poem. Nothing is stirring, not even a wife.

"How do you feel about working unconventional hours, say midnight to eight in the morning?"

I hesitated. So when would I sleep? Ten a.m. to six p.m. I could still visit Mom and make the Tuesday happy hour with Goode and Malcolm. Could even see Joanne, if she wanted to take up with me again.

Kempton explained that he wanted to extend service to twenty-four hours a day seven days a week. That seemed to be the going thing in the industry. Not much traffic would come in the door, but you'd spend most of the time handling big orders from the previous day. It was like free time to run the shop. He had two people already hired, youngsters really. It might help to have an older hand around. He asked my age and whether I had a resume. I told him that I'd worked as an actuary at the insurance company for over twenty years.

"Will they verify that?"

"They'd be delighted. They'd love to have me off the unemployment rolls."

"You know, Miller, you'd almost make more just collecting unemployment, to tell you the truth." He pronounced it troof. "But I do give benefits. You got any physical handicaps, chronic illnesses, allergies that sort of thing?"

I assured him benefits were no problem. I had no dependents. I didn't mention being blind in one eye.

Kempton asked me to stop by at his office the next day. I trotted out an old suit, though I didn't think one would be necessary on the job. Walt Junior had his father's prominent forehead and his mother's burrowing chin. He hired me, with the proviso that my references check out and I get a haircut immediately.

That was no big deal, I planned to get a haircut for the reunion. In case I decide to go.

❦   ❦   ❦

Kempton is right that he hires young kids. These two must be in their early twenties. The girl is short with big hazel eyes and pretty except for a large overbite. The boy is prettier than she is. They chatter constantly above the hum of the machines. My job is to take any incoming orders or phone calls, to greet anyone who comes in, and to monitor the youngsters. A coat and tie is not required but I wear a tie and a dress shirt anyway, which I feel confers an aura of professionalism, even at $5.75 an hour. The kids pay little attention to me. They discovered all they needed to know about me in five minutes.

The boy, Michael, studies acting and is appearing in a play at a community theater in some God–forsaken neighborhood. I bought a ticket. He is immersed in celebrity gossip and television, as is the girl. Melissa wants to be a journalist, presumably a famous one. To succeed, she will have to find an adjective to replace or at least alternate with "awesome."

A television plays in the back, mostly old movies and talk shows. There's a racket back there, what with the machines, the television and the high volume required of a conversation to be heard above the other two noises.

We get crackpots once in a while, and homeless people who come in for the air conditioning. Lonely people come in sometimes just to spill their guts, like to a bartender. Karen at the library used to handle these people well and I try to mimic the way she'd let them get to a transition between subjects and then cut them off. Gently but firmly.

Tonight is slow. I've started reading my dad's English histories again, books stashed in boxes in Lionel's basement for some twenty years. They're moldy and bedraggled by silverfish.

At the nursing home today Lionel told me again he thinks I'm crazy to work at the Lickety–Split. He predicts I will be killed in a holdup. He also claims you can get cancer from copy machines but I told him I let the kids handle most of that and anyway we wear goggles and smocks that protect us from the radiation, like those vests you wear when you get an x–ray. Lionel and I whisper because we don't want Mom to learn my new profession. It would confuse her.

Her condition is deteriorating. She alternates spurts of loquacity with stony silence, where she peers at the wall as if trying to decipher handwriting, or viewing a mural depicting technicolor tableaux of her life, a procession of her marriages with those arid stretches in between when she was literally unemployed, motherhood representing a meager offshoot of her vocation. Each new husband gave her a fresh start. For me, of course, the freshness went stale by husband number four. I don't think I'll ever give Lionel an even break. Doctor Bratz says she is "doing as well as can be expected." The ebbs will gradually increase and the flows decrease, and it will be all over. It could take years.

Lionel claims his support group helps him remain stalwart through all this. Today, at my request, he brought in my high school yearbook, exhumed from a box in the basement labeled Jared's. The poor man so hungers for activity that I think he actually enjoyed the assignment. As evidence of his excavatory prowess he also brought other treasures: a pencil box I made in shop, permanently redolent of shellac; a Saran Wrapped issue of Newsweek dedicated to the Kennedy assassination; a Swiss Army knife which must have been my dad's; a batch of letters I wrote to Mom during that semester away at college.

And then Lionel plucks from his pocket a little lavender jewelry box which contains, loose on a velvet plain, my mother's engagement and wedding rings from my father.

"Your mom wants you to have these. As part of your estate."

"My what?"

"And in case you find the right girl. You won't have to invest in the rings, like with that Sheila." Lionel finds my poverty amusing. "That Newsweek might be worth something," he added. "That's why I thought you might want it."

I had requested my yearbook as a favor to Goode. At his house the other night we went through his copy. I didn't remember half the people. Almost everybody wrote something in Goode's yearbook, mostly form letter stuff, like "Best of luck to a good good guy." I covered almost the whole back page with drivel, trying to be witty. Goode wants to see what he wrote in my yearbook. He is getting very nostalgic and Gloria loves it. She is wonderful. Son Mickey clucks like a chicken at the girls in their bouffant hairdos. For some reason he thinks they look like hens. He is awed by the football and basketball players, and the track and field team.

Tonight Michael and Melissa are watching a Henry Fonda movie. They grew up on Jane Fonda, of course, and this prompts the boy to start a contest in which they have to name current celebrities who are the children of celebrities. They invite me to join them but I pass, preferring a chapter on Disraeli.

They both study People and are steeped in entertainment lore. I hear names going back and forth. Kiefer Sutherland. Laura Dern. Drew Barrymore (disallowed, for some reason). Nastasia Kinsky. Isabella Rossellini. Bonnie Raitt. (They had started with actors only, but Melissa insisted they include singers.) Traci Nelson. The Nelsons, a gimme. Natalie Cole. Michael Douglas. Carrie Fisher. When Michael offers Mariel Hemingway Melissa cries, "No! Children of writers don't count. And especially grandchildren." "Writers are entertainers, strictly speaking and Hemingway was a celebrity. His books were all made into movies with Humphrey Bogart and Gary Cooper," replies Michael. "Okay, then Margaux Hemingway," retorts Melissa. "A gimme," says Michael. I feel like ducking in and telling them I remember the day Hemingway died and a man I knew cried like a baby. But I hold back. I've tried to put my two cents in before, and it only creates fifty dollars worth of cynical looks. Jeff Bridges. Beau Bridges, a gimme. Tatum O'Neal. Jamie Lee Curtis. Marlo Thomas. Larry Hagman. Emilio Estevez. Charlie Sheen, a gimme. Liza Minelli. Lucy Arnaz. Candice Bergen. Vanessa Redgrave. Lynn Redgrave, a gimme. Julian Lennon. Melanie Griffith, good one. Matthew Broderick. Timothy Hutton. Alan Alda. Keith Carradine. David Carradine, a gimme.

Goode could make mince meat of these kids. So could my mom, in her prime, just from TV Guide and Jack Paar.

At three in the morning Billy from the 7–Eleven bounces in to get a document copied. He says they plan to install a copy machine, five cents a copy, and we better watch out. Billy is about my age and worked for a trucking company that went belly-up last year. He says his feet have sprouted calluses but his ass doesn't miss the piles. Having the late night shift permits him to see as little of his wife as he did when he was a teamster, which suits him fine. Billy smokes constantly and in two minutes a nicotine haze permeates our small shop. Michael and Melissa start coughing loudly in the back room. "Sounds like you got a bad case of whooping cranes," Billy says. I don't appreciate the smoke, but Billy is a useful neighbor and in the interest of my shop I have to stay on good terms.

When Billy toddles away I phone Kempton's office to leave a message on his service: 7-Eleven will only charge a penny less per copy and it will be self-service, which nobody wants. At most they may get our overflow, but certainly not any of the profitable high-volume jobs. So we have nothing to fear. Kempton likes these communiques, which I bestow upon him several times a week. "It makes these extra hours all the more worthwhile, to get this kind of competitive feedback," he tells me. If I'm not careful, he might promote me to day manager.

Sometimes I read the stuff brought in for copying. An invasion of privacy, to be sure, but people who crave privacy should copy at their own office or use the self-service machines at the library or the 7-Eleven. Mario, a foreman in an envelope factory, brought us a TV script for a murder mystery that his wife wrote as part of a workshop at the university. He ordered fifteen copies at over three hundred pages each. He asked did I like it? I told him it was against the rules for us to read material we copy and besides I didn't know beans about TV scripts. My TV has been out of order since Johnny Carson went off the air.

His wife's script is godawful. The hero is a Mexican-American and there's a lot of Spanish dialogue, so I would think you'd need subtitles, unless there's a Spanish language station. All the women in the story fall in love with the private eye, a super-macho type who gets conked on the head three times in the first one hundred pages. You figure he should wear a helmet, the way bikers do these days. We never wore helmets. I used to pedal my Schwinn from here to Kingdom Come and never once landed on my noggin. Back then, only a sissy would wear a helmet, or somebody who lacked confidence.

Goode warned me it's dangerous working these hours but Kempton assured me we don't have to worry about robberies. There's next to nothing in the till. The manager makes a night deposit at the bank and what's left is barely enough to make change. A button under my desk supposedly trips an alarm at the police precinct office.

Also, a cop who moonlights as a security guard for this block drops in frequently. He's got a crush on Melissa. I told Kempton about it and he says as long as Melissa doesn't get too distracted from her work I should encourage the guy. Gordo is a nice kid in his twenties with a face full of potholes and a mouth full of chipped teeth. I can't imagine him drawing that gun and neither can he, from the way he walks with his right hand in his back pocket, as if his shoulder socket fit crooked. He is clearly under–qualified for Melissa, not nearly cute or educated enough, but I always summon her when Gordo comes in and he tries to make small talk. He wants to ask her out but he's shy.

Now that Gordo believes I have his romantic interests at heart I feel comfortable asking him about tracking down a guy I used to know thirty years ago. He excitedly jots down Byron's name and promises to file it with the missing person's department. When I call for Melissa Michael says she is in the john, but is there anything <u>he</u> can do for Gordo. The humor eludes Gordo, who promises to return shortly. I take shameless delight in using Melissa as a pawn. When you are in charge of something, even the titular way I'm in charge of the Lickety–Split, people lose their importance as individuals. Sheila was a master at not caring, so was Doug Curtis, the guy who fired me. Doug had on his desk a pencil box with the Kansas City Chiefs insignia, stuffed with ultrasharp pencils with the points aimed at the ceiling like missiles on a launching pad.

Managers. My father was a manager, I wonder what kind. I know nothing of what his days were like, beyond those pink, white, and canary requisition forms. I spent twenty–five years just taking my body someplace every day and this job is pretty much the same thing. A deathly livelihood. But I get an odd thrill out of being in charge, though I am kind of a manager by default.

I pass Terence and Randy leaving just as I come in. They greet me frostily, par for the course these days. I wonder if they're embarrassed that I witnessed Randy's fit and don't feel comfortable with me; perhaps his condition is a deep dark secret. Or maybe Barney's been bad–mouthing me. Our relationship was supposed to be confidential, but Barney doesn't play by the rules. Whatever, I need to find some way to make amends. I want to tell them life is too short to engage in these petty squabbles. I don't want to tell them that by actuarial assessment their lives are in fact destined to be exceptionally brief. I think if more people knew the odds they would commit suicide. Which would only jack up the odds of committing suicide.

I take out the yearbook, in pristine condition, as opposed to Goode's dog–eared copy. He says he runs into old classmates at the theater and it's fun to see what they looked like thirty years ago. I turn to the photos, a girl and boy in each, of the award winners for Best Dressed, Best Looking, Best Athlete, Best Dancer, Best Sense of Humor, Most Likely to Succeed, and (my favorite) Best All Around. Surely in a democratic society there should have been a category for everyone. One kid, Bobby Schultz, should have been cited as Best at Doing Nothing Well. Goode deserved recognition for his knowledge of movie trivia. Had anyone been able to read my thoughts I'd have been a shoo–in for Most Likely to Grow Permanently Sullen and Commit Some Kind of Second–Degree Felony. A prophecy as yet half–fulfilled, but with folks like Barney in my life don't sell me short.

Only five pages into this book and already I'm bristling with spite. I wish all but a handful of these people dead. No doubt a good number of the faculty have passed on. My mind concocts headlines from non–existent newspapers. VALEDICTORIAN ADMITS TO THEFT, AGREES TO DO COMMUNITY SERVICE. ALL–STATE HALF-BACK BARES BEEFY BELLY IN CHURCH. MOST LIKELY TO SUCCEED FILES CHAPTER 11. HOMECOMING QUEEN DISGRACED BY NUDE PHOTOS. CLASS PRESIDENT PEDDLES BRUSHES FOR FULLER. BEST LOOKING DISFIGURED, SUFFERS FIRST–DEGREE BURNS IN TOWNHOUSE FIRE.

I'm still not acclimated to this schedule, where I rise at ten–thirty at night, shower and breakfast and leave home by eleven thirty. While other people sit down to breakfast I am warming up a Swanson's turkey dinner. I'm not all that hungry. I had coffee and crullers for lunch at four a.m., courtesy of Gordo. It's like I'm living on European standard time.

I stuff the yearbook into a sack with the other relics and set them on a shelf in the hall closet. The book of Byron poems is here, but I can't find the baseball. I stand on my tiptoes and flail around with my hands, but it's gone. I can't find it on the floor, nor has it fallen in the pocket of my winter coat or rain coat or other clothes, which I now tear from their hangers and dash to the ground.

※ ※ ※

It seems only minutes later that shouting and banging on my door jolts me awake. My clock says five–fifteen and it takes me a moment to realize it's the afternoon. Five–fifteen p.m. is my middle of the night.

I groggily tramp to the door with a towel wrapped around me. Through the peephole I see the blurred figure of a woman who seems to be missing both arms. I hear a male voice.

"Jerry, listen, I caught her at your door, trying to sneak this. I know you've been having trouble," says Randy. When I open the door Randy hops before me with his jaw set and his fists clenched. He had evidently been restraining the woman from the rear with a double wristlock. The woman rubs her wrists. She wears a sleeveless lavender top and white cotton slacks.

"Do you know this woman?" asks Randy. "Do you want to call the police?"

"No. I mean, no don't call the police. And yes, I know her. Karen, this is Randy."

Randy looks disappointed. "I don't know her well, Randy. And you were right to do what you did. Thanks for all the trouble. I can take over now."

"Better check what's in that bag first," Randy says. At my feet lies a brown paper bag. It contains a bottle of scotch, with a typed note saying "J&B from J.B. Drink to me only with thine eyes."

I hand the bottle to Randy. "I only drink Jack Daniels. Share this with Terence or give it to a friend. It's the least I can do for all your trouble."

Randy would have preferred to see the woman manacled and booked but the bottle isn't a bad consolation prize. "Elevator's out of order, so I was taking the stairs." He holds the bottle up to the concentric fluorescent tubes that serve as our hall light. "Don't think this could have been tampered with, do you?"

"No, I don't think Karen would have done that. Hey, I've missed you guys," I call after him.

"Well, people change," he says.

Still rubbing my eyes I invite Karen in. The towel slips off and eludes my grasp. Karen gasps to see me in my underpants. Do I give her the third degree, scold her, or offer her a drink? The etiquette here equals my mental state for fuzziness. Whatever I do, I can't do it in my underpants. I ask her to sit on the couch while I go get decent.

I put on the kettle for instant coffee. Karen sits with her hands folded primly in her lap, her neck swiveling as she pans my apartment. "I almost forgot you have dwarfs in your building," she says, in exactly the tone she used months ago, the last time I saw her. "It's sweltering in here. How can you drink coffee?" She fans her face with both hands and I can see her unshaved underarms. She emits a sweaty odor that is not entirely displeasing.

"Can you get me something cold to drink? Anything."

"You brought me the Byron poems, didn't you?" This deduction had come to me as I zipped up my khakis.

She nods and explains that she had unearthed the book from an obscure stack, amid oversized volumes on seashells, Renaissance architecture and sundry other subjects. She thought of me immediately. In fact, she thought of me frequently since our date (a date?), but finding this book provided an inspiration for contacting me, however obliquely. I should be aware that she would never outright steal a book from the library; the Byron was noted as MIA since 1989, hence technically lost. She felt no compunction about using this to tease me as I had teased her.

"I never teased you."

"Ho ho ho."

"Certainly not intentionally."

"They're closing down the library. Lack of funds. The community held a protest. But public officials only care about numbers. We had a low circulation. So I guess you and I are in the same business now. Laid off." The blast from the tea kettle propels me out of my seat.

As I hand her a cup of orange juice Karen lambastes me for leading her on. I had glanced her way suggestively, spewed double entendres, caressed her shoulder and forearm, what did I take her for. That night I rebuffed her she sobbed for long hours thinking how I had seduced her just to get her help in my search for Byron, only to dispose of her the minute she delivered the goods.

I do recall an impulse to kiss her, and perhaps that fleeting lust had traveled to my eyes, or I had inadvertently pursed my lips. Perhaps our fingers had touched reaching for sugar packets at the coffee shop. I try to inform her that she had in fact not delivered the goods, that her printout was useless, and that I had never so much as flirted with her. Here I am defending myself against a woman who has invaded my private life and caused me anguish.

"So what have you done with my baseball?" I finally yell.

She sips from a plastic cup, which she cradles in her hands with the cracked part of the rim facing me. "What baseball?"

"You didn't get into my apartment and steal an old baseball? You might as well confess, Karen. The jig is up. Not that I would press charges or anything." I don't really suspect her but I've got to regain the momentum in this confrontation. I'm ninety per cent sure Barney stole the baseball, but I've been unable to find him. He quit the agency, absconding with some computer equipment. Even they can't locate him, and they're professionals. He's on the lam.

"You're accusing me of breaking and entering? I never even touched your doorknob. Go ahead, check for fingerprints."

She's almost glad they're closing the library. She is fed up with the weirdos and the lonely elderly and when school starts there would be the obnoxious kids. Some people in the community took the closing very hard. A fifth grader held a Save the Library carnival in his back yard, which netted forty dollars. Karen plans to leave town. She refuses to tell me where she's going.

The scotch cost thirteen dollars. She'll never forgive me for just palming it off on some scruffy midget. Yet as I close the door on her forever she throws her arms around my neck and squeezes so hard I'm afraid of intent to strangle. The scuff of her heels on the stairs, the final chord of our second final farewell.

CHAPTER 8

❀

The actuary in me cautioned that Goode was doomed to suffer a coronary, but I always assumed the first one would not be fatal. We hoped against hope. Gloria would joke about it. She said she would not have married a man who would up and die on her and she and Artie had a wager over whether he would make it to fifty. I often felt Goode's fatalistic talk was his hedge against evil spirits; the theory that the things you worry about never happen.

I dreaded being present at the scene of a Goode heart attack. I didn't know CPR from C.O.D. My own heart would hiccup whenever Goode put his hand chestward, to reach for something in his pocket or to scratch an itch.

Here at the cemetery, watching all the Goode widows, none of whom has remarried, I realize the odds were insurmountable. Several young male cousins join me as pallbearers and two of them exchange a smirk at the prospect of hefting this heavy dead man. I am too despondent to reprimand them. In any case, the inhabitant of this plain pine casket is not the real Goode, any more than it is my real mother in that nursing home. When the time comes ("Gentlemen, the casket," announces the minister) Goode is a light burden, as if his girth was more of spirit than flesh and the spirit has dispersed. There will be nobody to carry me. I should leave my body to science, like Victor.

The minister remembers Goode as a devoted family man who adored his mother, wife and child. A tenacious businessman. He loved God and his country in a subtle way. (So subtle I never heard him mention it.) The minister is a close friend of Goode's mother, an effective widow with snappy black eyes, who regularly visits New York, Santa Fe and other fancy places. She would not want to hear that Goode reserved his most solemn reverence for the movies of yesteryear and especially their recorded soundtracks, which trilled mystical melodies to him.

Or that the happiest day of his life, rivaled only by the birth of his son, was the day he opened his own movie theater. The building originally served as a streetcar depot and in fact old–timers still called it The Trolley Barn. It became a movie theater in 1937, showing only newsreels, which went out with television. It went through phases as a playhouse and then an arena for Pentecostal festivities; by the time Goode bought it the roof had literally caved in. He remade the place in his own image, which is to say the four hundred seat theater's physical capacity far outgrew its capacity for survival.

Goode had a sense of humor about everything except his weight. Only once did he make a joke about it: "I'd like to swim in the nude just once. Skinny dipping is the only thing I'll ever be skinny at." Kids used to sing "Around Artie Goode in eighty days/I searched for you/ Through the blubber too/To make a rendezvous." It must have especially stung to hear a movie theme translated into a personal attack. Guys humiliated him in the shower yet he forgave everyone, intending to absolve them publicly at our thirtieth reunion. He owned virtually every movie soundtrack ever recorded. He was my only true friend, and I his. He would have been my best man. Even though he disapproved of Sheila he never tried to dissuade me from marrying her. Maybe he had enough faith in me to know I'd come to my senses.

Too bad funerals lack that dramatic moment of the wedding ceremony, where the minister invites protestors to come forward or be still forever. I might have stunned the crowd. Then again, I'm no orator. I did propose a toast at my mother's last two weddings, but only under duress and buoyed by torrents of bourbon. I probably would squall if I tried to sum up Goode for my fellow mourners. My heart thwacks in my breast, a sensation much like stage fright, as if everyone expects me to play an important cameo in this ceremony—THE BEST FRIEND.

Rather, I am the unsung hero of this occasion. The minister didn't mention me. I am relegated to a pew that contains the projectionist and concession boy from Theater 50. Both look shaken, more from job loss than grief. Gloria, who knows that Goode and I were like brothers, leans on her father for comfort and for some reason averts my glance. I wonder if she has resented my closeness to her husband all these years. Gloria and I have hugged each other a hundred times on holidays and happy occasions but today when I tearfully embrace her she stiffens and moves on to the next mourner. Her father, a mill worker from Iowa, lays a bear hug on me; his stubbly face chafes my cheeks and I have a sudden insight into how coarse men must feel to the women they kiss.

When Gloria called to break the news her voice cracked, she sputtered "Jerry, Jerry," and no more. "I love you, Gloria," I murmured. "I love you, too, Jerry," she sobbed, in such hushed desperate tones that a casual eavesdropper might have construed this as a farewell of forbidden lovers. "One minute we were talking and the next minute a stranger was doing CPR," Gloria said.

At the funeral Gloria is beatific in her sorrow, as if the cosmetician who perfected her husband for burial had as a bonus ministered to the widow as well. Mickey pumps her hand. He is bored and wondering where his daddy is. He has never seen so many grown-ups crying. He just turned four, still at the pick your nose and eat it stage. In thirty years he will begin making anxious trips to a heart specialist. Perhaps by then genetic engineers will have figured out a way to rid families of hereditary curses. Maybe I should will my heart to the boy.

    Skretch and his wife stand ahead of me in the receiving line. His eyes are moist and his lips drawn tight. He and Goode never hit it off. He won't miss taking in a double feature of old movies every month. We shake hands but avoid each other's glance.

    Skretch is wearing a light blue tie with a busy pattern of equilateral triangles, a cluster of them amputated at the apex. Skretch buys his ties at a discount store that sells irregulars of designer fashions, and he used to defy us to detect the flaw. I could always find it, even with one eye under the dim lights of the Cattleman. Skretch withdrew from our Tuesday club after his rift with Caspary, and of course Caspary never returned. It has been just Goode, Malcolm and I for several weeks. Malcolm and I have agreed to meet Tuesday, if only in Goode's memory.

    In the cemetery parking lot I spot a familiar red sedan. Warren Caspary reclines behind the wheel with all the windows rolled up and the air no doubt turned up full blast. I can barely make out his face through the tinted windshield. The glimpse I catch is unsettling. Shorn of his sarcastic airs, with nothing to sell, he is a pun of his former self. The Skretches pass the car briskly without any greeting.

    I only have a few scattered photos of Goode, mostly from his wedding. It occurred to me when I was going through my yearbook that that picture of Goode is one of the few I have. His inscription beside that photo is the only written message I have. We never wrote, even when I was away at school that brief time.

    The day after the funeral I stroll past Theater 50, where the marquee in large black letters reads RIP A. Goode. He had joked about doing this, but evidently had the letters at the ready. The theater is closed. Malcolm has offered to help Gloria unload the property. As I gaze at the framed posters hanging on either side of the theater, reproductions of the originals for <u>For Whom the Bell Tolls</u> and <u>Mission to Moscow,</u> I think of how life is beating a hasty retreat from me, with my mom in LaLaLand, Sheila and Joanne (and Karen, if you must count her) estranged, and the men's club disintegrated. Even the Kapinski twins have inscribed me on their shit list.

❦   ❦   ❦

Out of our class of three hundred about fifty show up with spouses and allies. The affair is held at a posh equestrian club with the down–home name of Winsome's Stables. The clubhouse has broad lilywhite eaves and hunter green shingles. A flagrantly inebriated man whom nobody seems to know cavorts in a navy velvet sport jacket and white bermudas and asks everybody if they're Jewish and if so, why don't they go to Israel where they belong.

His attire must reflect the "casual elegance" prescribed by the invitation. I remove my tie, fold it into thirds and stuff it in the pocket of my sportcoat. We only had fifteen or so Jews in our class; I don't see any of them here. When I tell him to bug off he happily complies. A faint nausea rises in my stomach. The Nazis would have gassed me and this boor is the type to pull the switch. The reunion planners, the same go–getters who ran everything thirty years ago, have scored a major coup. They've lured The Silhouettes out of retirement. The Silhouettes were the premiere local rock band back in the early Sixties. Their appearance alone validated any occasion, even our prom, which of course I did not attend. The guys are all in their fifties, quite paunchy and two of them wear hairpieces. They play as loudly as ever, and as badly. Most people don't dance. Many drift out of the clubhouse and cruise the grounds, where the thumping beat, muted by distance, mingles with the chirp of crickets and the rustle of desultory talk.

I spend about thirty minutes going through the buffet, where conversation is fleeting. Few people know me and of those who do, few recognize me. My, how I've changed. I don't recognize most of them either.

At the buffet I harpoon barbecued beef, fried chicken, baked beans, coleslaw. A hail broad–shouldered fellow barks at me, "You know, they should've held this in the nude. It would save a lot of sizing up. Nobody'd be sucking in their midsection.

Hell, with somebody's bare tits staring me in the face I might be able to look people in the eye."

"Is that who I think it is?" somebody (who may not be who I think he is) asks me, pointing to our All–City halfback. Before I can answer The Silhouettes strike up "Louie Louie" and a stampede shakes the dance floor. "You can't not dance to this," yells one woman, who might be MaryLee Masters.

As I slink away, thereby disproving MaryLee's claim, I collide with a blonde who throws her arms around my neck and kisses me. It is Chrissy Carty, who thirty years ago was a daffy redhead with subtle bosoms. She says she's been divorced three times and has loved every minute of it. She's a lady of the Nineties. "You were a real sex maniac," she tells me. "You used to sit behind me in the sixth grade and snap the back of my bra. That's grounds for a sexual harassment charge nowadays, even at the grade school level."

When I look aghast she asks me my name. "Jerry Miller? Oops, I got the wrong man. I always get the wrong man, one way or the other. You didn't even go to our school, did you? Now who did you marry, that brought you to this crummy affair?" I tell her that I was indeed a classmate of hers. Mr. Strong, Biology, junior year. We dissected a frog together. "Mercy me," she says, shaking her head. "Then who was that little bastard that used to snap my brastrap?" "Maybe he was too ashamed to come," I say.

Those who remember me have very specific recollections. Didn't you used to have one eye or something? asks a woman. Her own eyeballs jitter as she tries to determine if I've got a glass eye. Several of the guys remember me as a baseball wiz and pepper me with trivia questions. Menzie Thorpe may have trained for thirty years dreaming of the opportunity to pit his knowledge of baseball statistics against mine: he looks crestfallen when I confess that time has completely erased my baseball database. Menzie can't resist challenging me with Bob Feller's won–lost record in 1937, which surfaces by some miracle of memory.

"He went nine and seven with a three point three something E.R.A.," I reply and, thrilled by Menzie's plunging jawline, I add, "Of course, Bobby was only eighteen, just off the Iowa farm." Menzie doesn't deserve it, but to help him save face with his wife, clearly bored with this pointless jousting, I toss him a hanging curve, the scores of the four–game 1954 World Series.

There is not a single black person at the reunion, which I guess is appropriate, because there were no blacks in our graduating class. I am disappointed, though, that none of those who may have married or befriended blacks has seen fit to bring them. I could have brought Malcolm, but didn't even consider it. Maybe it was for the better. God knows what that casually elegant anti–Semite would have said about a black.

I did not want to brave this evening alone. I called Joanne the day after Goode died and she wanted nothing to do with me. I almost wish Barney had sneaked away with her photos and cashed them in for a million. Sheila sent me flowers, along with a note saying all is forgiven, she's now engaged to a man she never would have met had she and I married. The colorful arrangement of carnations almost made me cry. Now wonder women are suckers for flowers.

The people at my long cloth–covered table are mostly couples and tend to talk with other couples about children. Nobody has much to say to each other beyond where do you live and what do you do. I tell people I'm a sales rep for a printing company, and some people give me their business cards and request one of mine. Viola Johnson's husband, a marketing executive, really grills me.

"So do you guys make color laser copies?"

"Oh, sure."

"How much for say, one thousand copies, legal size? What about slides, enlargements, setups, that sort of thing?" I nod yes, although I don't know what he's talking about.

"I may also be gathering some bids for a logo for a division of ours. You do logos?"

"Sure."

"How much you charge an hour? Bartleby's charges ninety–five an hour for three options. That sounds high to me."

"Me, too. I think we can beat that price. It will depend on the specifications, of course." Kempton always talks about specifications.

"Call me Monday with some price quotes. I think we can really help each other, Deron."

"Jared."

I write my name and shop phone number on the back of one of his business cards. "I like your style, Jared. Most sales reps hit on everybody at a function like this. Two guys even gave me

promotional pens, you know with their name and company phone numbers on them. Pretty tacky. The soft sell always works better with me."

So I triumph with Viola's husband but moments later I insult Harold DuMuth by assuming he took over his father's used car business. Harold flatly informs me that he's a jewelry salesman, and seizes his wife's hand (the rest of her remains absorbed in a debate at the far end of the table) to display a gaudy sample.

Why am I having such a lousy time? Would Goode and Gloria have salvaged it for me? I mention his recent death and a few people remark that they saw the obituary. Brian Kirk—who went on to become a prominent attorney and is serving as the Master of Ceremonies—does not include Goode in his recitation of the list of those in the class who have died. Maybe Artie died too late to make the cut. When Kirk leads us in a moment of silence I have an impulse to cry out Goode's name. That would earn me a striking cameo in the videotape being made of this occasion: "Remember Artie Goode!"

would be a highlight for generations to come. I should have worn a mourning band so that when people asked me who died I could utter his name.

But even if Goode had been here I would have had a lousy time. He was with me through high school and I had a lousy time and nothing has changed. I guess I had hoped at best this gathering would be a harvest of maturity, with maybe a tear or two for auld lang syne.

I hear that the 20th and 25th had more people. The planners would not have planned a 30th, except it was the anniversary of the JFK assassination, a focal point in so many lives. People glower at me when I remind them that the assassination actually took place five months after we graduated, thus rightfully belongs to the class after ours. For me senior year had only one focal point, my mother's inexplicable marriage to Victor. For Goode it was shaking hands with George Stevens, the director of <u>Giant</u> and <u>A Place in the Sun</u>, during a tour of local theaters to promote his new picture.

On the platform stage Jack Rowan, now a meteorologist on the Weather Channel, is making a speech. "Ladies and Gentlemen, My Classmates, My Friends...My Fellow Aging Boomers." Ninety half-hearted conversations halt in mid–sentence.

"We've been through so much together. Not exactly together, but at the same time. We've seen Pinky Lee, Muhammad Ali and Blondie come and go. Ditto the Cold War. We axed LBJ and we exxed–in Ronald Reagan. We sat in over Vietnam and sang hallelujah over Desert Storm. We now say downsizing with the ease with which we used to say out of sight. We've gone from designer jeans to fuller cut clothing. We pant in Gore–tex and lycra. We don't like any rock 'n roll after 1985. There's never been a song to top `Louie Louie,' the greatest hit of our senior year, despite the fact that nobody has ever deciphered the words. We've come to terms with our sexual preferences. We've quit smoking, except for the few light–ups I see around the room, scarce as lightning bugs in December. Most of us have made peace with our moms and dads, hopefully before we had the chance to mourn them. Some of us have nursed our children—in public or at the workplace. We've failed to get the jobs of our dreams and daydream on the jobs that we've got. We've experienced multiple relationships. Some of the ladyfolk have experienced multiple orgasms. We've developed ironclad prejudices against at least one minority group. We take some form of medication daily. Our son's don earrings; our daughters don't go out with boys, they go out for soccer. Many of us have moved from denial to recovery, with the help of support groups for compulsive eating, bereavement, divorce, our children's illnesses, substance abuse, child abuse, you name it. We're virtually carbon copies of our parents, granted the ink is smudged in some places."

Most of my old classmates stand enthralled. Many swipe tears with their index fingers. A hundred gulp in unison. Mates embrace. The man has struck a nerve. I don't know. To me nothing has altered a jot since June of 1963, as far as this crowd is concerned. I feel no solidarity; rather, I just feel stuck with these people, thankfully for only a few hours. I once again resent the popular kids and mildly disdain the losers, whether they now have graduate degrees or beautiful spouses. I pout when people snub me and cringe or lash out sarcastically when certain people approach me. Either my adulthood is an illusion or this reunion is. Deja vu is creepy enough when it lasts five seconds. This is an entire evening of it.

Following a resounding ovation for Rowan, the committee members present a series of skits satirizing members of the faculty. I don't get most of the jokes, but other people are practically keeling over with mirth. I have always hated seeing people laugh hard, so hard they close their eyes tight and slug their chests, gasping for sobriety.

Now they trot out Mr. Nolan, a much–loved French teacher who only just retired this year. He looks unchanged, in a bright red beret and the striped t–shirt of a lounge lizard. He makes a sardonic speech, sprinkled with French. I took two years of French from Nolan but can't even comprehend sprinkles of it.

On this note I prepare to take my leave when Naomi Fischgrund's mother materializes in the doorway. She's as beautiful as ever, but what is she doing here? She must be seventy but she looks forty. Of course it's not Naomi's mother but Naomi herself. She flits around little clusters of conversing groups, bouncing off them like a pinball. Her eyes meet mine and then instantly desert me, not out of shyness, but from either lack of recognition or absence of interest.

I tell myself never mind but do the opposite, weaving my way to her side to call out her name.

"Jared Miller?" she replies, perplexedly.

"Please don't tell me how much I've changed. I've been hearing that all night. I thought you were your mother."

"So do I, sometimes."

"Naomi, I remember…"

"Let's not talk about the past."

"Fine."

"And let's not talk about the present. Or the future."

My head jerks back as if from a left jab. Naomi bursts out laughing, her green eyes glittering in the dull light. "You know, Jared, I intended not to come tonight, but my mother forced me. I'm in town, in from St. Louis, helping my folks pack up for a move to Florida. Mom said I had avoided all the previous reunions so I should go to this one, as long as I was in town. I figured I could slip in in the middle of things and vanish unnoticed."

A suave man would say, "No woman as attractive as you could go unnoticed," but I don't have the nerve. Despite her stipulations we exchange brief summaries of our lives after high school. Unlike most people here she reacts neutrally to the fact that I have never married, to which is attached a greater stigma than even serial divorce. Suspicion, pity and bland tolerance surround an unescorted never–married male at a function like this.

"Would you like to dance?" I ask.

"No," she says, adding at my hurt look, "I mean, no thank you. I hate dancing." She raises an arm and scratches the nape of her neck. Even her elbow, momentarily aimed at my chin, looks irresistibly smooth and kissable. "Maybe I should circulate a little," she says.

Translation: get lost. But I can't. "Are you up for a promenade?" I ask, pointing vaguely to the path to the left of the platform, on which Muriel Somebody impersonates our American History teacher, Amarette Douglas, who used to perform birdcalls during final exams.

Naomi acquiesces with "Lead the way." We circle the clubhouse along a dark gravel path to the outdoor swimming pool, where specters from our common past posture on deck chairs and chaises, or stand rather too close to each other, all voices quiet, as if we'd contracted communal laryngitis from hours of trying to shout above The Silhouettes. Naomi and I park by the water at a canopied table, whose spreading parasol shields us from the glare of floodlights.

"Relax, Jared. Loosen up. If looks could kill you'd be a mass murderer."

"I guess it would be easier if I had come to the other reunions. This is just too much at one gulp."

"Speaking of gulp." She snaps her head toward the diving board, whose near end, draped with one of those old madras bedspreads, serves as a makeshift bar. "Jack Daniels on the rocks, with a splash of water. Preferably not pool water."

My hand shakes as I try to pour the drinks, I have to clasp my left wrist to my right hand to steady it. Addie Appleby, who is fixing a G and T beside me, politely averts her eyes, but emits an involuntary tch out of pity for Jared Miller's premature Parkinson's Disease. "Nice to see you, Jerry, how have you been?" she asks, surveying my jaws for tremors. Her voice sounds muffled, as if speaking to me through scuba equipment at the floor of the club's pool.

When I return with our drinks I find an intruder at our table. Pete McCrory grips my hand so hard you can hear a joint crack. "Naomi here tells me you're supposed to be Jerry Miller. Say a few words, maybe I can verify that by your voice." His nostrils collapse into a sniff every sixth word, possibly from an allergy or a reaction to the heavy scent of chlorine.

"You haven't changed a bit, Pete," I reply.

Indeed, Pete hasn't changed at all. He's a mass of hair and muscle, including above the neck. In gym I once saw Pete struck smack in the forehead, at ten paces, by a softball going at least eighty miles an hour and it affected him like a raindrop. He now operates a Jiffy Lube franchise in Wichita. He displays pictures of his wife and four children. Ray and Abigail were National Merit Scholars and both attend Ivy League colleges.

"That's truly unbelievable, Pete," says Naomi, with a sly wink in my direction. "Yes, unbelievable," I echo. Pete is clearly on the make. I feared at first that his opulent virility—the exposed hairy chest, granitic physique and gold neck chain—had appealed to Naomi. Pete would not have given her the time of day thirty years ago, but tonight he wants to give her the time of her life. He slumps back in the chair, whose frame disappears beneath his bulk, so that he appears to be levitating.

"The tuition is what's unbelievable. But I can handle it."

Naomi mentions that she owns a second hand children's clothing store in St. Louis, a basic fact she had not yet shared with me. She's igniting a glimmer in Pete's eyes, but when she raves about her husband as a successful surgeon and wonderful father the glimmer dies and the eyes retreat beneath the penumbra of bushy eyebrows. I feel worse than he does: the bottom has dropped out of my heart. She wears no wedding ring and I have enjoyed the fantasy that, like me, she has stayed single waiting for the perfect someone. Naomi finishes off Pete with a summary of her children's prodigious scholastic exploits.

Pete rubs his brontosauroid thighs back and forth. "I better get more chow while there's still some left." He shoves the seat under the table, banging my shin.

"I didn't realize you were married," I sputter.

"Divorced. But Pete McCrory doesn't have to know that. He'd probably sympathize with my ex–husband. Stan loved the Cardinals and Ohio State more than he loved me. Come to think of it, weren't you a baseball worshipper?"

"Used to be, but I hate it now. The game has gone rotten." Naomi squints at me, as if my repudiation of baseball displeases her. "I can see why Pete went into the lube job business. He's a slimeball."

Before I can ask Naomi about her career, Cara Fiori, with a frame as thin as a wick, glides into Pete's chair with her husband Tony in tow, his large hands seemingly attached to her shoulders. They talk to Naomi and me as if we are a couple, a "you two." Naomi scoots her chair away from mine. I gaze off into the pool, whose black swimming lanes resemble the spiraling waves in my mother's EEG. Tipsy couples wobble hand in hand beside the pool.

Legions of classmates stop by our table. "I had the biggest crush on Drew Morton," Naomi says of our latest invader, whose manly form has at last drifted from sight. "Forbidden fruit, since he wasn't Jewish. But he married a Jewish girl anyway. I remember, he and I walked down the aisle of the auditorium together at graduation ceremony, and I pretended it was our wedding."

I want to say something nasty about Drew, but actually I always liked him.

"At least they didn't call you the Black Widow," Naomi says.

"You knew about that?"

"Somebody made sure I knew."

"I got called Cyclops for a short while when we were reading the Odyssey sophomore year. I'm blind in one eye."

"Yes, I remember," says Naomi, her eyes roaming.

"I once had a dream about you."

"A nightmare, no doubt."

I shake my head. "Not one of those juicy erotic dreams?" I rub my forehead, my hand visoring my face. "I never wanted a penis but it did bother me that you guys were having climaxes in your sleep. God makes everything so easy for men."

I ask Naomi if I can bum a ride home with her. She consents; by sheer persistence I have established myself as her escort. There's ignominy in leaving an affair like this alone. She does request another bourbon for the road. She grants me permission to take a leak before I fetch our drinks. Before I duck in I look back to see her seated at one of the long tables with several couples.

In the john green formica barricades separate the urinals. The barrier hits me just above the elbow. I recognize my peeing partner as Frank Langston, the shoo–in for Most Talented Boy, who has starred in several skits tonight. He retains his long blond hair with the corkscrew bangs tumbling across a protuberant forehead. That forehead now sticks to the yellow–green tiles above the urinal. I wonder if he has passed out in mid–piss. I mumble words of praise for his fine performance tonight. "Yah, wiss," he grunts. He beats his head against the wall rhythmically every two seconds.

I leave Frank and stride over to the basin, which has those new-fangled spigots that shoot water when they sense a human is near. My reflection doesn't please me. My cheeks sag, there are patches of beard on my chin and over my upper lip, strands of hair stick up at the crown of my head, and my skin has an ocher hue.

I didn't bother checking myself in the mirror before I set out tonight—my way of demonstrating that I didn't give a damn about this reunion—but my negligence has backfired. I did not expect to fall in love. No wonder Naomi finds me so unappealing. I pat down my hair and pinch my cheeks, to little effect.

Mel Mulligan and Tom Dancer push through the door. "Howdy, Jerry, you seen Frankie...Oh, there he is." They each prop a shoulder under one of Frank's arms and drag him to a basin, where his bowed head triggers a double faucet attack. I can hear Frank blubbering a show tune as I head back out to the party.

I'm halfway to the bar when a monster in blue and white hovers over Naomi and blocks her from view. I speed toward him at full throttle with my elbows trained on his shoulder blades. He falls and I hurdle him and land in the lap of a woman who shrieks and shoves me to the floor. I raise myself on one knee like a fighter taking a nine count; my one good eye has momentarily failed, a clamorous darkness engulfs me, until strong arms hoist me up.

I'm terrified that I've gone totally blind—an old fear from childhood—but when vision returns I am sickened to see the widespread lips of my victim, whose velvet jacket is hardly rumpled, mugging for a camcorder whose lens now veers toward me expectantly. I cover my face, just like those arsonists and mass murderers when taken into custody. Spectators edge away as the Silhouettes strike up "This is Dedicated to the One I Love."

"What got into you, Miller?" says Pete McCrory. He was one of the lugs who had helped me to my feet.

"He insulted Naomi," I say. My right knee and right jaw are throbbing from my crash landing.

My right knee is bleeding—no, it's barbecue sauce, from where I swept that poor woman's entree.

"He can insult anybody he likes. Neal Painter. The guy owns this place," says a stranger. "That's just his sense of humor. He doesn't mean anything by it."

Naomi sits in profile with her arms folded, legs crossed.

"Are you okay?" I ask her.

"I can fight my own battles," she says.

"He's an anti–Semite bastard."

Now she glares at me. "You're lucky he's not pressing charges."

I try to take her arm but she pulls away from me and moves toward the exit. I chug along behind her. Carol McGee, a former cheerleader, eyes ablaze with turquoise tinted contacts, bids Naomi goodbye but ignores my farewell. I've put a damper on her party, just because I singlehandedly tried to execute a latter day Eichmann. She is making a mental note to delete my name from the invitation list for the thirty-fifth.

Naomi's car is comfortable and immaculate, and the night is cool enough that we can lower the windows. I cringe when the radio comes on, but as Naomi hums along to the classical music, a symphony or something, a peculiar serenity fills the car.

"You're happy, aren't you?" I ask her.

"As happy as the traffic will allow," she replies.

"I mean…"

"If you mean am I happier than I expected to be thirty years ago, given my godawful experience in high school, yes, I am. I love my children and my work." Silence for a while, then at a red light: "I'm getting along much better without a man than I ever thought I would."

"Would you like to go for coffee, or a drink?"

Without hesitating or looking my way she says, "I'm about drink and coffeed out. And I have to get up early tomorrow. Now, do I turn left or right on Harrell Drive?"

She doesn't even stop the engine when we arrive at my building, but keeps one hand tight on the steering wheel when we shake hands. I badger her for her parents' phone number. She will be difficult to reach, so many things to do.

"Maybe I can give you and your folks a hand, packing things up or whatever?" I ask.

The car jolts forward. She momentarily took her foot from the brake. "We'll see," she says.

❧ ❧ ❧

Love at second sight might be more intense than love at first sight, because it has to overpower preconceptions. Sheila was smitten with me, which flattered me to the degree that I thought I was smitten with her. The minute I stopped loving her I realized I never loved her.

But I do love Naomi Fischgrund. I love the Black Widow. I've tried calling her that, to rid myself of whatever's lacerating my insides. Billy brought me a three–pack of Tums, on the house, but it's not helping. It doesn't matter that Naomi doesn't love me, or that she lives in St. Louis, none of those reality factors are as real to me as the lava that courses its way through my once terminally tired system. I have spent hours staring at that horrendous picture of her in the yearbook, which I never even asked her to initial. She resembles a nine–year–old boy with a broken jaw. The old picture melts into a glossy image of the new and improved Naomi, like the overlapping transparencies in a history book that show how a country's borders have changed over the centuries.

I am once again the possessed romantic who forty years ago painstakingly penciled the lyrics to "Love is a Many–Splendored Thing." It's possible that my mother has bequeathed me this romantic penchant, along with partial blindness; and has also bequeathed her dementia, now kicking in precociously. Or was it my father—was this the way he felt about my mother, had to have her at any cost, under any terms?

From the moment Naomi appeared all sound but her voice had a muffled quality, all motion but hers slow motion. Her breathing, her heartbeat, drowned out the most raucous revelers. My whole body went novocain numb. I felt none of the joyful agony vaunted by songwriters, but only a blind resolve.

I will brook no opposition. I must have her. I have never wanted anything so badly; indeed, my life has been dedicated to the abolition of want. The last thing I ever really coveted was Byron's baseball. I will do anything she asks, except leave her alone.

I wonder what Goode would have made of this. Had he been on the scene he might have whisked me away, lest I make a fool of myself. He shared the universal scorn of the Black Widow, though he himself bore the equally demeaning moniker of Friar Tuck. Gloria, who tried in vain to fix me up with a procession of spinsters and divorcees, might have seized this opportunity to cement me to a female once and for all. I need to call Gloria in a week or so, just to see how she's faring in Iowa, and I don't think it would be insensitive to get her viewpoint Dear Abby style about how to make Naomi fall in love with me.

At the reunion Naomi told me I had been nice to her in the old days, unlike most of the guys. I smiled at her when I passed her in the halls and didn't avert my gaze in disgust. Perhaps my kind demeanor was a spillover, pardon the expression, of my erotic dream of her. Some unconscious mechanism must have forced a grin of amazement that this hideous creature had sneaked into the private preserve of my libido.

Michael and Melissa both had exciting weekends, which they share in detail. I try to distract myself with the career of Disraeli, my father's hero, who, I discover, idolized Lord Byron. Inhaling the mold from this volume's yellowed pages is giving me a sore throat. Perhaps I can bum free lozenges from Billy tonight.

Melissa has again brought in a workbook to help her prepare for the Graduate Record Exam. She wants to go to the University of Missouri journalism school, one of the best. I hear her asking Michael about the math problems and I've ignored this, not mentioning that I have a degree in math. Melissa brings the thick book with her every night, with an emery board sticking out to mark her place. I doubt the emery board has budged in two weeks.

I put aside the Disraeli and ask her for the book. I tell her I'm thinking of going to graduate school. Awesome! she exclaims. I am rusty but the old mastery returns after a problem or two. A quadratic equation here, some coordinate geometry there, and soon I'm totally absorbed, my pencil zipping deliriously over a legal pad. Square roots, means, medians, ratios. Kid stuff. For good measure I check the answers at the back: the editors flubbed a few, which I promptly correct, in case Melissa ever comes to use this book. It's been ages since I felt competent at anything. I could ace this test. Who knows, maybe I can win the heart of Naomi Fischgrund.

When I hear the clearing of a throat I realize that throat has already cleared three times, each time getting louder.

It's Barney, wearing sunglasses with reflecting lenses and a bright orange baseball hat bearing the logo of a local automotive repair company. I can hear Michael and Melissa whispering about the dwarf who has come in. Only Barney's head is visible to them from the doorway where I gather they are standing side by side.

"Michael," I call out, and I hear the guilty shuffle of weejuns. He makes me call him twice. I see my own twisted expression reflected in Barney's lenses. "Michael, I need to speak with this gentleman privately. Will you guard the front desk for a few minutes?"

I lead Barney out the front door into the narrow alley that separates the Lickety–Split from the 7–Eleven. It rained earlier and the alley is full of puddles. Barney's Nikes get wet and he curses and wipes them off with his handkerchief.

"Nice office you got here, Jer," he says. He hands me a plastic Revco bag.

I can feel the baseball rolling inside. I reach in and grip it with two fingers across the seams, the way Bob Feller readied his fastball.

"Hope you don't mind that I appropriated the ball," he says, offhandedly, as if we had spoken yesterday and he's adding a footnote to our conversation.

"I minded a lot. I tried to find you, to tell you that I don't enjoy being burglarized."

"Then get a Seagal lock. A chimpanzee could break into your place, especially with you away during the peak burglary hours."

His thumbnail picks away at a crack in the building's aluminum side. "This is the best you could do? You were that desperate to get back into the work force?"

"At least my boss doesn't have a warrant for my arrest."

"That's been all cleared up. A misunderstanding, was all."

"You mean appropriating the agency's computer equipment was like stealing my baseball. A no harm no foul kind of thing."

"Look, Jer, I didn't steal your ball, I borrowed it. And on your behalf. I just wanted to get it valued with this certain party I know in Independence. He used to work at the Truman Library. He knows the monetary value of everything. He says this ball is worth about a hundred dollars. I didn't expect you to be looking for it, not so soon."

"Why didn't you just take the hundred dollars?"

"Because it's your baseball. I tell you, I was doing you a little favor, to make up for that bit of malpractice when I was in your employ. I had this scenario, see: if the ball's worth over three hundred I consult with you, and if you want to sell, we go halfsies. You need money, obviously" (he lifts an elbow toward my building), "you need it as bad as I do. Any reckoning that comes in under three hundred, I just return the ball to you. As I have done forthwith."

"You stole the ball. You broke into my home and stole the ball."

"You wouldn't loan it to me. How come you broke up with that babe with the knockers? You haven't been there in weeks."

"Why in God's name are you following me around? And why are you wearing sunglasses at three in the morning?"

"They go with the hat. Look, Jer, I like you. I always follow up where my clients are concerned, even my ex–clients. She's fucking a professor, you know. Oh, and I found this."

He hands me an envelope containing photographs of a woman walking past my apartment building. "She seems to be casing your building. I showed the picture to Terence but he's never seen her. Randy doesn't speak to me, so I couldn't ask him. You recognize her?"

"No," I say, handing him back the pictures of Karen.

"I figure she might be an agent for this John Byron character. I may still be able to crack this case," says Barney.

I do get some of the old shivers, but Naomi has obliterated Byron. I am single–minded now. My mind can only accommodate one quest at a time.

"Jer, I can get you a year of <u>Swank</u> for $9.95. That's like an eight hundred per cent discount off the newsstand price. Real pictures of real women. All you got to do…Holy shit!"

A splatter of a puddle, the slap of Nikes on pavement, and no more Barney. Gordo stands at the entrance to the alley with his legs spread and arms akimbo. His thin frame fills the space, and his badge picks up a blinding glare from the streetlight right behind him. Gordocop, poised for retribution.

"Come outta there with your hands up," he says. His gun peeks out from behind his waist like a curious child.

"Don't shoot, Gordo, it's me, Jerry."

With a gasp of relief Gordo crosses his ankles and tilts against the 7–Eleven. "You ought not to be hanging out in a dark alley this time of night," he says, an octave below normal pitch. "Sorry, Gordo. Billy was in with his cigarette and the smoke was getting to me. I had to air myself out."

"Don't let it happen again, Jerry. You're a victim waiting to happen in a dark alley like this. Next time just hang out on the sidewalk for a spell. I'm glad I happened by."

I'm glad, too, Gordo.

CHAPTER 9

❀

"We're the only two who haven't made the papers," I say.

Malcolm swishes his drink in bloated cheeks. "I'm not about to bake a cockatiel and I'd rather not die of a heart attack. So that's two ways of getting publicity I'd rather not try. Actually, the realty is going to run my mug shot in some ads, along with fifteen other agents."

It's our third round, bourbon for me and vodka tonic for Malcolm. Lila told us all drinks are on the house tonight. She has seen our group dwindle and she says it's taken the oomph out of her Tuesday nights. Not to mention the drop in her revenue. "See, even a realtor gets a day in the sun," I say.

"Jerry, please don't say 'real–a–tor.' Why can't anybody pronounce my profession right? It's 'real–tor.' Two syllables. Dig?" His jaw relaxes. "Look, if you win over this Naomi you two might make the society page. They've started putting the groom in wedding pictures."

Malcolm wants to talk strategy. How do I propose to conquer a woman who reciprocates none of my affection? What dramatic action can I take in the three days remaining before she returns to St. Louis?

"St. Louis is not Bangkok, Malcolm. I can take a train there every weekend, shack up in a YMCA if I have to. My only strategy is persistence."

"Too vague," says Malcolm, who probably spends a half hour picking out tomorrow's tie. "From all you have told me she's going through a frigid phase. Withdrawal from men. I've seen it a million times. How long since her divorce?"

"Five years, maybe six."

"A younger woman?"

"I think."

"She either still loves her husband or is so bitter as to be unapproachable. Maybe she's a Lesbo?" I shake him off. "Maybe it's just bad timing, Jerry. Take it from one who's made a career of bad timing. How do you know this isn't just some tremendous crush?"

"I've had tremendous crushes."

Malcolm nods wearily.

"Remember the first time I hung out with you guys? Caspary had this theory about why women hated men. He said the two worst moments in a female's life are when she begins to menstruate and then when she hits menopause. Both those words begin with m–e–n, was Caspary's point. We had some debate about it and it made a real impression on me, the way you guys could talk about things. And then there was that time we all put on skinheads for that Yul Brynner film festival."

I don't want to reminisce about our group and especially not about Goode. The Cattleman, like so much of the space he used to fill in my life, feels bereft without him.

"Don't forget, free refills tonight, guys, just like Taco Bell," says Lila. I've never cared for Lila's loud bark, frizzy platinum do and trim, broad–shouldered build. She's the type they used to call a "dame." We request one more hit from the bar, thus tacitly agreeing to prolong the evening.

"I want to tell you something, Jerry, I never really intended to tell you," Malcolm says ominously.

But it turns out to be not so bad. Malcolm confesses that he hated Sheila. Malcolm's father had worked for over thirty years as a parking lot attendant at the county hospital. He was a steady, earnest worker, who knew everyone by name, garnered substantial tips, and lugged home a carful of loot from the docs every Christmas. Their family received a considerable amount of medical care on the house, including prescription samples. Whereas most attendants decorated their cubicle with pin-ups Malcolm's dad posted a signed photo of Eartha Kitt and pictures of his family.

Then one day he came home crestfallen. A woman had bought the parking lot and handed him a pink slip, no explanation, nothing. At fifty-one the man was too young for early retirement or a pension. Malcolm's mom had a civil service job, so the family remained solvent while he looked for work. Eventually he signed on as a doorman for a ritzy condo, but he never recovered from the humiliation. Malcolm had silently rejoiced when I dumped Sheila.

When I start to whine about Naomi again, Malcolm interrupts.

"Let's take a hard look at the situation," he says sternly.

"Work up a strategy. Every challenge like this requires a strategy. First, let's see what you have to offer."

He goes into his realtor mode: I am a modest two-story house in a declining neighborhood that has languished on the market for nine months. Despite my weakening foundation, unfinished basement, sieve-like roof, erratic plumbing, obsolete air conditioning, eroded wiring, termites, radon and a touch of asbestos, Malcolm accentuates my positives. "You're half-Jewish, which is better than gentile, right? You've got an engagement ring all ready to whip out."

"No. Sheila returned it and I pawned it."

"Moving right along. You and Naomi share a common past, those lazy hazy days of high school. You were nice to her during the worst years of her life. She owes you something. She's got a store. Could you help her with the store?"

"I doubt it. She has an assistant. And I don't know beans about children's clothing."

"What about her kids?"

"She's got a teenager at home and a grown son, in New York."

"Sometimes you can get to a woman through her children, but I don't see an opening here." His mind churns. Accentuate the positive. Focus on the still functioning fireplace, the fluted lintel, the built–in shelves, the spacious back yard. When God closes the doors he always leaves a window open somewhere. Who said that? Julie Andrews in <u>The Sound of Music</u>, Goode's favorite musical. He used to quote that line to Mickey when the kid got frustrated with Lincoln logs. Maybe Goode did love God, just as the minister said.

"And Jerry, never never forget one thing: this woman used to be ugly."

"But she's beautiful now."

"It don't make no difference. You never get over being ugly. You never get over being different."

As we part I slip Malcolm an envelope containing mail order pornography, which continues to clog my mailbox. Neither of us mentions next Tuesday.

❦   ❦   ❦

How can you be cocksure and jittery at the same time? I ask myself as I push the doorbell. Cocksure because I have dream–foretold destiny on my side. Jittery because destiny may not be enough.

You can't hear the doorbell from the outside, so after a polite interval I ring again, then rap on the door. When I peer through a square porthole into the empty vestibule, a little gust from my nostrils fogs up my view. A patter of feet, then Naomi's beautiful face fills the aperture like a movie close up. Only three inches of wood separate our lips.

We spoke an hour before and Naomi has had ample time to beautify herself, yet she appears dressed to the minus nines in a floppy denim shirt streaked with white paint, blue jeans with open–air knees, no make–up, and her radiant hair snuffed in a blue polka dot scarf. No matter, she's as ravishing as two nights ago at the reunion.

"What's so funny?" she asks as I cross the threshold into a foyer redolent of sweat and cardboard.

"Nothing," I reply, grinning at her delectable buttocks as she wends through columns of cardboard boxes into the living room, which contains two matching armchairs and an end table. Sunshine streams in through curtainless windows, casting tiger stripes across the pale boxes. Like my soul, this place is in transition between emptiness and replenishment. The walls are bare, save for large rectangular stains, the residue of framed art or mirrors.

"How is your father?" I ask.

"He's okay. Mom told him not to try to lift any of this stuff." She sniffs and her lower lip curls upward. On the way over I stopped at a department store and doused myself with a cologne from the display counter. I hope I didn't overdo it.

"My father can be so stubborn sometimes."

"Only sometimes?" says a man's voice, which has a slow moving man trailing it. He gives my hand a swift pump. "Melvin Fischgrund. Jared, I presume?" He pronounces my name to rhyme with dared. I rather like it, and him. Through thick spectacles his eyes loom large as silver dollars but hued the blackish brown of well–traveled pennies.

He swipes his backside. "I pulled something in my sacro–iliac. My wife accuses me of doing it on purpose, because I hate moving to Florida and I hate having to box up our forty years of life to parcel it out to the younger generation. My daughter, on the other hand, sees me as a stubborn old crow who couldn't resist one last chance to tote that barge."

"They're both selling you short, Mr. Fischgrund."

"Get this man a beer, Omi," he says. He doesn't ask me to call him Melvin, which means I have succeeded at some level of etiquette. His daughter does not find either of us amusing. She heads for the kitchen with a defiant shimmy, unwittingly charming me out of my mind.

Out of habit Mr. Fischgrund moves aside objects which are no longer on the mantelpiece before resting an elbow on it.

"I knew your dad," he says.

"You did?"

"From the shul. He would sit in the second row, fourth seat in from the left, every Friday night and Saturday morning. He was a fixture. He was always good for an *aliyah*, in case we were short one."

I don't know an *aliyah* from a Lear jet but I assume it's praiseworthy. Naomi produces our beers. "L'chaim," says Mr. Fischgrund to the clink of aluminum.

Two hours and several beers later I am dead on my feet. I have hardly seen Naomi. She and her mother, whom I've not yet met, have been wrapping objects and sifting through old photograph albums in the bedroom. I have been loading and lugging boxes, those with black slashes of magic marker to go to Naomi in St. Louis, those marked red destined for her older brother in Los Angeles.

My final assignment is the basement, which is suitably damp and basementy; the cement floor shoots a chill through the soles of my shoes. The walls are of chipping stucco, and lighting is provided by two bare bulbs suspended on cords from the ceiling. Boxes contain moldy articles caked with grime. On a large table sit fragments of an electric train whose works are rusted, the tracks dismantled or missing, the cars upended. As instructed, I disassemble it and stuff it into trash bags that I secure with twisters. There are boxes of old school textbooks, some of which I recognize, composition books, spiral notebooks, blue denim looseleaf binders with once colorful tabs. On wide ruled paper young Naomi Fischgrund lavished large wavy handwriting, the letters slanted at a forty-five degree angle, the T's crossed diagonally, the I's dotted with little balloons. Beautiful and clear, a foretaste of the beautiful, clear woman she was to become. My wife.

I am browsing through things that no one else ever saw unless they borrowed her notes. Intimate as diaries, they insulate me from blasts of mold. One notebook contains six whole sheets front and back with nothing but the name David. David Holloway? David Rubenstein? Maybe some David she met at one of those Jewish summer camps like my Miller cousins used to go to? Pangs of jealousy more intense than those produced by Sheila's incriminating slides surge through my breast. I page through copies of the school newspaper, programmes from plays and concerts, brochures from museums, coin collectors magazines, <u>Popular Mechanics</u> and sports magazines whose mailing labels bear her brother's name. I rip out at random a page from her biology notebook, headed Sphenopsida, Lycopsida, Pteropsida and covered with pencil sketches of what look like bulrushes, fold this one–of–a–kind artifact and stuff it in my back pocket.

I am about to slice off some packing tape and bury these remains forever when something catches my eye: a slew of little theme books and readers filled with writing I take to be Hebrew. I trace the characters with my fingers; they're like nothing I've ever written, and unlike Naomi's English cursive they are totally upright, austere, and thoroughly foreign.

Just then a figure obscures the light. "Mom has made some sandwiches. Are you about done down here, Jared?"

Naomi hovers over me as I sit spreadeagled, refrigerating my ass.

"You really want to get rid of these?" I ask, holding up a pair of Mickey Mouse ears.

"With one ear missing, yes. It's the Van Gogh model."

"And your Dragnet membership card and badge 714?"

"Those were my brother's. He combed through all this a few weeks ago. There's nothing worth salvaging. The mold alone is enough to bring on an asthma attack, even in a non–asthmatic."

Lunch is salami and mustard sandwiches on rye with potato chips and Archway oatmeal raisin cookies. At the kitchen table my eyes blur, my muscles have liquefied, I yawn as often as I bite. The draft from an air conditioner could knock me over. My rear end aches as if I have caught a cold in my ass from that cement floor. Mr. and Mrs. Fischgrund have just returned from the doctor, who diagnosed Mr. Fischgrund as having a mild muscle strain. He has gone in search of a heating pad.

"We've appreciated your help, Jared," says Mrs. Fischgrund curtly. Her lips are pinched, her eyes like Naomi's but with some of the green bleached out. She wears a navy blue kid glove on her left hand. "You know, we have to clear out of here tomorrow."

"Tomorrow?" I ask, a niblet caroming in my throat.

Mr. Fischgrund hobbles into the room with a heating pad strapped to his back like a drooping papoose. He takes without asking half of Naomi's sandwich, bites a chunk out of it and sets it on her plate. "Yeah, we're off to Fort Slobberdale tomorrow morning. You were our last inning relief, Jared. A closer, I believe they call it these days. God, I remember the Yanks had a guy named Joe Page."

My automatic memory mechanism kicks in with Joe Page's career statistics, including detailed highlights of his banner year, 1949. "That's remarkable."

"Joe Page is pretty basic." He names a few other favorites from his past—easy ones like Hoot Evers and Mel Parnell I'd give every baseball statistic for the most mundane phrase of Hebrew.

"I'd like to repay you for all your help, Jared."

"You mean with Joe Page's stats?"

The silver dollar eyes twinkle. "You have a safe drive home. Take some of these oatmeal cookies with you. You parked out front? I didn't see you drive up."

When I explain that I came by bus Mr. Fischgrund promptly instructs his daughter to give me a ride home. My heart sinks at her reluctant sigh. "Maybe just to Lockton Road would be fine," I say. Naomi grabs her purse from the kitchen counter and we're nearly out the door when Mr. Fischgrund hobbles after us.

"Wait! Jared, join us for dinner tonight, at the hotel. It's our last night, our farewell dinner. You can be a proxy for that California–loving son of mine."

Naomi flinches and Mrs. Fischgrund sweeps her gloved fingers across her forehead, but I accept.

Inserting the key into the ignition Naomi says, "You don't have to come tonight, Jared." She turns on the radio, then switches it off angrily. "Public radio, they're constantly groveling for money. Dad doesn't want to go to Florida. It's Mom's idea and it's the best thing for both of them. They've got friends and relatives there. He's been an asshole for days. I could swear he faked that back injury just to irritate us. Anyway, don't feel obliged to accept the invitation."

"I want to come."

"It's way out near the airport. We're all staying at the hotel. I don't have time to schlep you out there."

"I'll get a bus. I like your father."

"Right. I'm not flattered by all this attention, Jared."

The car stops on Lockton Road. I had hoped she would take me, schlep me, all the way home. Maybe we could neck in the car. I've never done that. My bus is just pulling up.

I'm so beat I doze on the bus. I desperately want to dream again of Naomi, an exact duplicate of that long–ago erotic dream only updated with the new Naomi. For over thirty years I've staved off that dream and now that I want it, it eludes me. I have to settle for a kid who resembles Sheila's nephew throwing paper airplanes that skim across deep puddles of water on a ruined street. The driver, a kindly woman with raspberry flecks in her close–cropped hair, awakens me as we approach my stop.

"Watch your step, now," she says.
"Thank you, I will," I reply, giddy with joy.

❦   ❦   ❦

Melvin Fischgrund has hogged the conversation over cocktails and appetizers and he's only just begun to wind down. Even though we're at a round table expansive enough to accommodate King Arthur's management team, we do not splinter into little conversational factions. Mr. Fischgrund is the focus. You either talk with him or listen to him. I suppose every family has its distinctive dinner table style. In my house my mother mostly talked. Dad often worked late so it was just the two of us. Dinnertime was the easiest thing to adjust to after he was gone.

So I've heard about Mr. Fischgrund's upbringing in St. Joseph as the youngest of nine children, his family's poverty, his scholarships to college and law school, his forty–five year law practice in St. Joe, the last forty of it spent commuting daily, his double bypass surgery two years ago, and the grudging capitulation to his wife over moving to Florida. Naomi, her mother, and Naomi's daughter seem to wince at everything the man says, but hell, a chapter of his life is ending and he obviously feels the need to tuck in his memories before he puts them to bed.

Maybe that's why he invited me. I don't care what his motives were. He is my benefactor and he can bend my ear till the lobe turns purple.

Naomi has scarcely acknowledged me. Her expression toward me is as deadpan as the Queen of Spades. Something about me repulses her and I'd rather not put my finger on it. Her daughter Leah, a teenager, is a plump redhead, thus breaking the tradition of slim brunettes among Fischgrund women. She pouts, impatient with us idiotic grownups. I sit between her and Mr. Fischgrund, which allows me to observe Naomi, who had no doubt hoped to achieve some distance from me by foisting me on her father, who presently embarks on another jag.

"I am a creature of habit. Why else would I commute ninety miles every day for forty years? I will be totally disoriented in Florida. Hell, I've been disoriented since Johnny Carson went off the air."

I nod, afraid that if I declare how passionately I agree with him about Johnny Carson I'll come across as a toady. Now I know how a hypotenuse feels: only if you squared me could I hold my own with the other two sides—one represented by Mr. Fischgrund, the other the three generations of Fischgrund females.

"Carson was one of a kind, Jared. Nobody else will ever be so good at it. It's like Ed Sullivan. Nobody could ever do a variety show like Ed Sullivan."

"There are no variety shows anymore," says Mrs. Fischgrund.

"Just my point. And there will be no late night talk shows in about ten years. Mark my words. And this Ed McMahon everywhere, hawking mail-order lotteries, life insurance, pretending to be Ted Mack. Ed McMahon. It's like losing the Lone Ranger and having to listen to Tonto all your life."

"You watch too much television, Daddy," says Naomi.

"Only when it's on," he replies.

"My husband always has to have something on," says Mrs. Fischgrund. "TV, radio, record player, electric toothbrush, anything. It can even be Paul Harvey. There always has to be something on."

"I like noise. I need a soundtrack."

"My mother's third husband was like that," I say, adding, "my TV went on the blink months ago and I never got it fixed. I don't miss it." I look to Naomi for approval. She is strangling a cloth-wrapped lemon over her trout.

This must be an ongoing family debate, trotted out either for a stranger's benefit, or perhaps to give people something familiar to talk about.

"How many husbands has your mother had?" asks Leah.

"Leah!" says Naomi.

"Five," I reply, adding, as I always do, "they all died, no divorces. Number five is still going strong."

"She must have trouble remembering their names," says Leah.

A perfect opening to announce that my mother hardly remembers anything, but none of the Fischgrunds, including Naomi, has even asked after my mother, and they don't pursue her now.

"You familiar with Deutschmann and Sons?" asks Mr. Fischgrund. When I say no, he tilts his head so far that his huge eyes seem to stand one on top of the other. "I thought you said you were in the printing business."

"Only a few months."

"Deutschmann and Sons is the largest printer in the tristate area. I did some legal work for them when they acquired one of my St. Joe clients. I know a senior vice president, if it would do you any good." He jots down a name on a spiral memo pad yanked from his coat pocket.

"What did you think of the reunion?" asks Mrs. Fischgrund.

"Jared spent the whole time in a stew," says Naomi.

"You weren't excited about going either, Omi. I had to twist your arm. I told you you would enjoy it."

"People were a lot nicer to me than they were thirty years ago. It helped my self–esteem, I suppose."

Her father karate chops the table, setting the flatware ajingle. "I'm sick of this obsession with self–esteem. In my day the words self and esteem would never have been linked by a hyphen, much less appear in the same sentence. Esteem used to be reserved for great public figures or institutions. Even God. It's out of all proportion nowadays."

"But Daddy, if you hate yourself…"

"Self–hatred is another thing. But if you esteem yourself so much, put yourself on a pedestal, you're bound to disappoint yourself. Let other people esteem you. Enough just to like yourself."

"Did your mother change her name each time?" Leah asks me.

"Naomi has every reason to esteem herself, Melvin," Mrs. Fischgrund points a gloved finger at him. This time it's a black glove. "She has created her business out of nothing and made a go of it. I never would have thought she would be a career woman. She wasn't brought up to be a career woman."

"Jared," says Mr. Fischgrund, "it occurs to me that there ought to be something you could do, I mean professionally, with your mastery of baseball statistics. Isn't there a market out there?"

"They use computers."

"Can't you be one of the guys who feeds statistics to the know–it–all announcers? It's incredible what they come up with. How many times a blond center fielder has grounded out to the left side of the infield against a right–handed Hispanic pitcher who hasn't shaved for two days. That sort of thing. It makes the law look superficial in comparison."

It's nice of Mr. Fischgrund to want me to better myself, even if his encouragement betrays a wish that I had made more of myself. I, too, wish I had made more of myself, if only to impress my future in–laws. Maybe because I'm so tired, his words are coming at me fast and huge, like those bullets and arrows in a 3–D western. Every word out of his mouth is an opinion. I haven't known any lawyers, so perhaps they all pontificate like this. I can see what Naomi was up against. Does she want a man who can hold his own against her father, or one who just sort of recedes?

Before I can blink he has changed the subject.

"This is probably a part of your family lore, so stop me if you've heard it already. The Shapiro <u>bris</u>?"

I shake my head.

"Your Uncle Jake could be a practical joker, as you well know. This goes back thirty plus years. Jay and Helene Shapiro were part of a big Jewish family and the <u>bris</u> for their newborn son, Barry, was a large affair held at their home. The house was packed, it was a fully catered affair. Every important Jew was there and even some important <u>goyim</u>."

"Do we have to talk about a <u>bris</u> over dinner?" asks Leah.

"Objection over–ruled. Jared, your Uncle Jake couldn't resist a joke on this solemn occasion. He brought a perfect pair of false teeth, which he planted in the first floor bathroom on that porcelain shelf behind the toilet. He wanted to see what people's reaction would be. I heard some people snickering about it and we were looking around to see if any of the older folk might have misplaced their choppers. We suspected Jake was behind it because he kept nudging people, asking if they'd seen it. With his reputation for pranks, we knew he was up to something. Now, if you've ever been to a <u>bris</u>…"

"Just my own," I say, not looking at Naomi but hoping she appreciates my anatomical correctness.

". . . it's a heavy–duty ritual, a joyous occasion that incidentally contains some nasty surgery on an infant's penis. Everybody's rejoicing and grimacing at the same time. Naomi's husband nearly fainted at their son's <u>bris</u>, and he was a surgeon."

"For a woman," says Naomi, clearing her throat, as I notice she always does when addressing her father, "for a woman, on the one hand you resent all this attention for a baby just because it's a boy. There's no analogous ceremony for a girl. Not that I advocate ritual circumcision for girls, as practiced by some African tribes, as a way of destroying female sexuality, among other things. Anyway, there's a certain satisfaction in having this male forced to undergo pain just because he's a boy, when we females have cramps and childbirth to contend with."

"I never felt that way," says Mrs. Fischgrund, raising her soup spoon with the gloved hand.

"This is gross," says Leah.

"So we are right in the middle of the ceremony, the rabbi is chanting a <u>broche</u> over God's covenant with man, the scalpel is raised when there's this blood–curdling shriek and Myra Waistblum comes charging into the room clutching her bleeding finger. The mohel puts down the baby and immediately bathes the finger in some water and wraps it in a bandage that had been readied for the baby. Mrs. Waistblum is assisted out of the room by her son and put to bed upstairs.

"Some of us suspected what had happened, though it wasn't really confirmed till the next day. Myra had retreated to the bathroom so she wouldn't have to hear the baby screaming in agony. She picked up the dentures and somehow they chomped down on her. Maybe Jake had inserted a spring in it or something. So she's the subject of gossip for months. I don't think she ever lived it down. Neither did Barry Shapiro. Even at his wedding people reminisced about his bris."

"Weren't the Shapiros angry at Uncle Jake?" I ask.

"They weren't happy. Of course, today there'd be major litigation, charges of negligence, the baby could have been damaged for life, the Shapiros and the Waistblums suffered mental anguish, some shyster would find grounds. Jake did fess up, apologized deeply and made a sizeable contribution to the shul in Barry's name. Still, he was never welcome in the Shapiro home again. I don't think he got invited to any more brisses either."

"You said this was a story about Uncle Jake and my father. What did Dad have to do with it?"

"Your father, may he rest in peace, felt sick with guilt over what Jake had done. So your father—and I only learned this from Jake one night when we were sitting shiva for your dad at Jake's house—your father swore he would make it up to the Shapiros. He got the opportunity a year later. Jay Shapiro's dad owned a pharmacy and one night he got held up and pistol–whipped almost to death. The store was in a bad neighborhood, and old man Shapiro worked nights because he couldn't find anyone brave enough to do it. Your dad visited old man Shapiro at the hospital and in Jay's presence volunteered to take over the evening shift at the drugstore. He knew the old man well enough to know that it was killing him to have the pharmacy closed during the very profitable evening hours, just because he was laid up with a busted head for a few weeks. So your father would work his full day at the shoestore and then put in another eight hours at the pharmacy. He refused to take a dime for his labors. He was a remarkable man, Jared. There must have been three hundred people at his funeral. That eclipse, it was one of the most moving things I ever saw in my life. We all knew it was supposed to happen but everyone was struck silent."

Naomi and her mother look solemn, Leah chomps on her t–bone steak, and I don't know what to say. Mr. Fischgrund has described a man I hardly knew, for whom fatherhood always seemed at best a chore. When Mr. Fischgrund reaches inside his coat I expect to see the memo pad again but instead he pulls out a wrinkled photograph and hands it to me.

"That was taken at our son's bar mitzvah. Naomi plucked it out of an old album we were packing up today."

It shows my father and Uncle Jake in full Jewish regalia, the yarmulke and the prayer shawl with the white fringe, flanking Mr. Fischgrund. My father is smiling gaily. The date stamped on the white margin is Jne 55. Where was I that Saturday? Probably on my bedroom floor, spinning away madly at All–Star Baseball.

I look gratefully at Naomi but she stares down at the carcass of a trout. Perhaps she just hates me instinctively, the way I hate Lionel.

Leah utters a bored sigh. "Now, may I be excused? I have work to do."

"School doesn't start for two weeks. What do you have to do?" asks Mrs. Fischgrund.

"The SAT's," says Naomi. "Leah is obsessed with the SAT's."

"All the kids are. It's the difference between getting into Brown and, I don't know, Boise State."

"Leah, you will do fine. She's practically a straight–A student," says Naomi.

"Not in algebra and geometry. And you won't let me take a course, like everybody else I know."

"A waste of money," says Naomi.

"And an insult to your intelligence," adds Mr. Fischgrund.

"Daddy would have paid for it," snaps Leah.

"I majored in math," I say, and all heads swerve toward me, as if I were leading a cavalry. "I'm rusty but I could give you some pointers."

"But we're leaving for St. Louis tomorrow morning. I need months of tutoring," the girl wails. In distress her eyes narrow to resemble those of her mother.

"Perhaps I can help. I doubt math has changed that radically in thirty years." Self–confidence based only on my foray into Melissa's workbook.

"When do you propose to conduct this tutorial?" asks Naomi.

"I have another commitment in the early morning. A meeting with, some possible clients. But what about right now?"

I have been worrying that after dinner Naomi would dismiss me. This way, I can at least hang on for a few hours.

Mr. Fischgrund claps his hands. "I bet I can arrange for a meeting room or an unoccupied suite. Jared, if you can rescue my granddaughter from the jaws of a sub–700 SAT score we will be forever indebted to you."

"This is ridiculous," says Naomi.

A spasm shakes my elbow. I see a small person clearing a table and for a split second I think it's Barney, disguised as a busboy.

"Don't worry, Jared, I'm sure I can swing it," says Mr. Fischgrund. "And don't worry about getting to your appointment. My daughter will be happy to drive you."

I can't tell whether Mr. Fischgrund is playing cupid or doing this to annoy Naomi. A hard man to figure, with his large eyes and non–stop mouth. Is he my savior, his daughter's nemesis, or both?

Leah grasps the basic concepts, but she's impulsive and refuses to double-check her work. She wants short-cuts. She's spoiled.

In exchange for a brisk synopsis of my mother's marriages she describes her parent's own turbulent relationship as a tango of bitterness and betrayal. She sides with her father, although technically he left Naomi for a much younger woman. She doesn't care for her father's new wife, but she considers Naomi uptight, much stricter than the other moms, and too caught up in this silly store of hers. I gather Naomi has had several near-serious relationships since the divorce, one with a younger man whom Leah might have craved for herself.

This time with Leah has given me a second wind. It's so gratifying to be good at something.

I now command a respect from Leah that I couldn't when I was another boring middle-aged dinner guest interesting only for the exotic marital history of his mother. I feel strangely at ease with someone of the teen-age persuasion. I think I would have made a good high school math teacher.

It's still way too soon to break it to her that one day I will be her stepfather, and I'll be better at it than Victor was. But right now time—measured rotarily or digitally—is against me. I have to be at work in ninety minutes and the shop lies a good forty-five minutes away. There are things I need to say to Naomi and one important thing I must give her.

When I deliver Leah to the hotel room she shares with her mother, Naomi answers our knock dressed in a bathrobe. Ready for bed, she is fragrant with talc and terrifyingly close to nakedness. A television plays in the background, and Naomi faces me at an angle with one ear cocked to the miniseries or whatever. When I plead for twenty minutes of Naomi's time Leah, now my booster, presses her to accept. Naomi agrees to meet me in the bar in fifteen minutes.

I also hear a television blaring in the background when Walter Kempton, Jr. answers the phone. He's watching the same program that's beaming on the bar's thirty-inch TV, and from this sound-muffling phone booth the bar TV seems to be lip-synching the sounds from Kempton's set.

"Hello, hello?" Walter shouts. I almost hang up. I hate lying so much. You're doing this for Naomi, I tell myself.

"Walter, I don't know what to say. You know my mother has been ill and she's taken a turn for the worse. The doctors say she could go at any minute. I've got to stay here at the hospital, at least for a few hours. I hate to leave you in the lurch."

"Look, Jer, I understand. I got elderly folks, too, and I know how that is. I could have used more notice, but tell you what. I'll let the kids run the shop for a few hours and put Fenstermacher on notice that he may have to go in early. You check in with those kids once or twice by phone. Fenstermacher can get in at six instead of eight. It won't kill him."

"Say, Walter, you know anything about Deutschmann and Sons?"

"You kidding?"

"I met this man at the nursing home, visiting his wife, and when I told him I was in the printing business he said he has a connection at Deutschmann's. He could put you in touch."

"Way to go. I can't believe that in a moment of stress you're thinking about the business. We could subcontract with Deutschmann, take some of their overflow. They're Jews, and I don't normally like to do business with Jews. But Deutschmann's son is not as slimy as his old man. You're a sharp guy, Jerry."

Nobody's called me a sharp guy in many a moon and I've got to admit, with all due respect to my future father-in-law, the past few hours have done much to elevate my self-esteem. I even like myself at the moment.

I seldom like myself in the present. I do, however, love myself in the past. I love the child with the ravaged index finger rewriting baseball history; the solemn genuflector before a bronze eagle; the actuary sleepwalking through a quarter century; the dutiful son of the beautiful mother; Sheila's jealous fiance, Joanne's unpenetrating lover, Barney's gullible stooge. Taken together they are my son, and I must come to love them, all of them, in time.

Naomi has changed into black stretch pants with those titillating stirrups, black pumps and a pink knit top. This is the best look she's given me of her figure. Her large breasts, grafted onto such a slender torso, look almost splayed. When she catches my wave from my nook in the bar she whirls a finger in greeting, then snaps into the swaggering gait she displayed at the reunion. As she moves toward me her hair, still damp from her shower, glistens in the ice blue streaks of neon zigzagging over the bar.

While I waited for Naomi the piped in music played "Someone to Watch Over Me" followed by "Moon River," coincidentally the wedding dance songs for two of my mother's weddings. The probability of this happening presents an actuarial conundrum I'd love to tackle someday.

The centerpiece of our table is one of those old diner–style red lanterns wrapped in white mesh. A large Budweiser clock is wound ahead to bar time, but that doesn't concern me because in lying to Kempton I've made my peace with time. A waitress arrives as soon as Naomi settles into a chair across from me. I am in mid–bourbon. Naomi orders a gin and tonic. The TV must be showing the same program Naomi was watching in her room, because her eyes rove high over my left shoulder.

"I shouldn't order a G and T," she says. "The quinine in the tonic gives me headaches. Jews are allergic to quinine. But I already have a headache, so what's the difference?" She steeples her hands in front of her face and I notice, yearningly, that the nails are long and painted red. "Does tonic water give you a headache, Jared?"

"You're really hung up on being Jewish, aren't you?" I am more fatigued than I thought. There's an edge to my voice she's never heard from me. It only encourages her own edginess.

"Most Jews are."

"Your first husband was Jewish."

"So?"

"So being Jewish wasn't enough to keep you together."

"What do you know about it? Don't tell me you grilled Leah, as you explored the mystery of obtuse and acute angles. You've made a great impression on my daughter."

"I would hope your son would like me too."

"He's a rabbi. Or studying to be one. I love Tommy Lee Jones," she says, her attention fastened on the bar TV.

"Why does your mother wear a glove?"

"Her hand got severely burned at this French restaurant in New York. They were making a raspberry flambe at the table and some flames went flying and scorched the back of Mom's hand. We sued the restaurant, of course, which covered the cost of plastic surgery. But she never liked the way the hand looked. One day she started wearing a suede glove and that was that." She laughs. "It's become an affectation. She has over twenty gloves of all different colors. She gives me the right ones and I use them decoratively at my shop. Like for finger puppets."

I mention how pretty Naomi's mother was and still is. "Mom never considered herself pretty. She had a dark upper lip that she thought looked like a mustache," says Naomi. "Dad never exactly doted on her."

"It was nice of your father to give me that picture. I've been thinking a lot about my father lately."

For the first time Naomi looks directly at me. "He was the most wonderful man. When we carried a Torah together at Simchat Torah he treated me like a princess, unlike all other males in those days, including my father, who teased me about my freckles and my figure, I mean lack of a figure."

I explain the Byron episode—omitting Karen, Barney, Walter Kempton Senior, and a host of other details—and how the summer of 1961 has haunted me. She listens intently, and when I am done she says quietly, as her long lacquered fingers enfold the lantern, "So you still haven't found this John Byron."

"I can't go on banging my head against a wall."

"But how can you just drop it?" she says angrily. Yet another Jared Miller personality flaw revealed: I'm a quitter. She has confronted adversity and has never given up, so why should I? her eyes challenge. Little does Naomi know that I've been rocksteady all my life, a faithful son, a dogged employee, a loyal friend. That I visit Jared's Eagle every Valentine's Day in memory of my father. All Naomi knows is that I renounced my beloved baseball, dumped my fiancee and bagged my quest for Byron.

"I gave it my best shot. I haven't told you the lengths I went to. Anyway, something, or someone else has become much more important."

"Like your career in the printing business? Jared, you're a terrible liar. You're lucky my dad didn't cross–examine you. What do you really do for a living?"

"What do you mean?"

"You couldn't sell cheese to mice. Even I have heard of Deutschmann and Sons. Being in printing and not knowing Deutschmann is like being in computers and not knowing IBM. They printed a little brochure for my shop. At a deep discount because of my father."

I come clean about the Lickety–Split.

She looks at the bar clock, about to strike twelve. "Aren't you going to be late for the graveyard shift?"

"I'm playing hooky. That candle in the kitchen of your parents' home, their former home. Is that in memory of someone? My father used to burn candles like that."

"It's called a Yahrzeit candle. Meaning the anniversary of a loved one's death. My father's mother died twenty–eight years ago this week. Why are you doing all this?"

"Doing what?"

"Jared, I live in St. Louis. I have a grown son and a nearly grown daughter. My business is my life right now. I'm the happiest I've been in twenty years. I can't wait to return home to the daily grind. Which reminds me, I have to be up at the dawn's early light. Six A.M. flight, then right to the shop to open up. I've got to be going." She starts to get up and I rise with her. My heart thuds in my stomach; my self-confidence nosedives into the flame of that red lantern.

"So who was David?" I ask glumly.

"What David?"

"The David whose name you wrote in a notebook a thousand times. About thirty-five years ago."

She shrugs her shoulders.

"Can you give me a ride to work?" I ask, tremulous.

"Afraid not, Jared. Let me take care of this," she says picking up the check, as if she assumes that if I pay I won't have enough for cab fare. "I can charge it to my father's room."

I have to hustle to keep up with Naomi as she strides briskly through the lobby to the plate glass doors at the entrance to the hotel. She shakes her head. "No taxis, I'll have them call you one," she says, charging the front desk while I, discouraged, plop down on a semicircular vinyl couch.

Naomi soon returns and in answer to my silent prayer joins me on the couch. "It'll be about ten minutes. I'll wait with you." I am too depressed or too exhausted to talk. A yawn starts at my big toe and ripples through my body to my jaws. The lobby is empty except for a bellhop gabbing to a maintenance man and, at the registration desk, a man complaining loudly about a lost reservation, which the manager steadfastly denies, as his assistant clicks on computer keys in search of a miracle.

"Why me, Jared?" asks Naomi.

A question I've not been asking myself. Falling for Naomi has come so naturally...too tired to analyze it now, I blurt out, "Because

I dreamed about you. You're the only woman I've ever dreamed about."

Her eyes blaze in disbelief. I don't dare elaborate with the thoughts that have percolated in my mind, that dreams contain prophecy, even so bizarre a vision that visited me in the summer of 1961. It's bigger than both of us, I want to say, but I have the impression that "it" doesn't amount to much.

Naomi turns sharply to the front drive of the hotel, where a minivan, not a cab, has pulled up. The fuming man at the desk has wrangled his reservation and tense smiles sweep the faces of the uniformed staff.

It is now or never. I reach into my pocket, pull out a little velvet box and hand it to Naomi. "What?" she asks.

"It's for you."

"You are out of your gourd, Jared Miller," she says.

My breath is like a pounding surf, "I love you, Naomi. Listen. This is the engagement ring my father gave my mother. It means nothing to me unless it is on the finger of the woman I love. I know you don't care for me and you may never learn to, but I'm not going to give up. Despite what you think, I'm not a quitter. I just never wanted anything so much. I ask only one thing. Take the ring. Keep it for three months. If, after three months, you can't entertain the idea of being with me, then you can dispose of it. I don't ever want to see it again except on your finger."

Dumbfounded, she shuts the case, which sits awkwardly in her palm. I fold her long lovely fingers over the case and press her fist tight. Her hand is so soft I have to struggle to release my hold. I should have run this idea by Malcolm.

"I can't do this, Jared. You should at least pawn it or do something practical."

A whoosh of tires and the cab pulls up.

Naomi marches after me, juggling the ring case like a sprinter trying to pass the baton. I bash her hand, knocking the velvet cube to the pavement.

"What do you have against me?" I shout.

"Ask your mother," she says. The bright lights of the hotel marquee turn her green eyes a cold jade. "Ask her about the shrine in memory of Joseph Miller."

The driver, intuiting urgency, floors it and I arrive at work a mere half hour late.

CHAPTER 10

❁

You're doing this for Naomi, I keep telling myself, all the while realizing I'm doing it for myself, to help me win Naomi.

Fortunately, it's a balmy September morning with a subtle chill that freshens the air like crushed ice in a mug of root beer. My pilgrimage has already taken an hour in a bus overstuffed with people headed for work, but only five of us remain for the last mile or so.

I move up behind the driver, who after humming a few bars of some ancient Top Forty hit asks me, "Now, if you don't mind my axing, are you of the Jewish faith?"

When I shake my head he says, "I wondered, on account of you wanting off at Brentwood Road. Not much there but one of those Jewish temples. A big one. And some shops. I took a busload of Jewish folks up there this morning and now these others. Today's their big day, you know."

As a large dome looms through the right windshield a man strokes the magnetic chime and ushers another man, two women and two children to the front of the bus. The doors open and I trail them out the bus and up some stone steps, to where a dense crowd mills before an enormous double-arched doorway shaped like the Ten Commandments. I run my gaze up to the building's large gray dome topped by a Jewish star and then down to the Hebrew letters etched in gold into the facade. Without the star and letters you could take this for a planetarium.

My father's old synagogue had stood in a bad part of town which today is even worse. The building was converted into a Methodist church catering, as Lionel would put it, "to the colored trade." Mr. Fischgrund dislikes the new synagogue. He says the rabbi lacks wisdom, the cantor lacks a higher register and the congregation lacks respect.

"People of my generation look back at the old shul with painful nostalgia. The new place could showcase the Mormon Tabernacle Choir, complete with organ and choirloft. It's not just a far piece from the old place, it's a far cry."

Somebody must like it, because waves of people arrive and soon I find myself at the midpoint of the line, even though I've hardly budged in ten minutes. Grown–ups babble while overdressed kids run amok. The men wear dark suits and many press fingers to their scalps to secure yarmulkes imperiled by the breeze. Most of the women wear silly felt hats with mesh veils. Everyone raves about the weather, several declaring that it augurs well for the new year. Two men behind me jaw about the pennant race as their wives discuss a talk show that featured adopted children in search of their biological mothers. The talk of baseball washes over me, harmlessly, for the first time in thirty years.

A familiar face approaches from way at the end of the line. "I know you," says a youngish fellow with a mane of black hair and an almond sized wart nestling in that little nook on the side of the nose. "But I don't know from where," he adds.

"I don't either," I say.

"You work out at the JCC?" he asks, surveying my physique. "No? You work in the National Bank building on Cherry Street?"

"I work at the Lickety–Split Copy Center on Conway." Now I recognize him but I leave the exaltation of discovery to him.

"Bingo. You're the folks that do the newsletter. And a great job, too. We are Don and Ellen Abramson. Honey, this guy works at the place that printed the family newsletter."

A lovely woman with full, luscious lips and a deep tan smiles warmly at me. "It was Don's idea. I gather all the information and Don gets it printed."

"It's a lot of work, but it's worth it," says Don. It's to his wife that I reply, "I'm glad we're able to help," She is too good for him, in the blatant way that Naomi is too good for me.

"Are you a member of this congregation? We only go a few times a year. Yom Kippur is about all we can take. So much to repent for, so little time. Your name is?"

"Jerry Miller."

"Well, good yontif, Jerry."

"Same to you," I answer. Don and Ellen have cunningly shouldered ahead of me in line; they have disappeared by the time I reach the double doors, where a man in a yarmulke and prayer shawl asks me for my ticket.

"No freeloaders. Members only or you had to buy a ticket."

I feel shoving at my shoulder.

"I have a seat, in the fourth row on the left. It has my father's name on a gold plate in front of it. Joseph Miller."

"Every seat has a gold name plate on it. There are one thousand seats in this synagogue."

"How much is a ticket?"

"We're sold out. Move aside. Herman, *l'shanah tovah*."

I make my way through the crowd. Conversations rumble in my ears, faces all look spiteful, and I hate all Jews, relieved I am not one of them. How naive to think my father's seat would be reserved for me after thirty years, as if by primogeniture. I didn't realize there were so many Jews in the area. Or maybe there aren't, it's just that all of them happened to gather here the one day I sought admittance to the faith.

An elderly gentleman, propped on the arm of his daughter (they have the same deep-set brown eyes), bats my shins with his cane. "Hey, there, young man, why so upset?"

"They're sold out. You don't have a extra ticket, do you?"

"No, but I'll tell you something, I bet a lot of these people would be glad to sell you their tickets at scalper's prices. That's what we have come to. All these High Holiday hypocrites, these Jews for a day. There should always be room in a shul for an honest Jew." His daughter looks off, embarrassed.

"I'm Joseph Miller's son. He died over thirty years ago."

"I remember Joseph Miller. There was a mensch. I only knew him a little while before he died, but I knew him well enough to know he was a mensch, may he rest in peace. There should be a seat for Joseph Miller's son. But let me tell you. You want to worship on Yom Kippur, am I right?"

I nod in the affirmative.

"And you can't afford to shell out a thousand dollars for the privilege, at this Temple Beth Mammon, right? Then here's what you do. My nephew, Leon Seligman, is rabbi at a congregation in Limebrook. You know Limebrook? He's holding services today and it's on the house. You a died-in-the-wool conservative? Limebrook is not for everyone."

"Daddy, the line is moving," says the woman, dragging the old man along the pavement. Puffy under her chin. A vision in red with a bright red two-piece suit with square black buttons and velvet hat to match. An excess of rouge flushes her bloated cheeks. She is dressed to kill, but she'd be lucky to wound.

"Charla, a minute, please. Now, son of Joseph Miller, take yourself to the Limebrook First Christian Church. That's right, a church. The congregation can't afford to build a shul. They can barely afford to rent a chapel in a church. They don't have much in the treasury and they'll solicit a small donation but they won't charge an arm and a leg. A donation would be nice."

"Daddy."

"I would go there myself, but I've got a long tie to this congregation. Also, I'm too old to sit in folding chairs and adjust my ears to a female cantor, which is what you get at Limebrook. But you head over there and you pray your heart out. Leon Seligman, my nephew, he's the rabbi." He taps my instep with the rubber tip of his cane.

The whole point of this expedition was to go to my father's synagogue, occupy his seat, drink at the fount of Judaism and report my baptism—or whatever you'd call it—to Naomi. I didn't realize what I was up against. I figured the perfect time to go was the high holidays and what a stroke of luck, the high holidays falling five days after Naomi's return to St. Louis.

"Ask your mother about the shrine in memory of Joseph Miller," she had said, unaware of how fruitless a task that would be. But with five intense days of reflection I think I've hit upon her meaning.

I recall that about nine months after my father died, Uncle Jake and other leaders of the synagogue wanted to establish a memorial to Joseph Miller. Mom told me, with disdain, that they planned to hold a ceremony at the synagogue and present her with a plaque which would hang in the corridor of the new synagogue, then under construction. Also the seat in which my father always sat was to bear a gold plate with his name.

My mother rebuffed them. "I can't worry about a shrine I will never see. His worthless religion couldn't prevent him from dying a terrible death." No sane person would expect my mother to take part in a Jewish ceremony, but Uncle Jake never spoke to her again, and most likely Naomi and her parents were part of this campaign and still hate my mother for this. But it's hardly fair to condemn me by association; hardly the spirit of burying the hatchet that Naomi espoused at the reunion. Her father has put it behind him, so why can't Naomi?

I know one thing: I will not quit. I will stay the course, inch by inch I will earn her trust, then her love. Five days have passed and she has not returned the ring. Every minute that goes by I regard as a reprieve And I will play one more card, whether a trump card or ace of spades, we'll see soon enough.

But I have no idea how to get to Limebrook. I just got off from work two hours ago and I am suddenly too fatigued to make a decision. A snippy telephone rep from the transit authority informs me that it will take two transfers to get to Limebrook. Her very rudeness reinvigorates me, as rudeness often does.

An hour later I saunter up a narrow gravel path to Limebrook First Christian Church, a foursquare orange brick building where people loll about the entrance like concertgoers at intermission. Several children climb a large pine tree and one seems to be ensnared between two gnarled limbs. A teenager climbs to the rescue; his yarmulke flies off and an older man retrieves it and presses it to his lips.

People are dressed much less formally than at the other synagogue. I weave through the crowd, most of the people talking about how hungry they are, which reminds me that I too am famished, this being my normal dinner hour. The wooden door springs open and I enter a cheerful lobby where streamers and Jewish stars overlay pictures of Jesus or whatever, and only a display case of Christian articles and a bulletin board cluttered with notices signify the true auspices of the building. It's as if a tiny country has managed to subjugate a giant one and festooned the landmarks with its foreign symbols.

Two women slouch behind a table littered with brochures. They could be the anti–abortion brigade at a shopping mall.

"I am here for the service."

"Welcome, and your name?" asks one of the women, her hands poised over a card file. I tell her she won't find me in there. "Then will you print your name on this?" She gives me a peel–off paper label and a blue felt tip pen.

"The chapel is that way. The Isgur service will begin in a few minutes, uh, Jared." She points to a plain glass door, through which emanates an amplified female voice. At the door a woman wearing a purple yarmulke greets me and hands me one like hers. It doesn't quite fit my head, but I take it anyway. Blue and white prayer shawls are draped across a folding chair, but the woman doesn't hand me one, so I don't ask.

"A seedur," she whispers and points to a stack of black books. "The Isgur service is beginning."

The chapel has wooden pews covered with foam cushions, not folding chairs as the old gentleman had said, and holds about two hundred but I count only about forty. I slip into the back row of the left side—where my father would have sat, only much farther from the dais, so I can duck out at the first hint of danger. A stout, ornately garbed woman tells us what page to turn to. Behind her stands what looks like a wardrobe with double doors, which reminds me of Kempton Senior's magical mystery outhouse. A large green felt tapestry bearing a gray Jewish star hangs suspended from the rafters.

The prayer book sits heavy in my lap. The right hand side displays Hebrew letters in boldface type, the left an English translation and some transliteration with many hyphenated words.

A headnote at the top of the page says this is a memorial service and I instantly see why so many people have fled.

It's grim stuff, lamentations about opportunities wasted, goodness insufficiently appreciated, affection never expressed, and just plain woe. I follow as best I can, but it's tough to read double pages in backwards fashion, with only one eye. I whisper along with the responsive readings in English, but I repeatedly drop a page or two behind. I do spring to attention when we come to "The Lord is my shepherd," which I never memorized but mouth it as if I know it, like at Goode's funeral. Thinking of Goode makes my eyes water. I want to mourn him, but the service seems to offer devotions only for a dead parent, spouse, sibling, children and relatives, so this portion passes without my giving Goode his due. I don't know if Dad and Uncle Jake are still eligible for remembrance, or if we're only to pray for people who died during the past year. I already paid homage at my dad's tomb last Valentine's Day. I play it safe and briskly read the prayers for dead fathers and relatives.

Maybe the prayer wouldn't count in the eyes of God, Goode being gentile, but I feel I've missed a one time opportunity to make a clean sweep, to utter one grand elegy for all those who have for all practical purposes died during the past twelve months: Mom, Sheila, Joanne, my career, Karen, Barney, Skretch, Caspary, Terence, Randy, and John Byron.

I have called Gloria twice in Iowa. She sounds brusque, as if she has put all her past behind her, and I suspect that unlike the other Goode widows she will eventually start to date. She will do what my mother did, get on with her life, as the saying goes, and Mickey take the hindmost.

The woman at the podium says "It is customary to rise for this prayer" and we all rise. I study the nape of a man's neck some five rows in front of me and pretend to read my father's name etched in gold on the back of his seat. Many are sobbing, including two small children who cling to their mother at either side. Another woman, swarthy and petite, leads us in song with a quivering soprano that reminds me of Joan Baez—eerily beautiful, but more suitable for a hootenanny than a hymn for the dead.

Once I accompanied my father to a Friday night service. Perhaps my mother was ill and wanted me out of the house. My father ignored me as if I were someone else's son. He gave me a comic book or baseball magazine to read. Jewish kids from school looked at me strangely. The satin beanie itched my scalp, as does the one I'm wearing today. I remember a glittering pulpit and chanting heavily dominated by basses and baritones, melodies that resembled "The Volga Boatmen," nothing like Christmas carols, the only other religious music I was familiar with.

A scrawny bearded man now assumes the pulpit. He has the wan, undernourished demeanor of Americans held hostage in faraway lands. He wears tennis shoes but also a highly ornamented yarmulke and prayer shawl, and I take him to be the rabbi, Leon Seligman. He surveys the hall and his eyes somehow fasten on me, to accuse me of gate-crashing.

What he does next is scarier still. He proposes to ask each person present to say out loud the name of the person he or she is mourning. He skips down three steps at the left end of the dais and pulls up beside mourners in the front row, much the way Johnny Carson used to dive into the audience and invite people to stump the band, for which they would win tickets to a restaurant. I always wondered if the restaurants were any good, or if they were greasy spoons and the whole thing was a put-on.

"I remember my father, Shimon Metzger," says one woman tearfully. "I remember my sister-in-law, Arlene Reinsdorf." "I remember my father, Samuel Lieberman." "I remember my uncle, Chaim Stoloff." Up and down the rows goes the old man's nephew, wrenching names from people. My scalp grows warm under the yarmulke. My mother would die deader than she is, if she knew. Naomi would call me a hypocrite, maybe a blasphemer.

Soon the rabbi is but five rows away. "I remember Sarah Weinberg, my mother." "I remember Marvin Lichter, my husband." "I remember"—it's the mother, who breaks down as she hugs both her sobbing children—and the rabbi softly says, "beloved husband and father, Howard Rogosin."

Now within two rows of me, he looks much younger, in his early thirties, and more wiry than frail. He peers deeply into the eyes of each of his mourners and I don't know if I could withstand the scrutiny, however compassionate its intent.

My toes point toward the exit but something cements me to the spot. The rabbi's tennis shoes pad softly up the aisle with the easy gait of a golfer strolling familiar links. I want to ask him why he wears tennis shoes on this solemn occasion and who is he trying to kid, because even with only one good eye I see they are Reeboks. Suddenly he is at my side and just stands there waiting. All eyes are on me, eyes wet with weeping for their loved ones and ready to weep for mine. "And you?" asks the bearded man. "And you?" he repeats, and something shatters in my chest, and I clear my throat and gulp and through parched lips comes a voice too clear and full–bodied to be my own, "I remember my father, Joseph Miller."

Tears come and I feel like a fool, standing here with genuine Jews imbued with their authentic grief, while I grieve a father I hardly knew for the sake of a woman I love in vain. Rabbi Seligman stands beside me: he is all dark brown eyes and pocked skin peeking beneath a beard's dense camouflage.

"Your uncle sent me here," I whisper. Is that all? his eyes ask bemusedly. A hush envelops the congregation. This guy might have ten uncles. He may not even be Rabbi Seligman. He extends his hand and when I hesitate he takes my right hand and cushions it between both of his own.

"Please stay a while. We can break the fast together."

He returns to the pulpit and softly entreats us to rise for Kaddish, a prayer for the dead. My blurry eye follows along in the transliteration. Pangs of hunger besiege my stomach. I have fasted by coincidence. The rabbi announces that at sundown there will be a special breaking of the fast, catered by members of the congregation. I don't know if I can hold out much longer, though I would like a free meal and I do want to talk to the rabbi. He senses that I'm a man with a purpose.

❦ ❦ ❦

We stand at opposite sides of the bed and talk over her as if she were a gulf between us and not the sole bridge. We keep things from her, the way parents protect a child from harsh truths—Hopalong Cassidy is going off the air, the president has been shot. Even now, an effigy of herself, Mom has the air of a woman who knows she's pretty. Naomi still doesn't consider herself attractive. Maybe Malcolm's right, you never forget.

I am reading a paperback edition of the Bible. Lionel regards me with some disdain, perhaps because he comes from a generation that equates "paperback" with smut. When I show him the cover Lionel asks if I am praying for Mom and I say no, studying. I do not reveal that the book is a loaner from a rabbi who assigned me the first five books, Job, and Ecclesiastes. Lionel and my mother must not know about Rabbi Leon Seligman. It would kill my mother—a merciful thing, actually—and create discomfort with Lionel.

Lionel looks weary and worried. The battery in his pacemaker needs recharging. I have not even dared to contemplate that something might happen to Lionel. He has always had such energy; to see him decelerate is a bad omen. He has stopped going to his support group and won't explain why. One of his sons is coming in from Arizona today.

The television drones on like a life support machine, even though Mom has lost interest in the soaps. She mumbles from time to time. The doctor says she is failing rapidly and there is nothing he can do. (I've never had much faith in Dr. Bratz and I don't believe there's anything he could do even in the simplest of situations, except hunch up his shoulders.) Physically she can last up to a year. I would not hesitate to pull a plug if there were one, but there's nothing to do but watch. Lionel has started referring to her in the past tense, which unnerves me even more than his more typical Hubert Humphrey gusto.

Lionel does perk up when his son arrives. Roger is a big, strapping man, a little younger than I am. He barely glances at my mother, whom he regards much as I have regarded Lionel, as an interloper, a necessary evil. He dislikes having to worry about his dad. His voice bristles with an annoyance I recognize as similar to my own, at the doctors, at Lionel, at the cab that brought him from the airport.

Roger struck it rich as an accountant in Arizona and before Mom fell ill he had pleaded with Lionel and her to join him there. I can see why Lionel declined. The son obviously considers his dad a fool and snipes at everything the man says. Granted, Lionel utters the most snipable things. Finally Roger kisses Mom absently on the cheek.

Roger is intrigued to see me reading the Bible. Like Lionel, he assumes I'm reading for spiritual sustenance.

In truth, I'm doing homework. Rabbi Leon and I have met several times at his office since my Yom Kippur debut. He has adopted me, possibly as a "subject" or "control" for some arcane study of the kind Joanne used to conduct. When I mentioned my interest in history he recommended that I read the first five books of the Bible, which chronicle the history of the Jews and purvey an unending cavalcade of characters, power struggles, battles, a dollop of sex. Or so Rabbi Leon said. On the whole, I'd rather read about Cromwell or the exploits of Lord Nelson.

I was pleased to discover that Jared, who occupies maybe six lines of Genesis, lived to be nine hundred sixty-two—presumably without vitamins or a dialysis unit—only to be bested a few paragraphs later by Methuselah, who tallied nine hundred sixty-nine. The Bible can hardly be called history when a man's lifetime approaches a millennium. Not to mention the havoc those lifespans would wreak on actuarial tables.

The dreams, however, have piqued my interest: Jacob, Joseph, and the others invariably have their dreams fulfilled, albeit in a cockeyed fashion, which makes me feel like less of a fool for maintaining to my dying day (nine hundred years from now) that Naomi awaits me, in naked expectation with bosom heaving, in some dark alley, just as in my soggy adolescent nightmare.

On the bus this morning I started to reread Ecclesiastes, to see if what Rabbi Leon argues makes any sense: "Read between the lines. Try to look at the words from God's point of view."

"Isn't that blasphemy or something?"

"Nope. Imagine you are all–powerful. You have created a magnificently ordered world, whose rivers all run into the sea because that sea is limitless, whose sun rises and sets with stunning regularity, whose seasons come and go. And here is your finest creation, man, kvetching…"

"What?"

"…complaining. Now, deep down, we Jews are pro–life in the broadest sense. When we drink we toast L'Chaim, Hebrew for `to life.' I wanted you to read the most cynical part of the Old Testament to show you how faith shines through. All is order. Yet to man it seems meaningless, dreary, devoid of novelty, chaotic. He is always kvetching. He sees only chaos."

"So do I."

"You look at the world and you say it must be flat. You have to go to outer space to really see for yourself that it's round, from the heavens. That's what we have to do. We have to give God a little credit, take the world on faith, go with the flow. You're a mathematician. You take all those square roots on faith, don't you?"

"So why is Ecclesiastes in the Bible?"

"In my humble and not particularly learned opinion, it's there to show us how petty and cloying lack of faith is. The speaker of Ecclesiastes is a pipsqueak gifted with manifest eloquence. He is as seductive as the serpent who tempted Eve. Some of the most inspired wisdom of the Old Testament is essentially glorified kvetching at God."

"But what's the point of k…k…complaining to God?" "Because God just might be listening. The interesting thing about Judaism is its immediacy to God. There is no middleman, no Savior to intervene on your behalf. No Mohammad. Just you and God. We rabbis don't hear your confessions and we cannot absolve you of your sins. We can listen and advise, educate, perform at weddings and funerals, but in some ways we're just cheerleaders trying to stir up the faithful."

Rabbi Leon wants me to attend Friday night services regularly at Limebrook, but I felt queer the one time I went. There were thirty or forty people there, some of whom I recognized from the High Holiday service. The widow and her two children did not show up, which surprised me, but several black families did, which surprised me even more. A couple of women had that unattached and available aura, that mournful expectation I misread with Karen. Do they regard the Friday night service as more of a dating service? Good women are so easy to find. I have not told Rabbi Leon about Naomi.

If Rabbi Leon is right, that nothing is random, then I might have a shot, since Naomi and I came together so randomly. I knew with John Byron when enough was enough, but I'm nowhere near that point with Naomi. Ten days, sufficient time for even fourth class, and she still hasn't returned the ring.

"You're not becoming one of those born agains are you, Jared?" asks Roger.

"It wouldn't hurt you to read a chapter or verse or two, son,," says Lionel.

"That's great, coming from you, Dad. I never saw you crack a Bible, much less go to church. Mom always took us on Sundays."

"I was working on Sundays. It sent you to college."

My mother moans softly and we all turn gratefully to her. She has picked up Roger's voice. She looks right at him and asks who he is. "Oh, so it is Roger. How nice of you to come. My son used to come but he stopped. Haven't seen him in months. My own real son doesn't have time for me."

"I'm right here, Mom," I say, taking her hand.

"Did you get married yet?"

"We broke up, Mom."

"No great loss," she says.

I want to tell her that her bigotry has cost me the woman I love. I will tell her when we are alone, if I can shake Lionel. There's always a husband between us. I want to tell her I am taking baby steps toward becoming a Jew. The words may not even register and even if they do they will soon be lost in the maelstrom that passes for her mind, but I want the satisfaction of popping off. Perhaps in her subconscious she will repent.

    As Mom dozes off I ask Roger about his wife and kids. He used to whip out his wallet and display photos. Either that enthusiasm wears off at some point, or maybe the pride does. Mom has always held Roger up to me as a model: he's a successful CPA, nice kids, wife, a palatial house with an outdoor hot tub and so forth. The fact that he's a jerk who despises and probably cheats on his wife and spends virtually no time with his kids has never affected Mom's opinion of him. He says the accounting profession has become a rat race, the tax laws are absurd, clients are assholes. His wife Alice had a lump removed from her neck last year.

    Lionel and Roger leave for lunch at a coffee shop across the street. They invite me to join them but I decline, as I would rather read Ecclesiastes and watch my mother sleep than endure the way Lionel slurps the bowl of soup he unfailingly orders for lunch. I can easily visualize Mom dead. At the Yom Kippur service I had the impulse to recite a prayer in her memory, or better yet a prayer in memory of her memory.

    Dr. Bratz tiptoes in for a cameo. Shrugging his shoulders he exhorts me to keep my chin up. As he takes Mom's pulse he gripes about having to endure one more autumn without a World Series in Kansas City.

    On his way out he bows to Mrs. Western, who is entertaining her oldest son, a nice fellow about my age with an effeminate lisp. Lisp and all, he teaches speech at a boy's private school in east Kansas. I hope he doesn't get into trouble. So many teachers get indicted nowadays, twenty years after they have allegedly molested a student.

    I kiss my senseless mother on the cheek and take my leave, thrusting the fat paperback into my jacket pocket. Something about the cover always provokes scorn or adulation. On the bus the other day a woman sitting far down the aisle cried out to me what a fine man I am, to which a woman with a Pro–Choice button replied that it's people like me who blow up abortion clinics in Wichita. I've never been to Wichita, I said timidly.

I used to see countless people reading the Bible—lots of them at the unemployment office—touching each word with their fingers, and I dismissed them as religious fanatics. It never occurred to me that a normal person would read the Bible.

As I stroll through the waiting room, steeling myself as always against the phalanx of wheelchairs, I notice a young boy sitting on the floor with his back propped against a couch. He has a math textbook in his lap and nibbles at his upper lip.

"Having trouble?" I ask.

He looks up at me, undecided whether to admit defeat or do the manly thing and say no sweat. He must be nine or ten. "I can't do this," he says. "I have a mental block against math."

"There's no such thing. Math anxiety is a myth invented by math teachers, just to torture students. Anyway, only girls are supposed to suffer from it. You're not a girl, are you?" His face brightens a bit. "I know a thing or two about math and I'd be happy to help, if you'll let me."

"Sure, I guess so."

"First thing, you have to get up off this floor. My bones are too stiff to get down there with you."

We sit together on the couch and I instantly see the crux of his problem. Long division, nothing more. After a whole morning of waxing helpless I suddenly brim with capability. The boy is no wizard but I can teach him enough to survive the next few nights of homework.

"Daniel, who is this?" says a man standing so close that his shins brush the boy's knees.

I rise to my feet. The man eyes me suspiciously.

"I was just helping with a math problem."

"Daniel is not supposed to talk to strangers. Can't I leave you for fifteen minutes without something happening?" Daniel does not look at all bowed. He returns his father's stern gaze.

"He's a math teacher," says the boy, looking hopefully at me to corroborate his fib.

"It's my fault," I say. "And I am a math teacher, of sorts."

"Where do you teach?"

Well, I've only just started putting ads in the neighborhood paper. (I've become the last member of my men's club to get himself in the paper.) Math tutor, all grades, will make house calls, inexpensive hourly rates. Rabbi Leon suggested it.

"But I hated school," I told him.

"School is different when you are the teacher. It's like being a rabbi. Everyone assumes you know all the answers."

I don't have any pupils yet but somehow I don't think I am long for the Lickety–Split.

"I'm a tutor," I tell the man. "I'm here visiting my mother, in room 205. My name is Jared Miller." I offer my hand.

The man draws back. "Come again?" he asks.

"Jared Miller?"

"Robert Varden. I'm sorry, did you say Jared Miller?"

"Do I know you?" I ask.

"Geez," gasps Daniel, who stands up, dumping his math text on his foot. "You're the Jared Miller on Easton Street?"

I nod yes.

"Dad, can I ask him? Can I?"

"Certainly not, Daniel. Mr. Miller, this is crazy. Daniel and I are visiting from Columbia. We come up almost every weekend to see my uncle. He's…"

Daniel seizes his father's belt. "Please can't I ask him, Dad?" he shouts.

"No!"

"Mr. Miller, you've got the ball and I want it! Please, please, please," says the boy, pumping my wrist. The force of his hands and my own amazement almost topple me. I put my hand on the boy's head to steady myself. "You don't want it, do you?" he wails? "You haven't sold it have you? Can I maybe buy it from you? I have $16.75 of my own money."

Robert Varden subdues his son and the three of us sit on the couch, Robert acting as a buffer between me and the agitated boy. Robert explains that eighteen months ago he helped move his Uncle John, John Byron, to this nursing home. Several boxes ended up at the Varden home and lay neglected in the basement, until Daniel went scavenging and unearthed the baseball from a box that contained silver platters, flatware, embroidered napkins and other stuff that had belonged to John Byron's mother.

Daniel pleaded for the ball, but a note inside the box specified that the ball must go to Jared Miller at such and such address. Daniel threw a fit but Uncle John was adamant. The ball had to go to Jared Miller. They had to promise Daniel all sorts of movies and video games as a consolation, but finally placated him.

"You can have the ball, Daniel," I say.

"I'll pay. Anything."

"It's yours. It belongs in your family." Daniel moves to hug me but his father fends him off.

"I would like to see your Uncle John if that's possible." I explain that I have been searching for him for months.

"Uncle John never had a listed telephone number. He lived as a kind of hermit. We never imagined you would want to track him down. He instructed us only to leave the ball, that you would know who it came from. He said it would close a circle. It was mysterious, but Uncle John has always been peculiar, even more so in old age."

"So when do I get the ball, Mr. Miller?" shouts Daniel.

"I don't know. You have to earn it. I'll make you a deal. I'm going to write down ten difficult problems in long division and if you get all ten of them right, the ball is yours."

"You want to see Uncle John now?" asks Robert Varden.

"Very much. But ask him first. He may not want to."

"That's true. There's no telling with my uncle." Robert leaves and I sit down beside Daniel. I take his spiral notebook and jot down ten problems, easy ones.

"Why did Uncle John give you the ball? You love baseball?"

"Not as much as you do, Daniel. Which is lucky for you, because otherwise I might not be so willing to part with it."

"It's got Dizzy Dean, Frankie Frisch. Guys from the Hall of Fame, my dad said."

"You like the old–timers, do you?"

"I read a book about some of the great pitchers. Dizzy Dean was funny. I collect baseball cards mostly. I play second base for my Cub Scout team. I've seen three Royals games. And the Missouri U team, but that's not the big leagues, of course. Actually, I like soccer even better than baseball."

I ask Daniel to name his favorite ballplayer. Roberto Somebody, I never heard of him. The boy asks me again and again if he can really have the ball, until finally Robert returns and says that, yes, Uncle John would be delighted to see me.

I see the nameplate outside a door I have passed hundreds of times. The man who slithers to a sitting position in bed has thick silver hair, all now the color of that once skunklike shock. His eyeglasses are so thick he seems to peer through a row of overlapping mirrors.

"Well, if it isn't my old lunchmate, Jerry–Jared." Instead of a handshake he taps me on each shoulder, like a king dubbing a knight. His hands are delicate, untarnished by age. The voice has hoarsened, but what strikes me most is the mouth.

John Byron smiles and taps his teeth. "I always longed for immaculate dentition. Once I got on Medicare and it absorbed so many of my medical expenses, I couldn't resist splurging on a new set of choppers." Sliding into a chair beside his bed I notice a stack of books on his night table.

"I see you're still an avid reader."

"My reach far exceeds my grasp, I'm afraid. Or is it that the spirit is willing but the flesh weak? Whatever, I tire easily. I rarely meet my quota of one hundred pages a day. I falter around page fifty–seven, and have to implore the nurses to read to me, but they butcher things, no expression, and I feel infantile being read to." He speaks slowly, but he always did. A clock radio plays classical music, which evokes Naomi. Perhaps she would think better of me for discovering Byron, however inadvertent.

"You look very healthy, John," I say, awkwardly. I don't believe I ever addressed him by his first name, nor do I remember calling him Mr. Byron. I probably couldn't decide what to call him; in those days, I couldn't even decide what to call myself.

"I look healthy for an invalid," he says, pointing to a wheelchair against the wall behind me. "Spinal stenosis and assorted other difficulties, too intricate to detail for you right now. I tried a cane for a while. With major surgery and a convalescence the length of an elephant's gestation period, I would have a twenty per cent chance of walking again. I elected to go into the chair rather than under the knife. I understand your mother resides in this vale of antiquity?"

When I tell of my mother and her condition he expresses no sympathy, which I find refreshing. He always did have a different slant on things. He contends that Alzheimer's is a myth, that people just reach a point where they decide to mentally withdraw from life. Which would come as disconcerting news to Doctor Bratz and Mom's health insurance carrier.

"The codger in 117 is a Jerry, though it's a derivative of Jerald. He plays a mean pinochle, albeit at a sluggish tempo. We've been on the same game for three days. The poor soul has pancreatic cancer, so I might win by default. I'd give my left leg for a competent chess partner. You don't play chess, do you, Jerry–Jared?"

I shake my head. "Thank you for the baseball."

I detect a glimmer behind the translucent shutters. "You had it coming to you. Still a baseball fanatic? No? Sorry to hear it. Mind you, I personally consider baseball absurd, but it's important to feel passionately about something." He grunts over the word "important," and for a moment I fear he's choking or in pain. But the problem subsides.

I ask his permission to turn the ball over to Daniel.

"You had right of first refusal. I promised to bequeath it to you what, over thirty years ago, and in my book that promise was binding. Daniel's a fine boy, but exceedingly acquisitive. He begged me for that ball but I felt he needed a lesson."

I've been searching the obscured eyes, the supple voice for any signs of rancor toward me, but as I find none, I navigate into the past. "John, I never had the chance to thank you for all of your, guidance, that summer at the Chicken Coop. My first job, and all."

"My last job," says Byron. God, how I hated that mandarin, what was his name? Puker? Kuker. And then there was Hickey. Poor excuses for human beings. They're both deceased and I confess that I read their obituaries with unconscionable delight. Now, don't look shocked. People always say one of the depressing things about growing old is that you outlive those you care about. Well, there is also a morbid satisfaction in outliving those whom you detest. Sound vicious? So be it. I'm an invalid, I've been punished enough already."

He nods toward the other bed in the room, now vacant. "I've also outlived six roommates in three years. I expect a new one to be deposited any minute. There's a waiting list the length of eight columns in the White Pages. I only hope the next inmate abhors television. People don't really live longer nowadays, they just take longer to die. But enough of these ravings. My bark is worse than my bite, despite these superlative dentures. What have you been doing the last thirty years?"

He really doesn't want to know about me, he just asks out of politeness. I can tell it's a hoot for him to have an audience. It always was. I am an indulgent, sympathetic ear, or at least a fresh one. I whip through a summary of my past three decades in about five declarative sentences.

"Take heart, a pink slip can be a carte blanche in disguise, Jerry–Jared. Getting fired from the Coop was the best thing that ever happened to me," he says. "Of course, it took me months to get over the humiliation. I scarcely budged from the house. But eventually I was able to cast off my guilt at being independently wealthy and shed all pretense of proletarian integrity. I traveled—visited every place Hemingway ever lived, all over the world, retracing the footsteps of his life. In chronological order, mind you. It took me over five years and entailed considerable zigzagging and jet lag.

"Oak Park, Illinois is one dreadful town. Hemingway's first, irremediable mistake was to be born there. The town in Idaho where he killed himself was no paradise either, though it's fun to be in a place where the principal minority group is the American Indian. Can't complain about France and Italy, or the Florida Keys, and obviously not Kansas City. I loved Madrid and its environs so much I stayed there seven years. I enjoyed the bars and the bullfights, the only sport that ever appealed to me. I tried running with the bulls in Pamplona but sprained an ankle. I did have one important gap in my peregrinations, Cuba, because of those execrable communists. I still cling to the hope that they'll overthrow Castro and I can set foot, or wheelchair, on Cuban soil.

"I read Hemingway over and over. It may sound odd, but what I love about him is his consummate lack of wisdom. I don't think he knew what he was talking about most of the time. I find his posturing endearing. All these biographies have come out, imputing latent homosexuality and whatnot. Anybody who knows Hemingway knows he was incapable of latency in anything. That was part of his problem. If he had been latently suicidal, like so many of us, he might still be alive. Theorizing about historical figures has gotten all out of hand. Lord Byron, they say he was manic–depressive. I'm glad we're not related. I hear it runs in families. You're not listening."

On the contrary. I savor his soothing, civilized voice—if you can savor with your ears. I can't believe I ever found anything threatening in this man; whether he is, was or ever has been a "fairy" is assuredly beside the point. He may be crotchety, but he always was. He smiles with his new teeth and that mollifies his harsh pronouncements.

So I am listening, but my eyes have wandered to the ceiling high bookcase, where Byron has evidently salvaged his most prized volumes. What a contrast to my mother's room, reduced to a red armchair and Lionel.

"So are you reading Hemingway now?" I ask, strumming the pile of books on his night table. "The Sun Also Rises. That's from Ecclesiastes."

"Good title for a book about despair."

"I know someone who thinks Ecclesiastes is about the silliness of despair."

"Do tell, Mr. Miller."

But I don't tell, because John Byron is drifting off to sleep with my name on his lips.

In the waiting room I see Robert helping Daniel do the math problems, so I slink past them to pay a call on my mother. I forgot to ask Byron why the baseball had meant so much to him. Who gave it to him? I will save that story for another time. Not necessarily the next visit.

Lionel and Roger have not yet returned. Mom is sleeping, as is Mrs. Western. Had my father lived he would be at Mom's bedside, or perhaps occupying Mrs. Western's bed. (Not with, but instead of, Mrs. Western.) My heart flutters as I wonder if some similar fantasy might this minute be percolating with Mom as her eyes twitch in a sleep of vivid memory or violent forgetting.

Her once thick chestnut hair is now a gauzy white with patches of pink scalp. The flesh of her slender white arms, which have never known a tan, even when she traveled near the equator, has grown slack. A tiny oblong black mole on her right upper arm used to make me fear for cancer, though Mom insisted on calling it a beauty mark. It seems to have doubled in size. Seeing her edge toward death, I wonder what good it does to nurse this resentment. So much of my life has turned on betrayal—by my mother, my Ex–Fiancee, my employer, the whole sport of baseball. At least, I've always considered them betrayals. Did I really betray John Byron or did I provide the passport for his Hemingway travels? The baseball I took for retribution was a pledge fulfilled. Is Byron a fool or a noble soul? Maybe I can figure this out by next Yom Kippur, when like a good Jew in one bold day I'll make my peace.

I must have fallen asleep in my mother's old armchair, because the next thing I know Roger is yanking my left arm as if I were a slot machine. The nurse taps her toe impatiently at the foot of Mom's bed, holding a cellophane covered tray of food. Lionel awakens Mom with a kiss and the blue eyes spring open. Her lips curve upward in a smile, a totally spontaneous, involuntarily blissful return to the land of consciousness.

"Laura, you put your poor son to sleep with all your lively conversation," says Lionel.

"Jared works too hard," says Mom, looking directly at Roger.

"It's the schedule, not the job," says Roger. "I just read an article about it. People who work in the wee hours, their mental and biological clocks get all out of whack. It's no coincidence that all the major man–made catastrophes, like Three Mile Island, the Chernobyl explosion, the Exxon oil spill, they all happened at night during the graveyard shift. People who work those weird hours…"

"Roger," I interrupt. Obviously Lionel has not told him that we are concealing my new career from my mother.

"…I mean, people who work those hours are liable to all sorts of weird sleeping disturbances, emotional disorders and what have you. Sleep–deprivation, the article called it."

The crisis fades when Lionel spoons an omelet into my mother's mouth. They have tuned out Roger, who accordingly raises his voice. "These people lose all sense of time."

"Time!" I cry, looking at my watch. "Christ, I've got to run," I say, and I hastily pat Roger and Lionel on their backs, kiss my mother and bolt toward the door.

I am relieved to find Robert and Daniel still in the waiting room, sharing one of those plain Hershey bars with all the little squares, which Daniel breaks off one at a time and slips into his father's mouth. When he sees me Daniel jumps up excitedly. He hands me a sheet with the math problems, now freshly smudged with chocolate. I screw up my eyes, clear my throat, act gruffly pedagogical. Robert winks at me. I have always enjoyed being winked at, perhaps because it means that for a split second the winker and I share a semi–blind state, we're on equal footing.

Daniel aced the test. I flash him a thumbs–up, which triggers a broad smile with not a crinkle in it. He must not take after the Byron side of the family. I invite Daniel to pick up his reward at my place and after much begging Robert agrees to stop by later on their way back to Columbia.

"I'm afraid I'm not very good at giving directions," I say.

"Oh, we know where you live, buddy," Daniel says menacingly, probably in imitation of a cop movie or TV show.

Through the window of my bus the landscape droops with the onset of autumn. Fall never got me down. Mom couldn't understand it. She always expected me to sadden as the baseball season hurtled to its close, the diamonds abruptly stilled as if their green energy had been transmuted into the doomed, resplendent leaves. But the season that really mattered played unending in my head and would only cease when I told it to. It will be nice to have Robert and Daniel over. I'll need to nap an hour or so beforehand; they will probably show up at the equivalent of my midnight. But I've at last been able to put the fans into storage, and, if Daniel will only control himself, I expect the three of us can sit and talk comfortably in my living room.

I can't wait to see Daniel's eyes.

About the Author

A native of Kansas City, Missouri, Richard Rabicoff has published a volume of short stories, Tough Customers (1994) and more than 200 articles in newspapers and journals. He lives in Baltimore and works in public relations

0-595-21415-0